ASHES

ARISING

Stephanie Welch

Printed in the United States of America

Published November 2021

Published by:
Southern Willow Publishing, LLC
1114 Highway 96,
Suite C-1, #340
Kathleen, Georgia 31047

Cover Art by Victoria Hawkins

ISBN: 978-1-956544-04-6

"Out of suffering have emerged the strongest souls; the most massive characters are seared with scars."

The finale of this trilogy is dedicated to my sisters-in-ink. Alasen for helping me bounce ideas (and all other forms of conversation), for Olivia who braved the first edit, and the women of Southern Willow Publishing who made this possible.

CHAPTER ONE

GABRIEL

Never in his immortal life had Gabriel seen this level of chaos erupt so quickly. As the carriage carrying their most precious possession, their fiercest weapon, ambled away with Michelo's laughter soaring over the skies, he felt his eternal heart sink. Gabriel looked down at Heretia, the love of all of his lives, bleeding heavily in his arms.

"Hold on," he whispered, and rose to fly her back to Purge where she could receive the lifesaving care she so desperately needed.

The sword Michelo had planted into her petite shoulder before shoving her back forcefully across the magically warded barrier was still buried almost to the hilt. Heretia shivered as if cold, but he knew it was from the immense loss of blood she had endured in the mere moments he had spent watching Amelia Vida Wardman, the all-powerful Druid, give herself up to save her parents.

Theodeus Varillian, Mia's lover and Pair, the one person attached to her in heart and magic, still raged at the invisible wall. His fingertips were bloody from scraping at it. Mia's father continued screaming at the top of his lungs to recover the beautiful brown-haired daughter he had been willing to sacrifice his own life and happiness for. Clarisse, Mia's lovely mother, crawled in her weakened state to her husband's side. She pulled at his pants to hoist herself up and cried tears of grief.

"Theo!" Gabriel shouted above the noise. Theo didn't turn at first, but he couldn't be sure that Theo had noticed Heretia's state. "Theo!"

Gabriel shouted again, this time so loudly that his auburn hair fell into his sweat soaked eyes. "We have to go!"

Theo turned in anger, the mere thought of leaving Mia behind incomprehensible to him.

"We can't! We have to get Mia back!" he roared, the Earth quaking beneath their feet from the force of his Earth magic. It too was losing control, and the rocks and sand beneath them undulated from his might.

"Heretia is dying!" Gabriel fired back, lifting her in his arms and presenting the wounded High Queen of the Ancient Kingdom with her flowing white hair now stained by blood for Theo to see.

Theo was briefly concerned, having become her friend in their journeys across the five kingdoms after hating her false identity as the mad Queen of Purge for so long. Concern for the small woman dying before him and the anxiety of being parted from his Pair warred within him visibly. The internal battle played out in the storm of his green eyes.

"I can't leave her Gabriel! I can't leave Mia here," Theo bellowed.

He threw his hands out in the direction the carriage had driven off in. It had gone straight back to the line of tents and smoke that made up the camp of the Second Uprising, the army of Cannibals that were somehow growing in numbers and influence each day. War was coming, and instead of fighting and possibly losing countless lives, Mia had bought them time by offering herself as a sacrifice. It wouldn't stop it, but it was slowing the tide of events, allowing the High Rulers from the other kingdoms and their armies to arrive. It also allowed for the potion to cure the Cannibals to be created, a job Heretia was spearheading. Gabriel glanced back down at the woman, with her now blue lips.

"Theo! There is nothing we can do. Mia didn't just give herself up to lose it all because you won't come back," Gabriel begged. He tried to reason with the aching man, but he was losing time. Eventually, he would just leave the sorrow-stricken Earth Sorcerer if it came to it.

Theo turned and threw a few more blasts of magic at the wall, all of it for nothing it seemed. Finally, Gabriel nodded and took off into the air with Heretia cradled against him for warmth.

"Almost there, my love," he whispered again, but Heretia was beyond responding.

When Gabriel flew straight into the South gate with Heretia now barely moving, the entire castle sprang into action. This was their High Queen and she was wounded. The few healers left were called for and the potions masters ordered to switch from the cure to anything that could help the Queen.

Gabriel raced to Heretia's chambers and gently laid her on the bed, barely stepping back to give the witches room. They went to work stitching and reforming everything that had been damaged by the assault. Thankfully, one of the assistants noted aloud, nothing vital had been hit, but there was significant blood loss and that was her greatest danger. The Water wielders began working on that specifically while Fire and Earth worked on her physical body.

Medeis, the world in which they all lived, hadn't seen a Life Sorcerer in over twenty years before Mia had come along, stumbling through a mirror portal, and upending everything they knew. Only a Life Sorcerer could heal a wound like this quickly. A Life wielder, such as Mia's friend Esmerelda, could certainly help with this greatly, but the Ancient Kingdom, the least liked and trusted of the Five Kingdoms of Medeis, hadn't even seen one of those in just as long.

Almost two hours later, Gabriel was happy to hear that Heretia was going to be okay. With a sigh of relief, he flew back out of the Castle using his Death magic to launch him into the skies. He squinted and saw Theo riding in the distance with Mia's parents in tow.

"Good," Gabriel muttered to himself. "Idiot finally got his wits about him and headed back. Mia's parents need medical help too now that we finally have them."

Clarisse and Daryl Wardman, the banished Princess of Suravia and her Pair, had been captured by Michelo some weeks prior. They were the catalyst to this whole debacle. When they had realized they were pregnant, and that Mia was a Druid, they had prayed to the Mother Goddess for help. Gabriel, the magic of Death, had answered.

He had granted Mia not only Death magic, but himself completely, in hopes that she was the reincarnation of the last Druid, Meloni, whom he had loved so much that he had been willing to give up immortality. By the time he realized how wrong he had been, it was too late. Clarisse and Daryl had panicked and left Medeis altogether for the Original World, known as Earth to the mortals who inhabited it. There, they had raised their only daughter in peace and ignorance, never once telling her where they were from or who she was. An ill planned decision, it turned out to be, because the trouble they had so desperately tried to protect her from had inevitably found them. In haste, Daryl had shoved poor magicless Mia through the same portal they had used over twenty years prior and dumped her into Medeis.

Gabriel had been with Mia, throughout her life, a constant presence inside of her soul, but he also had made a fatal mistake early on as well. Not wanting Mia to be found either, he had locked away all of her magic from the time she was young, making Mia and her parents believe she was magicless. It wasn't until Michelo showed up and kidnapped the two parents that horrible night that Gabriel, as the Death magic, had seen the error in his ways.

Mia had to struggle to unlock her unused magic time and again. It was only in fits of uncontrolled emotion that she had been able to peel away. Layer by layer, she had grown more powerful, Gabriel didn't even think she understood how much magic she wielded. But she had been mastering it beautifully, until today.

After a journey across the Ancient Kingdom to speak with the Mother Goddess, something that only Mia and Gabriel could do, they had come home to a letter from Michelo, and the piece of Daryl's body to go along with it as a threat. In her fear and haste, Mia had given herself up in exchange for them.

Gabriel thought again as he came closer to the threesome still wandering in the desert to fly someone back first. He hoped that for the time being, Michelo would be so enamored with having Amelia in his clutches, that Gabriel could formulate a plan.

"Who needs to get back next?" Gabriel called out as he hovered over the riders, all silent in their sorrow.

"Take Clarisse," Daryl Wardman finally croaked out. His once fluffy, bright white hair was now limp and dirty, with sand and mud caked onto his head.

"No! Take Daryl, he's the one badly hurt!" Clarisse countered. She pointed to the dirty rag unceremoniously wrapped around Daryl's injured and missing finger. Gabriel nodded at Clarisse and swooped down to grab his cargo.

Daryl spluttered against the movement and reached back for Clarisse who shouted back to him, "Go get fixed! I'm coming, I'm right behind you!"

She kicked her horse into a faster pace, leaving Theo behind before he realized what was happening and spurred his into movement, too.

Gabriel didn't fly as fast with Daryl as he had earlier with Heretia. Daryl wasn't in any immediate danger, but his hand did need tending to. Mother only knew how long ago the finger had been removed and infection was a terrible possibility.

"You should have taken Clarisse!" Daryl protested loudly, but Gabriel just rolled his eyes. He understood the concern all too well. It was the Pair bond that everyone who shared felt. Pair bonds were rare; only about ten in a whole generation would ever have one, and so far, Gabriel was now facing his third set since becoming a part of Mia and leaving Medeis.

First had been Clarisse and Daryl themselves. It was a quiet, simple, and easy flowing type of love they shared. Gabriel had seen it through Mia's eyes growing up, so his concern for her parents was not all manufactured.

Then came Mia and Theo's, which Gabriel had not seen coming. Lastly, and most recent, was that of Heretia's Captain of the Guard, Jeremy, and the lovely, yet high spirited and impish, Wyndetta Lily, lovingly known as Wynnie. That one had knocked his socks off. Wynnie had hated Jeremy from the moment they met, an instant signal to Mia that something was up. She refused to go near him, speak to him, or touch him. When Mia, ever the fixer, had confronted her about it, Wynnie had admitted she didn't know what it was, but it was different, and she didn't like it.

Mia had begged Wynnie to just hang in there and deal with it until the war ended. Then she would never see the man again. Wynnie had agreed, after assuring nothing inappropriate had happened to make her feel that way. Jeremy was gallantry personified. Then, unforeseen by everyone, Wynnie and Jeremy had finally touched hands during the journey to see the Mother Goddess, and the Pairing became known.

Gabriel had enjoyed watching the drama unfold as Wynnie battled the Pairing and Jeremy yearned for her. It was like one of those mortal soap operas that Clarisse used to watch when Mia was a baby and she didn't think anyone was looking. Finally, Wynnie had accepted the Pairing. It only took her almost dying to do it, but there it was.

To admit that he was jealous of such a thing was a bit of an understatement. Gabriel was now going through his second life in

5

human form with the woman he loved more than life itself, and they weren't Paired. First it was with Meloni, a long and happy life. Now it was Heretia, Meloni's reincarnation, but at least this time Heretia had been promised eternal life, though not immortality. It was one of the things the Mother Goddess put in place over and over to make sure the balance was never upset. So, it seemed that while Heretia would stay her age forever, she could be killed, a fact that Gabriel was not thrilled about as he carried the injured man into another room and called an Earth Sorcerer in.

When the woman came running into the room panting, Gabriel pointed at Daryl. "This man is the father of the Druid. He has been mutilated and needs assistance. He is an Earth Sorcerer himself, so I figured between you and some healers, you all could get him taken care of. The Druid's mother will be here shortly, as will Theo."

The witch nodded quickly, her eyes bulging with excitement at getting to care for the father of the Druid. Gabriel stood to leave, but stopped just as he walked by her. "Anything happens to him, you will deal with me first, and then the Druid," he warned.

No matter how distant he tried to be from some things, he had been living with this man in a way for over twenty years. He liked Daryl, and he meant his word to the witch. If the pain of losing Daryl didn't kill Mia first, after all she had been through, she would make sure she found a way to kill an immortal magic herself.

Gabriel rushed to settle back in at Heretia's side now that everyone with pressing medical needs were attended to. Upon entering, they all bowed away from the still motionless figure.

"We need the Druid to finish our work," one woman mentioned quietly.

"Where is she?" another of the women asked.

Gabriel didn't know exactly what to say. Did he say she'd been captured? That she'd leveraged herself? Did he say that she was gone? Squaring himself against the loss of hope he wanted to feel, he looked the witch straight in the eye and commanded, "Finish doing what you can for your Queen and only worry about her right now. I want someone with her at all times if I can't be. Prince Theodeus will be here soon with the Druid's mother. Her father is already in the castle and wounded greatly as well."

He knew it didn't answer anything. In fact, it may have just made everyone even more worried, but he had nothing else for them. A few minutes later, with Gabriel still next to the unconscious Heretia, Theo came running in.

"We need to talk, now!" he shouted.

Gabriel's mood darkened at the demanding tone. "You need to lower your voice and cool your temper, young man. You are in the sick room of a High Queen," Gabriel growled in response. Yet he rose from his seat and stormed out into the hallway.

Theo rounded on him as soon as the door was shut.

"We left her!" he shouted, throwing his hands in the air.

Gabriel hissed through his teeth and gripped the idiot's arm, yanking him to Heretia's private study, and slammed the door.

"Are you trying to cause a massive panic throughout the entire castle!" Gabriel roared to the dark-haired, green-eyed fool.

Theo crossed his arms and widened his stance. "If that's what it takes to get someone to go back with me and rescue my Pair! I'm only doing what you would do if it were Heretia!"

Gabriel picked up a chair and in a fit of uncontrolled anger, slammed it against the wall. It shattered into a thousand wooden pieces that rained throughout the room.

"Do you think I don't know that? Do you think I knew what she was planning to do? Obviously, Mia had known this was going to happen and she chose this route," Gabriel thundered.

He paced back and forth, anger emitting from every pore in his body. Yes, he was worried about Heretia, insurmountably so, but he hadn't forgotten what was really at stake in the long run with Mia's actions. He knew that their best chance at squashing the Second Uprising had just willingly offered herself as a hostage and possible sacrifice to the enemy. Without Mia in the battle, they were doomed. He let Theo know his thoughts about this as well.

"Then we go get her," Theo answered slowly, repeating himself for what felt like to Gabriel the one hundredth time.

"We can't Theo. You saw those wards! He's concocted some bastardized version of natural elemental magic with that damn amulet of mine, and no one, not even I, can get through it," Gabriel sighed.

He slumped into a chair and grabbed his hair tightly. Maybe if he yanked them out by the strands hard enough, the pain in his head and heart would go away. It was his go-to method of getting through a raging headache caused by his human condition. It had been so much easier to just be an element of magic where there were no emotions;

just work and his power. There was silence in the library as both men tried hard to find a light at the end of this seemingly hopeless tunnel.

"Heretia got through," Theo suddenly whispered from his seat.

Gabriel looked up from his hands and gave the other man a blank stare of surprise. Theo kept going, not even looking at Gabriel as the thoughts came flooding back to him.

"For a moment there she got through. You saw it, even Michelo was shocked. Something about her blood magic was strong enough," Theo mused.

Gabriel remembered the momentary sight of Heretia breaking through the ward that surrounded the Second Uprising camp before Michelo flew to sink the blade into her shoulder and shoved her back. She had been able to do it.

"You're right. Her blood magic did get through. Whatever Michelo is using must be a form of blood magic. He had to have seen Heretia use some while he was living here in Purge all that time and figured it out by himself. We just need to decipher what spell it is and maybe we can break it," Gabriel's mind began to spin with ideas.

Gabriel stood up and moved to open the door, his heart racing with excitement. They had a way to rescue Mia! He was beaten to the door by a messenger stumbling through from the other side.

"Sirs!" he panted and leaned against the knob. Gabriel's heart skipped a beat. Was it Heretia? Daryl? Mia?! The last thought gave him some hope that maybe there was news about her sudden escape and she was already coming back.

"The initial envoys from the other Kingdoms are at the gates. Elevetia, Maravette, and Lotho. There is also news that the armies of all four kingdoms are making their way here. Even Suravia is finishing gathering its troops for departure to our borders."

While this was fantastic news, it was also troubling. These envoys were here to see the Druid, as she was the one who had called for them and they had quickly Transported in to see her themselves.

"This is moving faster than I expected. I guess Wynnie, Tim and Will didn't need to convince them much," Theo mused.

Mia had only sent the three Elite Guardsmen away to their respective countries as proof of Heretia's good will the previous afternoon. The High Queen's past had been one hidden in mystery, and the rest of Medeis and its four other kingdoms had always considered her mad and evil. It wasn't until Mia had come to the

Ancient Kingdom for herself that the truth revealed that Heretia was not only completely sane, but she was the only line of defense left standing against the Second Uprising that had been amassing.

"What do we tell everyone about Mia?" Theo asked as the two men made their way towards the Throne Room. Not having the Druid that summoned them was not going to go well with the envoys, nor their High Rulers themselves. "And what do we tell them about Heretia?"

Gabriel grew dark for a moment. What indeed? For so long it seemed the two women who were unable to be present had held everything together, and now it was up to them to keep it going. Theo and Gabriel. A Prince and Death himself. What would they tell them all?

"We tell them the truth," Gabriel finally replied.

CHAPTER TWO

THEO

Captain Jeremy was waiting for them as they entered the Throne Room. The cool and gallant demeanor the two men were used to in the typically well put together captain was suddenly gone. As soon as they opened the door, he swooped down upon them in a seemingly blind panic and grabbed Gabriel by his shoulders.

"Where is Her Majesty? What has happened?" he frantically asked, slightly shaking Gabriel.

Gabriel, who wasn't a huge fan of being touched to begin with, shoved the man's hands off of him and took a step back.

"She is with the healers now. They assure me that she will recover, but she hasn't woken up yet. There was an incident when we met with Michelo to obtain the Druids parents." Gabriel looked down on the ground and sucked in a breath. It was time that the rest of the world knew.

"The Druid is now a willing hostage of the Second Uprising in exchange for her parents safe return, which has occurred. The High Queen was attacked during the exchange and was struck with a blade in the shoulder."

Jeremy's face paled. "So," he started, and then stopped. His face slowly turned from white to red as the realization of what was going to happen next sunk in. With a tremendous shout, he yanked his glove off his hand and threw it on the ground.

"I *knew* I should have gone with you! Her Majesty wouldn't tell me exactly what you four were doing out in the desert, but I knew deep down something was wrong." He kicked the glove across the Throne Room.

"This is all my fault. All these years I have been so hypervigilant on her safety and that of this city and when I'm needed most, I'm not there because I'm some lovesick puppy over my Pair being gone for a day." He hung his head in shame and buried his fist in it.

"I was being stupid and decided to distract myself with preparations that I didn't even think twice when she asked for those horses."

Theo made a move forward with both hands out, attempting to calm the raging man.

"Listen, we get it Jeremy. We are not thrilled about this either. My Pair is a hostage in the enemy camp, the closest thing Gabriel will ever have to a Pair is lying unconscious in her bedroom surrounded by blood and healers, and the envoys from the other kingdoms are gathering at the gate. On top of that, we still have Mia's parents to deal with and get Daryl healed."

Jeremy's ears perked up at this. "Mia's parents? Why are they here?"

Theo looked to Gabriel for direction. "Did Heretia really tell you nothing when she asked for the horses?" Gabriel asked cautiously.

"All she asked for was four horses and that they be ready for the desert. She mentioned something about scouting and that I was fine to carry on my work getting ready for the other kingdoms to arrive," Jeremy recalled.

All three men went silent.

"You may want to sit down then," Theo sighed. He motioned to the steps leading up the dais. Three wooden Earthen chairs appeared, and all three men sat down heavily.

"A messenger box came last night and all that was in it was a severed finger and a message from Michelo to meet if Mia wanted her parents back," Gabriel started. Jeremy didn't even flinch at the beginning statement, leading Gabriel to believe that the man had seen enough evil in his life living amongst the Cannibals in this city that a severed finger wasn't new to him.

"The finger was Mia's fathers, Daryl. She lost control and sent that pillar of magic into the sky last night in response to Michelo. I'm beginning to believe, however, that it was a distraction for us so that we couldn't realize her real thoughts. Mia went headfirst into that meeting ready to give herself up with the idea that it would get her parents back. Michelo took the offer, and in the struggle, Heretia was attacked with a sword through the shoulder. This all happened about two hours ago and now we've got the other kingdoms lining up at the gate asking to be let in to see the exact two women who we either don't have or can't move right now."

Jeremy looked over at the grand doors to the Throne Room, the same doors that Theo had barged in through less than two weeks prior. He had come with intentions of rescuing Mia, but had learned quickly that she was there on her own account and wanted to stay. Theo thought back to the feelings of relief when she had run to him with her arms outstretched. She had looked like an angel in the white kaftan as she descended upon him with tears of joy. Now she was gone, and he had no way of knowing if he was ever going to see her again. He wanted to take up his swords and rush back to the Second Uprising camp. He wanted to storm its wards like he had the city of Purge, but it seemed impossible. Mia had handed herself over, so what did that mean for him? Was he supposed to just let it happen? Was he to wait? Or was he meant to be actively planning a way to get her back? Theo groaned roughly. This was Wynnie's domain, not his. They would just have to wait for Wynnie to return with the High Rulers from Maravette, her home kingdom, before any move could be made to secure Mia and get her back to their side of the upcoming battle.

Jeremy was suddenly up on his feet. "Seems to me, we need to just keep going for now," he announced and called for a guard to come forward.

The young man was familiar to both Gabriel and Theo, but they couldn't remember his name.

"Reggie, escort the envoys from the other kingdoms straight to the Throne Room. We will meet them here and explain everything," Jeremy commanded.

Reggie nodded and raced off out the doors towards the city gates. It would be a while before he could get every emissary into the Castle and settled.

"Let's get ready. This isn't going to be pretty, but maybe they will stay long enough to listen to us before giving up and going back home," Jeremy barked.

He turned and shouted orders to servants and others to bring in chairs and tables, enough for the visitors and anyone they had brought with them. One scout announced that the three kingdoms present had sent around nine people total for the meeting, including a few of the High Rulers themselves.

"Relay this information to the maids and footmen and ready a room for each one. If we can't give them the Queen and Druid directly, we can at least give them that type of treatment. Maybe it will be enough for them to hang around until we can get this mess figured out," Gabriel nodded, before grabbing Theo's arm. "We need to go check on Daryl and Clarisse. We're going to need them as a sign of goodwill."

Theo agreed, and together they headed toward the room Gabriel had left Daryl with the Earth witch. Gabriel knocked lightly before opening the door and smiled when he saw Daryl sitting up with Clarisse by his side.

"You look much better, sir," Gabriel commented before giving a small bow of his head to Clarisse. The older woman was still a Princess of Suravia after all.

"Where is my daughter? Where is Mia?" Clarisse asked hurriedly, ignoring the gesture. The color hadn't returned to her face yet and the damage of over a month worth of captivity was showing. Her hair was messy and dull, her skin sunken in and her pallor sickly.

"We're going to get her back, Clarisse. I promise you that," Gabriel reached out to comfort the small, beautiful woman. Her eyes widened as she looked him over fully for the first time.

"Who are you? How are you involved in all of this?" she questioned.

Daryl sat up further in his bed. "He has to be a friend of Mia's, dear. Otherwise, he wouldn't have helped us get back here." He tried to reason, but Clarisse shook her brown head again.

"No. I don't know these men and I don't like this anymore. Ever since we were forced back to Medeis, everything has seemed off. First, the Cannibals. Then Mia feels different, and she does something so stupid and irrational. Now these two men are here, and everything feels wrong," she said tearfully.

Theo could see Gabriel's heart breaking.

"Princess," he began, causing Clarisse to suck in a quick breath at the title. "I am Theodeus Varillian. You've known me since I was born. I believe I am the Prince you sent your daughter to find, and she did."

Daryl's face softened.

14

"Almost immediately, I might add," Theo said. He scratched at the back of his head, the memory of his and Mia's first tense meeting in the forest of Suravia still so real in his mind. "She is my Pair and we have worked very hard to rescue the two of you from Michelo."

Clarisse still wasn't having any of it.

"So, you knew she was going to do that? You knew she was going to give herself up for us?" she accused, but Theo shook his head.

"No," he continued calmly. "We didn't. No one but Mia knew she was going to pull that move on us. In fact, if I had known she was, I would have forbidden it. I don't presume to tell Mia what to do in anything, but that I would have gone down fighting over."

Daryl seemed to understand, but Clarisse still held back. She moved to return to her seat next to her husband.

"While it is good to see you again, Theo, you've got to understand our view in this whole mess. We were happy with our Mia back in the Original World, away from all of this, doing our best to protect her. Now we've been held hostage, my husband mutilated, and our daughter has thrown herself into the same situation we have been in. To say we aren't happy with this is an understatement," she breathed. She looked down at her husband's arm and stroked it gently as she spoke.

"I can understand that Your Highness, but" Theo began, Clarisses' gaze snapped up at hearing the title spoken for the second time.

"Don't call me that. I haven't been that since I gave up this life and this world to protect my daughter." She cut Theo off abruptly.

"I'm not sure you understand what we went through back on Earth to do that, to hide Mia and protect her from Heretia. The same woman, who by the way don't think I didn't notice, is the same one who was stabbed by Michelo as he took my daughter away. Someone want to explain to me what's going on there?" Clarisse demanded. She planted her hands on her hips and Theo witnessed Gabriel fighting back a smile.

"There's a lot we need to explain, Clarisse. Maybe I should start from the beginning, and then I'll let Gabriel jump in for the rest. Well, at least the part where his physical body shows up," Theo smirked and gave Gabriel an accusatory glance, which left both Clarisse and Daryl even more confused.

An entire hour went by before finally both men felt like they had explained everything carefully. It was good practice for when the envoys were ready to hear it as well. Clarisse and Daryl had only interrupted once or twice for small questions that were quickly answered with the story. They both sat quiet and drank it all in.

"Mia sounds as if she has been very brave," Daryl finally spoke, reaching to take his wife's hand and squeezing it.

Theo nodded solemnly, agreeing with him. She had been that for sure. Not just when she had given herself over as a hostage but since the moment she had fallen through the portal.

"So, what do we do next?" Clarisse had certainly cooled her temper during the narration and was back to her normal calm and practical self.

"Next, we meet with the envoys from the other kingdoms that are almost here. We should be getting back. We have to tell them all of this as well and just hope they accept the explanation as well as you have," Gabriel concluded.

With a grunt, Daryl swung his feet over the side of the bed. "Sounds like you need us in that regard," he winced. He found his footing.

Shoes were quickly slipped onto his bony feet. The two of them had already changed into decent clothing. A simple shirt tucked into cloth pants for Daryl, so as to keep him comfortable. Clarisse had been given a camel-colored kaftan that reached to the floor and opened at the sides to allow for cooling air. Daryl's finger wasn't able to be reattached. Not even the Druid could have accomplished that after all the time it had been removed, but the Earth Sorcerer and healer had closed the wound with stitches for now and cleaned it. Even with all of this nursing, Theo still worried that it was too much too soon. They weren't aware yet of the extent of starvation and mistreatment the Pair had been through on behalf of their daughter.

"No, you need to rest. You two have been through a lot and you need to recover," Theo cautioned.

"Nonsense," Daryl waved him away. "The fastest way to end this whole thing and see my daughter home is to get involved and make sure the other kingdoms commit to helping. From what you tell me, Suravia will have no choice but to commit because we are safe. Lotho will join for sure. Elevetia will take a bit of convincing, but those Fire hearts will eat up war if given the chance, so they will only pretend to hold out. It's Maravette we're going to have to work on, and you'll need me for that. I still have some family over there, and I'm sure they will want to hear from me if they can."

Theo wrinkled his brow over his green eyes. "Family? Mia never mentioned family in Maravette."

Daryl waved him away again. "It's really my mother's family. My father died when I was young, and they didn't approve of her marriage, so they didn't talk to her. We made it our own way, with my mother working as a librarian for the Royal Family. She wasn't the most accomplished witch, but she could move books around with Air magic that were high above her head. It was good enough to keep a job and food on the table," Daryl explained and reached for his wife. They turned to head out of the door, arm in arm. "About once a year I'd get to go see my cousins, but they were always too rich and uppity for my blood. The connection may come in handy now, however. I bet that old bastard cousin of mine has even more money than I remember."

Gabriel and Theo looked at each other as they walked down the hallway. It was like watching two light bulbs slowly flicker to life as what the wounded man was saying started to become clear.

"You don't think," Theo started to ask, pointing at Daryl and Clarisse's back. "There's no way!" He was too stunned in his thoughts to finish the sentence yet again. Both men ran to catch up with the mysterious Pair in front of them.

"What was your mother's maiden name?" Gabriel called out.

Daryl didn't even turn around as he answered the name that stopped both men in their tracks. "Lily!"

CHAPTER THREE

MIA

I was led by both arms into a dirty tent staked into the sandy ground. I tried to pull away but the Cannibals, though seemingly weakened in their state, held their grip firm. The wards all around the camp seemed to be draining not only my physical strength, but my magic as well. I felt as if my magic was wading through a swamp of mud to surface. In an effort to conserve what I had, I pulled back, forcing it to be still.

Michelo and Gregor both had gone ahead of me into the tent and were standing around a long table with no chairs in sight as the flap was pulled back. Nothing else seemed to be present so I was quite stunned when out from under the table Gregor pulled two sets of heavy iron chains. The Cannibals moved me closer to the ugly aged man with breath like the dead. I flinched away when he snorted a sickly laugh, clapped the chains onto my wrists, and bent to do the same to my ankles.

"Now that I have your undivided attention, Druid. We can speak more candidly," Michelo began.

He walked around the table to take up the space that Gregor was limping away from in front of me. I pulled at the chains to lightly test their strength, but they were firmly bolted to the table and it was certainly heavier than it looked.

"What in Medeis could you possibly have to say to me?" I hissed between my teeth, trying not to let my anger show and failing miserably.

Michelo chuckled as he traced his finger amongst the swirls of the wood. It was an absent-minded movement, but one that made Michelo seem all the more predatory as he stepped into my personal space. I moved to back away from him, but the chains were tight, and I could only manage turning my body away in the end.

"I have quite a lot to say, but that can be for another time. For right now I just want to lay down some ground rules for you during your extended stay with us," he offered.

I grunted through my nose, the only type of response I would deign to give him.

"First, no magic from you. I have magic of my own design set up to where you will, over time, be weakened to the point of a human. Saving your magic won't help, like you're trying to do now," he pointed out.

I hid my surprise at his statement concerning my reservation of magic. I remembered that he had been able to not only see it, like I could, but had also been able to touch it. The feeling had been horrible, and the memory almost made me shiver. Another person, other than Theo, touching my magic and then strangling it was enough to make me sick.

"Second," he continued. "If you do try and use any before it is gone, I will snuff it out completely. Lastly, and certainly not least, there will be no escaping. No one can get through my wards, and no one is coming to help you."

He snatched my arm and I struggled against him, but his grip held firm. His hands were like vices as they tightened around my slim appendage. Though I had grown stronger during my time here in Medeis between training with Wynnie and Heretia, it was nowhere near enough to take on a powerhouse of a man such as Michelo.

"You will die here, Druid. Get that through your head now. There will be no Mother Goddess to save you and no portals like last time," he advised.

I hardened my resolve and stared back into his icy blue gaze. The scar that ran down his face was atrocious and had obviously been self-healed. No half-decent Life wielder would have left a scar so mutilating on what seemed to be a once handsome face.

"You mistake me as someone to be intimidated, Michelo. You forget that while you may have an amulet that has Death magic and you may wield some aborted version of magic, I am still the Druid. I

20

was born and sent by the Mother Goddess specifically because of you and this shit show you call a Second Uprising. So, get this through your head," I spit his words venomously back at him. "You have a chance to end this now and let me go, or, when I do get free of here, there will be hell to pay."

I took a huge chance and stepped into his personal space. I was done being afraid and intimidated by this man, but Michelo only chuckled.

"Spirit. I like it. I was a little worried when I saw the look of pure terror on your face the first time I saw you. I thought you would make this too easy and take the fun out of it, but I am happy to report I was wrong. You, little Druid, are going to be a lot of fun," he grinned.

On those last words, he shoved me away from him, causing me to stumble over the chains wrapped around my ankles.

"Rest up now, because I will be back later," he called over his shoulder as he and the giggling Gregor left the tent, leaving me alone.

As soon as the flap was back in place, I began to scramble against the chains, pouring any type of magic into it that I had but it only got harder to reach out as I tried again in vain. After a few more minutes of physical struggling, I realized that it was useless. I assumed there was at least one Cannibal guard in front of the tent who would immediately alert either Michelo or Gregor if I started crying out or making too much noise, so I remained silent as I took in my surroundings.

It was completely empty, save for the singular heavy wooden table that I was chained to. There were no chairs, nor other smaller tables with anything on them that I might be able to use. The ground was sand beneath me, no flooring or covering in sight. I could hear the sounds of the camp around me. It was much like the one that had been in the Forest. Repetitive and futile. They were all just mindless Cannibals performing menial tasks to keep from going completely weak, but the tasks had no purpose or end in sight. With the sun still high in the sky, I could catch a glimpse of shadows at certain intervals. I tried to keep track of the movements, hoping I could find a pattern to exploit, but there was none that my untrained eye could see from this standpoint.

I stood back up and began to pace back and forth, attempting to calm myself down. My magic was even slower now. I had to find a way to keep it strong, even with all this broken and disgusting magic

21

weighing it down. I took a moment to study what Michelo claimed to have created and it felt so wrong to me. It was greasy, contrived, and unnatural. Even when Heretia had performed Blood magic, it felt better to me than this. I reached deeper into it and discovered it did feel slightly similar to hers, but it was so altered and grotesque that I couldn't keep sifting through it.

At some point in his stint under her rule, Michelo must have realized that Heretia was magicless, save for the ability to wield a very ancient form of Blood magic that was present even before the elements had given themselves up to the witches and become part of them. All except Death of course, who had made the decision to stay its own entity and not grant its gifts to mortals and witches. That Death magic had eventually found a companion it was willing to sacrifice its immortality for in the last Druid, Meloni.

That magic was now Gabriel, the human incarnation of Death. He still wielded all of his Death power, but in a more limited and human capacity. At Meloni's own death, he had reverted to the Death magic again and wiled away until she was reborn as Heretia.

Unfortunately, Death had mistaken my birth as that of the reincarnation of Meloni and attached itself to me, granting me Death magic, but also subduing my own power up until the point where I returned to Medeis that horrible night Michelo had kidnapped my parents.

When I had finally made my way to the Ancient Kingdom, where Heretia was the sole High Queen, she had been able to return him to his human form and they had been reunited. I, however, had been stunned to learn that it was Gabriel making me feel inferior my entire life, thinking I was magicless. Fortunately, we were past that and he had become one of my closest allies. Gabriel had been there when I offered myself as payment for my parents and had joined in the desperate attempt to stop me.

I hung my head in shame. I felt horrible for not telling anyone what I had planned to do. But it had been Gabriel himself who had counseled me that one day, as the Druid, I would have to make a tough decision that would alter the course of this war. Whether this choice had been right or wrong, it was what I had chosen. Now I had to find my way out before it was too late.

As I continued to think through my situation, the tent flap reopened and Gregor hobbled in, barely holding on to a tray that he was carrying now. I raised my eyebrow, curious as to what they would feed me here. As he gently set it down, my curiosity turned into horror. It wasn't food that rested on the tray, but one neat little row of vials, all filled with different liquids I couldn't identify off hand. I was never particularly good at potions and hadn't even begun to learn while I was in Lotho or Purge. I didn't want to hazard a guess at what Gregor was going to try with those, so I remained silent until he spoke first.

"I've been working on some new magic that incorporates what Michelo has started here. I was extremely intrigued when he proffered me the position of his Master Magician," he wheezed, after setting the seemingly light tray down on the table.

"I always wanted to be free of the constraints of known magic, and with Michelo's guidance and knowledge, I certainly have been set free of MY chains." He annunciated the second to last word while making a knowing face at the chains clapped firmly around my own wrists.

"These are some of the most recent concoctions I have come up with," He waved his hand to signal the vials before us.

"I'm testing a theory that a witch can change their magic gifted to them with the right ingredients." I paled at what he was trying to unfold before me, and my breath caught in my throat. "Mother no," I whispered. I returned my gaze to the five bottles before me, their varying colors suddenly evident: White, Blue, Red, Green, and Yellow.

"But first," he lifted his crooked finger for attention. "I need to find a way to harness that actual magic from a witch that wields it so I can give it to another."

My heart began to hammer in my chest as the realization of what he was going to do became clear. I thrashed around in my chains, blasting them with spell after spell to get them loose. I had made a horrible mistake in coming here. I had been given one chance to do the right thing for Medeis, and this wasn't it.

Gregor clucked his tongue and wagged the gnarled finger that was still raised.

"I would stop trying if I were you, Druid," he crooned and lifted the red vial, Fire, from the tray.

"You're going to want all your strength. Luckily, while the wards on the camp may dampen your magic, it doesn't weaken it within you. Which is great for my experiments because it gives me full license to do what I need without risk of being hurt, or without risking losing the magic altogether before I take it from you."

I dropped to the ground as he rounded the table with the red vial and began kicking at the legs, hoping to break it loose. Panic was welling up inside of me.

"This isn't right! You can't change a magic gifted by the Mother Goddess!" I shouted vehemently, still lashing out with everything I had. "It will destroy the witch, you know this, so why try?" I grunted heavier against the kicks, throwing as much weight as possible into them.

"That's what the Mother Goddess wants us to believe," Gregor chimed and uncorked the bottle.

Wisps of red smoke flew up from the neck.

"It's true! Witches have tried in the past and failed miserably, losing not only their magic, but their minds in the process. It tears them apart from the inside and they become vegetables," I screamed.

I thought back to what Wynnie had told me of her cousin, Remus, who had denied his Water magic at the Rite and now was basically a shell of a person, never fully whole and never able to wield any magic. I was horrified at what this experiment of Gregor's might do to me in this process. I knew it would fail, but to what extent? Was I going to lose my mind as well as my power, too? Gregor just smiled as he saw the thoughts and fears dancing across my face.

"We can only hope that you, being the Druid, are strong enough to survive these trials. I will have my bottled magic, little girl. So, hold still and let me work," he said icily.

He reached forward with the vial, but in a last-ditch effort, I stood up and reached for the tray myself, attempting to hit him with it. Instead of fully grabbing it, however, I just knocked it over, and all the vials, along with the silver tray, fell with a muted thud on the sand below. For a moment, I thought I had made a good move, destroying Gregor's precious vials, but as we both looked over the edge of the table, my heart sank. All four vials were still intact and unharmed on the bedding of sand beneath them. The tray was now well out of my shackled reach and I was out of options.

Gregor moved again, but I struck out, trying to spill the red liquid before he could get it inside of me. Gregor was faster than I expected, however, and snatched it back.

"Guards!" he shouted over my shoulder, and my stomach turned to liquid as two Cannibals came barreling in and reached to subdue me. They forcefully shoved me to the ground and one of them pried my mouth wide open for Gregor to pour the contents of the red vial down my throat. I gagged against its bitter and burning taste.

"Keep fighting, Druid. You will need your heart racing for it to work effectively. Fear is a fantastic emotion that guides almost everything else in our bodies. It causes our heart to beat, our breath to quicken, and magic to work faster," he laughed.

He muttered almost as if to himself as he hovered over me and waited for the last drop to fall. The Cannibals didn't release me until I swallowed every ounce of it. It didn't take long before Gregor pulled them back to stand on either side of me. I scrambled to my knees, gagged slightly against the taste, and waited.

At first, nothing was happening. It was just a useless, horrible liquid that was sitting vilely on my stomach. I looked up at Gregor, panting from the strain of my fight. I was shocked to find him grinning like a wild man, the feral delight evident in his gaze. I opened my mouth, planning on giving Gregor some nasty retort, letting him know that he hadn't accomplished anything except pissing me off. As I sucked in my first breath to say the words, the screaming began.

CHAPTER FOUR

THEO

To say that Theo was stunned into complete silence as he continued to gaze upon his Pair's ever astonishing parents would be an understatement. Never in another thousand years would he have guessed that the fluffy white-haired man with the bronze skin and wizened bright blue eyes was a Lily. He was too kind, too loving, and earthly. Absent was the money hungry, scheming, and power mad traits that seemed to be embedded into every Lily he had ever known, excluding Wynnie of course. Wyndetta Lily had run away from her family only a few years prior and had begged to join the Elite Guard as a means to get away from the life that had always plagued her with sorrow and insecurity. It still did, as evident by her borderline alcoholism.

Wynnie's only and recent hope had come in the form of her newly found Pairing with the dashing and ever sturdy Captain of Heretia's Guard, Jeremy. Wynnie had fought the pull of the Pair Bond at first, but after a horrible run in with a Wild Beast, she had finally accepted it, and happiness still radiated off her in waves. Jeremy was accepting of Wynnie, her talents for stealth, and her terrible temper and rakish tongue. He found it endearing after his own sorrow filled life within the walls of a city, cut off from the outside world and filled with death, despair, and hopeless Cannibals. Theo still grimaced at the idea of a Wynnie that could be found sweet and charming, but Jeremy saw that in her and who was he to judge?

Other's would claim he was crazy for being madly in love with a fledgling Druid who could possibly be a ticking time bomb, in a relationship that would forever put her life in danger and his heart in jeopardy of being crushed. Just like it was now, but the Mother Goddess chose how she chose, and he wasn't going to fight it. Mia had been the best thing to come into his life after dealing with the repressive and exhaustive life of perfection demanded of him by his father. He had, like Wynnie, attempted to escape it as well by running off and joining the Elite Guard, but even that hadn't fulfilled him.

It wasn't until Mia had fallen through the mirror on top of that hill in the Suravian forest that day that he had finally felt whole. It had shocked him at first. He had even fought it a little, too, unsure of what he was feeling and why, but after Mia was almost killed in the garden at the High Castle, he decided he was done fighting it. He had fallen head over heels in love with the woman the Mother Goddess had chosen especially for him and never looked back.

Now here he was, in a strange kingdom he had been raised to fear, standing next to a man who wasn't supposed to exist, getting ready to convince the High Rulers from all the other Kingdoms to join him in a battle that could destroy this world, all for that same woman.

Such was life. He gazed towards the doors that were about to be opened to a group of people that were now his job to convince to stay and fight. The noise was growing, evident even through the thick wood that separated the wave of people from Theo, Gabriel, Clarisse, Daryl, and Jeremy. All five stood at the foot of Heretia's dais, no one daring to ascend it without her present.

"Alright everyone. Shoulders up and chin out. It's time to let in the hounds," Gabriel directed with a small grin across his face.

Gabriel, ever the comedic relief, found his job to be particularly important at these most inappropriate times. Theo rolled his green eyes in slight disgust. However, he did as told and widened his stance against the onslaught that was approaching. Jeremy waved his hand, directing the two guards waiting at the door, spears in hand, to open the doors for the envoys waiting on the other side.

Silent on their hinges, despite their massive size, the doors were thrown aside to reveal a group of nine people all staring in awe at their surroundings. The fear and anticipation amongst the crowd was evident. No one moved at first. Finally, one figure broke from the crowd and approached Theo swiftly, a hand of greeting out for him and a smile on his large and handsome face.

"Theo!" Thomas boomed throughout the Throne Room, his voice bouncing off the rafters.

Theo's face broke out into a huge smile as he moved to greet the man halfway. The High King's sweet petite new wife, Alyssa, trailed right behind him. Her own smile was just as bright and inviting as her husband's. The men met with a loud clap of palms and Thomas pulled Theo in for a quick hug before releasing him to greet Alyssa with a deeper, yet much gentler hug.

The other seven emissaries began to trickle in behind the happy threesome. Theo led them all forward to exchange greetings. However, as with every large gathering, there was always one in every crowd.

"Where is the Druid? Where is the High Queen Heretia?" a demanding little man from Elevetia, the fire kingdom, shouted above the noise of introductions and pleasantries.

Clarisse, who was hugging a woman she had known years ago from Maravette, looked around to see who the interloper on the tepid level of peace was. The crowd began to grow anxious once more and she stepped forward to take control.

"Ladies and Gentlemen!" she called above the group, raising her hands for attention. "If everyone could please be seated, everything will be explained."

Theo took charge of guiding those from Lotho to the chairs set up for them in the middle, Clarisse moved to help those from Maravette, and Gabriel attempted to assist the few delegates from Elevetia as well, but the small man wasn't done.

"We are here at the request of the Druid. Not some hodgepodge group of witches from Mother only knows where. Where is she? Where is Heretia, this suddenly benevolent High Queen who has loomed over our borders for decades and terrorized our people?" he shouted.

Gabriel bristled at the attack on Heretia's character, but thought better of it and just walked away instead. It was Thomas who spoke first.

"We came here to hear them out, not attack anyone, Gilroy. Why don't you give them a chance before you burst your panties into flames?"

A small chuckle from a few of the guests could be heard throughout the large room. The small man frowned, and his ears turned red at the light insult.

"Be that as it may, shouldn't the all-powerful Druid and Queen have greeted us? They are the ones who demanded out presence. They are the ones who sent our own people to talk us into this and raise our armies," he countered. He sat in the nearest chair and placed himself next to a particularly lovely young red-headed woman who couldn't have been more than nineteen years old.

"Gilroy, give them a moment. We all just got here. Let them speak first," the woman counseled.

Gilroy bristled once again, but sat back, apparently chastised by the young woman. Theo turned and began introductions. He began with Elevetia since the member from their delegation seemed to be the loudest. After calling on her, the young woman stood first.

"I am Giselda, High Princess of the First Throne of Elevetia. This is Miranda, our finest scholar in the kingdom. The members from Lotho will know her daughter, Jersica, who has been working in Lotho for a number of years now recruiting newly Rited Fire Sorcerer's from their Kingdom in an effort to grow relations between us. We in turn have been sending willing newly Rited Water Sorcerer's to them as well. Our other member, who you all have now heard his thoughts, is Gilroy. He is our army's finest tactician, strategist, and trainer."

Giselda took her seat and nodded back to Theo. He then motioned for Lotho to continue.

Thomas stood and introduced himself, his wife Alyssa, and Dryan, the scholar who had helped discover that Mia was a Druid and had been her Water teacher while in Lotho.

"I also consider all three of us friends of the Druid, so we come on a more open and trusting understanding after her call," Thomas smiled. He placed his hand over his heart and bowed his head to Theo, relinquishing the floor.

Finally, it was Maravette's turn. A tall, stately man stood and cleared his throat, a move which made Daryl raise an eyebrow as he took him in completely.

"I am Eric Lily, eldest son of the Lily family in Maravette and brother-in-law to the High King of the Third Throne. With me I bring two of Maravette's finest. Helga, our foremost warrior," he motioned to a gruff looking beast of a blonde woman. "And Henry, our most brilliant Air Sorcerer and personal Councilor to the High Rulers."

A younger looking fresh-faced brunette man gave a jaunty wave from his seat. The man couldn't have been more than thirty to hold such a title. Theo gave a brief glance at Daryl, to see if he would say anything upon meeting a relative of his for the first time in so long.

"I am Daryl Wardman," he announced, staring at the young man who hadn't sat down yet.

"I am Mia's father and my mother's name was Francesca Lily."

Everyone, save for Helga and Eric, gasped in surprise at the revelation and looked to see what Eric would do with this information. Daryl explained further.

"My Mother was a sister to your grandfather, but she left the family after marrying my father and lived outside of the city until her death when I was eighteen."

Eric looked to Helga briefly and holding her hand up, she nodded, stopping the young heir from speaking.

"What he says is true Eric. I knew Francesca well in my youth. She was slightly older than me. This man is truly who he says he is. He is a Lily. I had kept up with him even through his marriage to the Princess Clarisse, who was a favorite of mine," Helga smiled. She winked at Clarisse again, who smiled and nodded her head. Eric turned to face the distant Uncle he had never been aware of. By Theo's calculations, that made Eric and Wynnie second cousins. He waited to hear the man's answer to the announcement.

"Well," he coughed into his hand to clear his throat, "While this is news to me, I am heartened to hear that we have relations to the Druid and I will hazard to guess that this will definitely alter how our country and our military view this meeting."

He sat down quickly and drew into himself, trying to puzzle out what it all meant. Daryl gave a solemn nod to the young man before looking to his wife.

"I am Clarisse Robur Wardman, Princess of the Fifth Throne of Suravia. My brother is High King Michael. My daughter is Amelia Wardman, the Druid you all came to see," she spoke.

Theo winced at the royal title that fell heavy off of Clarisse's beautiful lips. He wasn't sure she was really allowed to use such a stylus after technically being cast out of the kingdom and slashed from its history. Clarisse may not know all of that, however, as she had vanished right before the decree was given.

Jeremy stepped forward and bowed deeply to all those present.

"I am Jeremy, Captain of High Queen Heretia's Guard and Pair to Wyndetta Lily of Maravette, sister to Mr. Lily who represents their home country."

Theo could have sworn he heard Eric snort in derision, but Jeremy apparently was choosing to ignore it. It was no good fighting Wynnie's battles for her, she could handle herself if she felt like it. Theo raised his head, it was finally his turn.

"Most of you know me, I am Theodeus Varillian, Prince of the First Throne of Suravia, Elite Guardsman, and Pair to the Druid Amelia."

There were more small bows of the head, and then finally Gabriel stepped forward with a cocky grin spread across his face.

"Oh, please don't," Theo muttered to himself, terror gripping his heart at what the idiot might say to relieve the strain.

"I am Gabriel, and I am Death," Gabriel announced with a booming voice, seemingly meant to strike awe and amazement with the group before them.

He waved his arms triumphantly in the air, as if ready to accept a round of applause and bow for it. No one moved, they all just blinked back at him, confused. Theo fought the overwhelming urge to smack his hand over his eyes and shake his head in disgust. Gabriel glanced around the room expectantly, and when no one responded he dropped his open arms.

"Really? Nothing? I honestly thought that would get some kind of reaction. Well, okay then, have it your way." He waved them off and within a blink he had lifted off the ground and black smoke emanated from his body. His golden eyes blazed bright against the darkness he was creating as it crept into all four corners of the room. The air became thick with electric charge and the shadows began to spin around the audience beneath him faster and faster. All nine heads turned sharply upward, combined with gasps and screams of varying levels from each one. Even Helga, the unmoving old woman, jumped slightly at the sight of Death incarnate.

"That's more like it!" Gabriel whooped in triumph and landed gracefully back down on the foot of the dais.

"Who in the Mother are you?" Eric Lily shouted from his seat. He had practically crawled up into it in fright. Theo shook his head at the pathetic display.

"I told you already. I am Gabriel, the human incarnation of Death. Heretia, through the grace of the Mother Goddess, gave me a body to encase my ethereal form and make me human for a time. I am here as a guide to the Druid, as she has been the only mortal in the history of time to be granted my power by me alone."

Gabriel was eating this up. He was a showman at heart, and this was his wheelhouse. A captive audience that he could flaunt and strut his power before. No one moved for a moment as they soaked in the information being thrown at them from all directions.

"I think it's time we explain the entire situation," Theo announced. He stepped forward to calm the tension and launched into the story that he had rehearsed just moments before with Mia's parents. He allowed Jeremy and Gabriel to jump in every now and then. Jeremy could explain the situation with Heretia, the city of Purge, and her lifelong attempt to contain the Second Uprising in secret until Mia could arrive.

Gabriel was there when it came time to report what he and Mia had seen in the Forest and the encampment the Second Uprising had erected there. When all three men were finished, silence rang out amongst the group. It was Alyssa who spoke first, the only one brave enough to move the conversation forward.

"So, is Heretia going to be okay? And do we have a plan to get Mia back?" she asked.

Her heart was evident, and it was clear why Thomas had demanded she join him on this journey. Not only did he love her immensely, but she was a wise and considerate council. Gabriel turned to her with a smile.

"Heretia should be fine once she wakes up," he began, but a snort, from the ever-negative Gilroy, interrupted him.

"You mean, *if* she wakes up!"

Gabriel shot him a dark and foreboding look which quelled the man's speech for a moment.

"When it comes to Mia, however, that's a different story," Theo jumped in, attempting to squash the verbal assault Gilroy was about to receive from the increasingly upset Death magic that sat beside him now. "Everything happened only a few hours ago and we haven't had time to even begin assessing what Mia's hostage situation might mean for this upcoming battle, that is, if you and your kingdoms agree to joining us."

Theo pointedly gave a moment of pause to let that sink in for the emissaries. Henry, the Air Sorcerer that had accompanied the group from Maravette, cleared his throat and scooted forward in his chair.

"I am curious as to why your own Kingdom, Prince Theodeus, is not present?" he pointed out, a talking point Theo was loath to answer at this moment.

The messenger had mentioned the Suravia was readying its army, but how much of one? Had the letter Mia sent just the night before made it in time to ensure the size was sufficient? Jeremy twisted in his seat.

"My intelligence, meaning the messenger who delivered the letter via Transport, leads me to believe that the Princess Esmerelda of the Third Throne of Suravia was able to amass everything and is heading for us as we speak. She had to, ahem," Jeremy glanced at Theo for a moment, "Collect a few more items that the Druid had asked of her. We should be seeing the entire Suravian force arriving within a week."

Even Theo's dark eyebrows rose to his hairline in astonishment as the entire crowd gave gasps of surprise.

"Everything?" Giselda asked in an airy voice.

Jeremy nodded with a brilliant smile, causing the young woman to blush deep enough to match her fiery hair color. Theo snorted inwardly. Thank the Mother Goddess Wynnie wasn't here to see that. She'd have the girl's head for breakfast.

"Everything." Jeremy repeated, the grin now unable to be wiped from his face. "While the Ancient Kingdom doesn't have much of a standing army to speak of it does have a few well-trained guard units who can also be used as foot soldiers and we are ready to offer them, as well as my own sword."

High King Thomas of Lotho stood from his chair resolutely, the determination written on his strong face. "Lotho is also prepared to offer everything it has. While it may not be much for our island Kingdom, it will be not only our army force of soldiers, but our top Sorcerer's in every element we can spare. Our general, King Ludwig, has been granted the control of our military and is readying as we speak. A word from me and they will be on their way."

Theo nodded in thanks to the young man who had looked after Mia for the two weeks they had been apart. The two sitting on either side of him were just as much to thank in that endeavor, and Theo would always appreciate what they did for his Pair.

"I don't expect an immediate answer from either Maravette or Elevetia, but I do expect some sort of answer in due time. With Mia in captivity, we have been granted a sort of reprieve, but in the same hand, none at all. As soon as Wyndetta Lily returns from Maravette," he looked to Eric wondering why he hadn't brought his younger sister back along with him. "We will begin plans to rescue the Druid and see her safely back with us."

Eric didn't even flinch. Clearly his sister was not a topic he cared to discuss. Theo wasn't sure what Wynnie had to do to get the delegation from Maravette to even show up, but whatever it was had worked. Jeremy was also staring the young man down. The concern for his Pair was written across his own face. He, too, was worried why the beautiful and spunky Wynnie hadn't led the charge back to Purge with her weakling brother in tow.

The three from Elevetia began to whisper amongst themselves quietly as Jeremy moved to instruct the castle help in showing everyone to their rooms. Theo was turning back to the still silent Pair of Clarisse and Daryl when a small hand tapped his shoulder. He turned abruptly to see Giselda, the fledgling and soft-spoken Princess from Elevetia standing there, wringing her hands together.

"May we speak?" she asked and motioned to move to a more private location.

"Certainly," Theo said. He ducked his head in the direction they could go, a small alcove that was tucked only slightly away from earshot, yet not view. She quickly made her way to the place he had indicated and then whirled on him, eyes wide with an emotion Theo couldn't place just yet.

"I want to thank you for calling everyone here," she began, her voice low as if she needed to whisper.

Theo blinked a few times. He was not expecting that type of start. He clasped his hands behind his back and leaned down just slightly so he could hear her better.

"No, it is I that must thank you, Princess, for coming. All of Medeis will thank you and this meeting may very well be written into the history books of where the beginning of the end of the Second

Uprising began. I'm glad that you were able to be a part of it." He tried to instill how important all of this was to her before she could even continue. He had a gut feeling she was pulling him aside to inform him Elevetia would have no part.

"It's nothing really. Honestly, my kingdom has been itching to go to war with Heretia for some time, and while it seems as though we won't get to see her on the field of battle as planned, we will get to see battle. To my father and the rest of the High Rulers, the idea of war alone will be enough."

"So, Elevetia is agreeing to commit its forces and join us?" Theo prompted.

Giselda gave a short high-pitched laugh and nodded.   "Oh of course, that was never a question. Don't mind Gilroy. He's an old coot that just likes to stir trouble. He plays the nasty devil's advocate all the time. Honestly, he can be a bit of a bother, but he does make good points at times and that's why we keep him around." She glanced over her left shoulder to the small man that was being herded away by a plump looking maid that he had taken a fancy to. It was Miranda, however, that watched the two of them from the corner of her eye. Like a mother hen she bristled as Giselda took a step closer to Theo. He inadvertently shifted backwards.

"No, what I wanted to speak with you about was something much different than the war. I wanted to speak about the Druid herself."

Theo raised an eyebrow, not understanding where all of this was heading.

"What about her?" he asked cautiously.

"Well, I was wondering what her plans were for after the Second Uprising is defeated. In the history books, the other two Druids rearranged the power hierarchy, and I was questioning what her plans in that regard was."

Theo cocked his head to one side, glancing at Gabriel in an attempt to catch his eye and plead for help in extricating him from this situation.

"I'll be honest with you, Princess. No one has thought that far or even considered it a necessity. Why? Are you worried about losing your future throne?" he prodded into her questions with his own.

Giselda bit her small lip and looked away from him. "No, not exactly. I was hoping I could speak with her when she gets back about possibly getting rid of the Five High Ruler set up that we already have.

See, Elevetia is having some trouble at the moment with producing heirs and I'm not sure if you know," she began, but Theo interrupted her.

"I am aware that you and your cousin, Judas, are the only two heirs alive at the moment. You to the First and he to the Third. But I'm not sure why that would be a concern to the Druid. We have a war to fight and your parents are still young. So are the other three High Rulers."

Giselda shook her head. "No, the other three can't have children. They have been trying for years and nothing has worked. And Judas," she looked around the room carefully before reaching up on tip toes. Theo leaned just ever so slightly to hear her better.

"He's missing."

Theo almost stumbled backwards. This was shocking news that he wasn't sure he had a right to be privy to.

"How long?" he finally was able to stammer out in his surprise. He attempted to collect himself, but the situation in Elevetia was far worse than what little he had ever known.

"Six months. We believe that he may have either left and joined the Second Uprising or was lured there. He left on a hunting expedition and never returned. He had claimed to be looking for Tailong, the Wild Beast made of Fire. A dragon so large and ferocious no witch has been able to control it. We all knew it was hairbrained and he would eventually come back empty handed, but the more time went on, the more concerned we grew," she admitted, the story spilling from her lips like water.

Theo's mind spun. He remembered that Mia already found out that Michelo had Tailong under his control. Maybe he had taken Judas with him, or Judas had brought it to him. Either way, Prince Judas' missing status was a game changer for the kingdom. No wonder they were ready to pounce into the war. They wanted to find their only other heir and get him back.

"Are you prepared for the idea that he may be a Cannibal?" Theo asked her after a few moments of uncomfortable silence. Giselda nodded weakly.

"I love my cousin, and while he was always a little wayward, he was a decent man. If he is safe and just imprisoned, I want him back. If he is gone forever, I wanted to speak with the Druid about Elevetia's future. Which may all now rest on me." She hung her head with a heavy sigh.

No wonder such a strong kingdom, who prided themselves on power and presence, had sent such a small woman as their mouthpiece. She was all they had at the moment. Theo blew out a heavy breath.

"This can't be kept a secret. While I'm happy to know Elevetia is now invested in this war as much as we are, it also comes with a heavy price and I'm sorry for it. We need to let the other Kingdoms know so they understand the seriousness of this."

Giselda looked back at the waning group, thinking through the idea of outing her kingdoms heaviest current secret. Eventually, however, she nodded her ascent.

"You're right. Let's do it. They need to know, and we need to do everything we can to find him."

Theo gently guided her over to Gabriel and broke the news.

CHAPTER FIVE

MIA

What felt like hours later, the burning and spasming in my entire body abated for a split second. I caught my first full breath of air into my lungs and whimpered. My throat was raw from the screaming over the last thirty minutes. The liquid had made its way through every inch of my physical being. It had poked and prodded, ripped, and nipped at my magic, but to no avail. My Fire magic was still solidly within me and Gregor hadn't won this time.

With a grunt, the broke-backed man stood from the stool the Cannibals had brought him to wait on and he hobbled toward me, looking over my weakened state.

"Pathetic. The potion almost killed you the first time around. I really thought the Druid would be stronger than that. It also seemed to have not been enough to take it from you." He twisted an empty vial in his hands. I still wasn't sure what form my magic would take if it could be stolen from me, but I was almost certain it wouldn't have fit in a vial that size. From what I felt, it would take at least an ocean to contain it.

"Oh well. We will try again tomorrow. I clearly need to tweak the ingredients for strength. I was hoping we could start with Fire magic as we have a Prince of Fire here among us that has been immensely troublesome to control. I thought between his magic and yours, we could fuel at least fifty warriors with new Fire magic for the coming war, but no matter. We will try with another magic tomorrow."

He flipped the vial back on to the now righted tray and took it out of the tent with him.

"Good night, Druid. Get your rest. I'm guessing Earth won't be quite easy to take from you either, but I'm going to tweak these just a tad and see what we can do tomorrow."

A tear fell from my cheek as the tent flap descended behind him. I still couldn't move from the fetal position on the sandy ground. I waited for as long as it took me to get feeling back in my hand before I even attempted to right myself. I pushed down on the ground, but with a mighty shake, my elbow caved in and what little progress I had made ended up being my downfall as I collapsed heavily back down onto my side.

"Ow," I whispered breathlessly into the cool sand beneath my face.

I stayed still for a while longer and focused as much of my Life magic as I could into healing the aching muscles, but the pain had been inflicted magically. There was nothing physical for it. I reached deeper still into the wounded part of me and eventually I began to feel it soothing itself. The tension that still racked my legs and shoulders relaxed and I was able to lie flat on the ground after a time.

When I eventually opened my weary eyes, I noticed that the sun was almost gone from the sky and there was nothing left to draw energy from to continue to heal my poor body. I choked out a small sob of desperation and reached out to try and gather the last of the filtered and muted light that I could, feeling the tiny tendrils do what they could to help my aches and sores.

It was well after the sun had finally set that I was able to fully move myself into a sitting position and begin to look around again. The continuous movements of the mindless Cannibals surrounded me, but no one came into my lonely tent. There was still no one to ask for help. They couldn't help if they wanted to anyway. In fact, they didn't want to. Michelo had altered them, took away their minds and bodies and left them shells of the witches they had once been. I hadn't been able to gather numbers in my head when I was thrown into this tent, but from the sound, there had to be at least fifty or so just within earshot. I buried my head into my arms and rested them on my bent knees.

No one was here except me, Michelo, Gregor, and the Cannibals.

I was wallowing in my despair when something donned on me. A nugget of information that Gregor had dropped just as he was leaving. He had mentioned a Prince of Fire causing trouble in the encampment. Was it one of the Princes from the Kingdom of Elevetia, the fire kingdom? Why was he here and how could he be causing trouble?

There had to be some reason if they had left him unchanged. My heart sank at the thought of another witch suffering as I did, and he probably didn't have a choice on coming here like I had been given. My heart gave a small leap when footsteps approached my tent and I scrambled to stand as best I could to greet my captors yet again. Gregor had promised it would be tomorrow before he would come back, so who could be here now?

A young man, no more than eighteen entered the tent, heavily shackled as I was and carrying a tray. He was just as stunned as I to see someone who wasn't a Cannibal standing before him, chained as he was, and immensely weary.

"Who?" he began to ask, almost dropping the heavy wooden tray filled with food, but he stopped himself and looked over his shoulder. Obviously, he had grown paranoid of others overhearing him and maybe even thought this a trick to get him to bend.

I took a hesitant step forward, my hands out in peace and spoke first. "I am Amelia Wardman, I am the Druid. I am here as a hostage in exchange for Clarisse and Daryl Wardman, my parents. Who are you?" I asked him, trying to ease his suspicions.

"I," he began, but faltered. Regaining his composure, he set the tray down, his chains clinking and dragging heavily with his movements.

"I am Judas, Prince of the Third Throne of Elevetia. I'm here because I'm a pompous idiot who accidentally let myself get captured hunting Tailong for stupid glory."

My stomach turned, realizing that I had been right. There was someone else here, but he was truly kidnapped. From Elevetia too, but how had Michelo gotten him here? Wasn't his kingdom looking for him?

"How long have you been here Judas?" I asked and motioned for him to join me in sharing my bread and water that had been sent. It was meager but it was enough to pass between us and from the skin and bone looks of him, Judas needed all he could get.

STEPHANIE WELCH

"I'm not sure, but a good handful of months. Maybe five or six. I was out in Elevetia, tracking down Tailong to capture and return with some token to show I was a man. I was an idiot and stumbled right into Michelo tracking the Wild Beast as well. He kidnapped me and then used me to lure the Wild Beast out. Tailong is a very noble creature and it wasn't going to stand by and let an innocent get hurt."

I nodded, remembering what the Mother Goddess had said about Michelo tricking Tailong into taking the potion so he could control the Wild Beast of Fire. Tailong sounded as if it were a Wild Beast I would like to meet, but now probably never get to, given the circumstances.

"I'm sorry Judas," I muttered and bit into my bread.

"Why are you here?" he dropped his voice to a whisper.

He obviously knew something I didn't about others overhearing conversations, so I dropped my own voice to match.

"I told you, I gave myself over to save my parents."

Judas grunted and ripped into the bread, sloshing down a big gulp of water before handing the cup back to me. I greedily drained the rest of it.

"Yeah, but if you are the Druid, why didn't you just incinerate this whole camp once they were safe?" he waved around us.

"Because everyone would have died and that's not what I'm here for."

Judas nodded conspiratorially. "So, you are just here for information and then you'll escape afterwards. Can you take me with you?" he asked quickly.

I hesitantly shook my head. "No, I'm here for good. I mean, I'm not going to give up on trying to escape, but I didn't come here for information. I just wanted my parents safe and I am going to figure out the rest as I go." I took my last bite of bread and sat back on my haunches.

"YOU HAVE NO," Judas began at a shout and then quickly dropped his voice, looking around. "You mean to tell me you're the Mother fucking Goddess Druid and you have no plan?" he hissed between his teeth.

I shook my head in response. "I had no time!" I tried to explain. "Michelo severed my father's finger and I was given only a few hours to decide if I was going to make the switch for them. I couldn't ask for help or let anyone know what I was doing because they would have stopped me."

42

"You're damn right they would have stopped you. Any sane person would have. If I were your friends, I would have locked you in the deepest dungeon until I figured out how to get them myself before I let you hand yourself over," he sighed and shook his head in defeat.

"So, it's hopeless now. Michelo has the only weapon we had against him and there's no stopping him from continuing his madness and changing people into the mindless fucks I have surrounding me day and night. Everything is lost."

He slumped back against the table and groaned into his hands. I winced at his words but felt the need to defend myself.

"Hey now, I'm figuring it out. And if I don't, Theo will. He probably has Wynnie in some room right now concocting a scheme to free me and get me back to Purge where all the armies of the kingdoms are converging."

This seemed to pull the young helpless man out of his despair, and he sat up, quickly pouncing to his knees.

"You've united the kingdoms for war? Finally!" he shook his fists in the air in a gesture of victory.

"I've been trying to get Elevetia to make a move on Heretia for years. That mad bitch has to go down for causing all of this."

I waved my hands out in front of me to stop him. "No, you've got it all wrong. Heretia didn't start this. She's the only reason it hasn't gotten past the Ancient Kingdom so far. She's not mad, nor is she evil. In fact, she is the reincarnation of the Druid Meloni."

I tried to explain further, but heavy footsteps were coming closer and Judas sprang to his feet, chains scraping against each other and against flesh as he stood. Michelo threw back the flap and his wicked and crooked smile broke out.

"Good to see you've met our newest guest, Judas old boy. How do you like my new play toy? I might be too busy with her to come have our fun time, won't I? Good news for you, huh?" Michelo cackled.

Judas winced at the questions but said nothing with his dark brunette head bowed. I stood to defend him, but Michelo kicked at a chain around my ankle and my backside came crashing back down to the ground with a thud. I cried out lightly and moved to ease the pain.

"She's the illustrious Druid everyone has been talking about. You know, the one I tried to go collect myself a while back. She got away from me once, but it seems all I had to do was wait and she handed herself in," Michelo continued.

Judas didn't move, nor did he respond. He was eerily quiet.

"What could you two have been talking about? Oh, I know, what about how I came to collect the little Fire Prince for myself?" Michelo punched Judas in the shoulder. Judas stumbled forward and braced himself for the fall to the ground, his hands catching him before his face could make contact. I crawled to help him up, but my own chains prevented me from reaching him.

"How sweet. Once a Druid, always a Druid. Trying to comfort the lost soul, are you?" Michelo reached down and yanked me backwards.

I gave a shout as I was unwillingly pulled backwards. Judas moved to reach for me as well, but Michelo stomped on his hand. Judas screamed in agony as the boot twisted over his palm and crushed it into the sand.

"Stop it!" I shouted and stood.

Michelo quit moving, but didn't remove the boot. "What do you think you can do about it?" he taunted.

My anger was boiling inside of me now and my magic struggled to respond in its sluggish state. I pulled and pulled at it, forcing it to surface when finally, I felt the heat beneath my fingers grow.

"Fuck you, Michelo," I spat and threw the ball of flames that I had collected in my palm.

It was larger than I expected as I stomped down with my left foot and thrust my right palm forward as I had seen Wilhelm do weeks ago on the boat to Lotho. He was the Captain of the Elite Guard, my friend, and a Fire Sorcerer. When we were attacked by Cetus, the Wild Beast of Water, he had used the same movement to shove fire into Cetus' path in an attempt to stop its onslaught.

The ball of fire raced from my grasp, and in a flash, hit it's intended target. Michelo roared in anger, shielding his already damaged face from the attack, and stumbled backwards off of Judas' hand. I reached for Judas as he looked up to me in shock, and I motioned for him to get behind me. He scrambled as fast as his wound would allow, and as his hand touched mine, my Life magic instantly began to heal his shattered bones.

By the time Michelo had snuffed out my flames, Judas was completely together again, no indication that Michelo had ever hurt him.

"You will regret that, little Druid. My wards are still working on you and that may have well been your last hurrah of power left. Glad to see you wasted it early," he breathed.

He was seething with anger as I moved Judas behind my body, blocking him. This was the only other sane witch left in the camp and I wasn't letting him go easily. Michelo closed his eyes, breathing deeply. I gasped when the black amulet around his neck began to glow and smoky tendrils of Death magic floated out from around him.

"Forgot about this little trinket I picked up back in Purge didn't you?" he chuckled, his voice deeper and more concentrated than just moments before.

The Death magic inched it way forward across the ground. I moved to scramble away from it as it came near, but I couldn't get far enough away. The black smoke passed by me however and moved straight for Judas.

"No!" I shouted in alarm, but I was too late and too unprepared.

Judas screamed as the black smoke snapped around his chains and dragged him across the ground out of the tent and far away from me. I tried to run after him, but I was held back by the heavy shackles. Judas' screams continued as he was dragged away out of sight until I could hear him no more.

I snapped my attention to Michelo who was still standing in the exact same spot, now grinning from ear to ear. "Don't you dare hurt him!" I threatened.

Michelo shook his head before slowly shuffling to the exit. His leg was obviously wounded from my fire attack, but he was trying not to show it.

"Just a reminder of the situation you are in, Druid. Try nothing more. No more magic, no more spells, and no more making friends with the other prisoners," he warned.

My ears perked up. Prisoners? There were more than just me and Judas?

"Oh yes, there is more. I have to keep my army happy, don't I?" he chuckled, and I paled as I realized what he meant. They were called Cannibals for a reason.

"This latest acquisition is the best. Newly acquired, just two days ago I came across an orphanage outside the city of Purge on my way back from the Forest. The matron was asleep, and it didn't take much to dispatch of her, but the prizes inside were bountiful. I took all of them with me as a sacrifice for my army. I have to give them something every now and then. It stirs morale, you see."

My bowels turned watery and I almost vomited up the little bit of food I had ingested only a few minutes before. He was talking about children! He had kidnapped helpless children and he was going to murder them all. As my thoughts raced, I couldn't hold back my disgust any longer and I emptied the meager contents of my stomach on the ground at the end of the table. I could only hear Michelo's laughter as I came back up shaky from the aftereffects of my actions.

In my despair, I sank to my knees and wailed. I was useless. This was out of my control and far beyond my abilities. I couldn't even save myself. How was I going to save those poor babies that were hidden somewhere in this camp that were probably terrified and unknowing of their fate. I screamed through my pain over and over until finally exhaustion claimed me and I passed into the darkness of unconsciousness. My dreams were littered with images of children bloodied and thrown across the ground that would haunt me the rest of my life.

CHAPTER SIX

GABRIEL

To say Gabriel was shocked to hear that a Prince of Elevetia had been missing for six months and no one outside of the kingdom had known was an understatement. Theo had recalled every single person who had left to see to their accommodations back to hear Giselda's announcement.

The people from Lotho had gasped all at once, Alyssa and her sweet soul being the loudest. Everyone from Maravette had paled at the knowledge, and those from Elevetia had hung their heads in shame.

"So, this is as real to your kingdom as it is to ours and Suravia's?" Gabriel finally spoke when no one else had the courage to do so.

Giselda nodded but held her head high. The entire gatherings attention was on her, and she was playing her part wonderfully.

"Elevetia is announcing its full involvement to not only find and retrieve the Druid, but our lost Prince Judas as well. We will see this Second Uprising crushed, or we will all die in the attempt," she declared grandly.

Gabriel grunted, squinting his eyes at her. Something inside of him screamed 'Showman.' He didn't think her a liar, but she wasn't exactly sincere, or at least it seemed that way to him. Pushing the intuition aside for the moment, he turned to face Maravette, the last holdout.

"Please inform your High Rulers, of every other kingdom's decision and let them know they would be wise to follow." He dismissed the crowd to whisper anxiously among themselves.

Gabriel pulled the five he had entered with aside and led them down the hall to Heretia's private study. As they passed by the High Queen's room, Gabriel waved them forward.

"Go ahead and be seated, I'm just going to check on her real quick," he called over his shoulder.

Clarisse gave him a sad look of understanding and clutched her own Pair tighter. "If there is anything we can do, please let us know," she offered.

Gabriel's hand hovered over the door handle for a moment before he finished his reach and entered Heretia's room. There was only one witch sitting by her now, a good sign by his standards. To him, that meant that Heretia was out of imminent danger and attention was not as necessary.

"How is she?" he asked in a whisper, so as not to disturb the tiny woman still lying prone upon the massive bed.

The witch set the cloth she was wiping the Queen's forehead with to the side and made a low bow.

"She is stable, sir. She still has not woken, but everything that can be done has been. Really, she was quite lucky. The weapon didn't hit any major part of her and it's been cleaned up nicely. Only infection and not waking up are the main concerns. I was just cleaning around the wound for her next set of bandages." She motioned to the shoulder that was swollen and bruised, unshielded by cloth. The stitches were wonderfully drawn together, but they still looked hideous against Heretia's porcelain skin.

"I will be in her study next door with the Prince, Captain, and the Druid's parents. If she wakes up, come get me. I want to be here," Gabriel said.

The witch nodded and gave another bow for him. Gabriel turned and left. It was hard to see her so feeble and helpless, but there was nothing he could do for her in that moment. If something bad were to suddenly happen, he as the magic of Death would feel it. Just like he was making sure his magic kept its feelers out for anything to do with Mia, he would know.

The foursome was waiting patiently for Gabriel to join them again in the study, everyone but Jeremy sitting in plush chairs and making themselves comfortable.

"I think that went as well as could be expected," Jeremy began and moved to begin unrolling a large map of Medeis and then a more detailed map of Purge and the desert beyond.

"I agree, however, I'm still nervous about Maravette holding out. Hopefully your revealing your relation to the Lily's will stir up some feelings. Mia is technically their family after all, and that wouldn't look good for them to abandon the Druid in her time of need," Theo mentioned to Daryl, who had remained quiet since he had introduced himself earlier.

The older man nodded, but still said nothing. It was Clarisse who seemed ready to jump in with both feet.

"So, when does Wynnie get back? I want to rescue my daughter as soon as possible and hold her again," she said.

Gabriel looked to Jeremy for that answer. He only shrugged. He may have been her Pair, but he wasn't her keeper.

"My guess is that she is staying to continue rallying the forces and lead them back here herself. Eric didn't seem inclined to talk about her much, which is ridiculous as it is his sister. She's twice the witch he could ever hope to be, and yet he acts like she doesn't matter in the grander scheme of things," Jeremy scoffed at the insult it meant to his Pair that her own brother was so nonchalant about her presence.

"That's the Lily's for you," Theo began and then righted himself, throwing Daryl an apologetic look. "Present company exempt of course."

Daryl waved it away. It wasn't like he had been raised with them. "From what little I knew of my cousin, Eric's father, I wouldn't put it past him to play a few games first before helping Maravette commit to the war. Little runt had a way of getting what he wanted all the time." He scoffed at the memory of the eldest Lily that must have been hidden away in the deep recesses of his life.

Jeremy suddenly looked to the door and reached for the blade at his side. Gabriel stiffened as well and turned just as a light knock came from the other side.

"Enter!" he called, hoping it was the witch that had been watching over Heretia. It was just the same messenger from the night before. He was exhausted, his brow sweaty and his clothes dirty.

"I've just returned from Suravia," he wheezed.

Clarisse was on her feet, reaching for the poor boy and helping him up.

I Transported as long and as fast as I could, but I had to run the last mile. My magic was too spent," he attempted to explain.

Clarisse clucked like a mother hen and reached for a decanter of water on the desk. She filled it to the brim and handed it to the messenger who guzzled every last drop.

"Suravia is coming?" Theo sat on the edge of his chair, keen on hearing what he had to say.

The messenger nodded through his panting. "They are. Princess Esmerelda received the letter I had in my possession and she asked me to stay for a while to make sure I had the right message back for you."

The man produced a single document and Gabriel snatched it away, with a scornful look from Clarisse. He reddened with embarrassment in the ears and mumbled a quick apology before ripping the letter open.

> *Mia,*
>
> *I got your message and I've already got everyone working on it. Every Life Wielder in the kingdom is rounding up every last Moondate to bring with us and Transporting them as fast as they can to the docks. The ships are ready to go, don't worry. I'm coming and I've got everyone with me. Hugo has enough for three months on hand, with more coming later. Mom isn't thrilled, but honestly, what can she do at this point? Your Uncle is doing much better, I wouldn't have left him if he weren't. Tell Theo that we should be docking in two days' time. We leave this evening. I'm paying the messenger extra to push his Transport as much as he can so this can get to you today.*
>
> *Ez*
> *Lead Medic of the Suravian Army*
>
> *P.S. Like the new title?*

Theo gave a small snort through his nose, having been reading the letter over Gabriel's shoulder, before handing it to Jeremy. He relayed the message to Clarisse and Daryl. They both sagged with relief, knowing that all the help they were going to need was truly on the way. As soon as Jeremy finished, he began barking orders to the soldier who stood in the hallway.

"I want every wagon and available foot soldier to make their way immediately to the docks on our Eastern port. The Suravian army is coming and bringing enough supplies for three months. They will be here in two days, but I want to make sure we get there early to greet them. We move out tonight, no excuses."

The soldier nodded and ran off.

"This is good news. No, this is excellent news! I'll have a few others stay behind to ready a camp for their army to base in."

He rubbed his hands together excitedly. This was the job he was trained to take on and never able to do. He was meant to lead armies and command logistics, not just train and wave swords around in front of mindless Cannibals.

"There's no room in the city for them. They will have to be based just outside the Southern wall in the desert. Close enough to the castle to not only defend it, but receive safety from it. Yet far enough out so they can spread out as need be," Gabriel offered.

Jeremy nodded in agreement. "My thoughts exactly. I'll go let my men know and get them working." He hurried from the private study, eagerness written all over him.

"Well, I'm glad he has a job," Theo muttered darkly.

Clarisse was still helping the young messenger relax in the chair on the other side of the desk.

"Are we done with him? He needs to get home and lay down," she asked.

Gabriel nodded, and with a smile, paid the boy handsomely again before he left the room.

"We all have a job, Theo," Daryl suddenly interjected into the conversation.

Everyone's heads turned in a little surprise at the statement. Clarisse moved to stand next to her husband.

"Well of course he does," she smiled brightly. "His job is to go get our daughter back."

Theo shook his head, "I can't do that just yet. We need Wynnie for the actual rescue. This is her area of expertise and she needs to be heading this. I also want to wait on Will and Tim before we make any moves. This is going to take the whole Elite Guard to pull off and it has to be done right," Theo said.

"Who's talking about me?"

A strong feminine voice emanated from the door. Everyone turned in astonishment as the sprightly and beautiful white-haired Wynnie pranced through the doorway and jumped into the center with her arms out. She had a childish grin plastered on her mouth.

"Did you guys not think I was going to make it back in time for the fight? I only stayed behind a little longer than the rest because I wanted to tell my parents that I had a Pair and he was wonderful, and they sucked," she snickered.

She wiggled a little finger close to her face. The joy that had surrounded the young, troubled woman since finding Jeremy was more than evident. She was less gloomy and found ways to make jokes more often.

"Hello?" she turned, suddenly noticing Mia's parents next to her. "I don't know you two."

Gabriel noticed Theo visibly wince. Wynnie could be suspicious of new people and sometimes came off as scary or even crazy. When she had first met Mia, she had offered ways to torture her for the truth of who she was. Luckily, Mia had worked past that and they were best friends. A lot of that had to do with Mia not giving up on Wynnie in her alcoholism caused by a traumatic and depressing childhood with the aforementioned Lily family.

Daryl finally stood up and reached his hand out. "I'm Daryl Wardman, Mia's father, and if I'm correct, your uncle once removed."

Wynnie's mouth fell in surprise in the middle of the offered handshake. Her eyes raced over the man. Gabriel looked between them and couldn't help but see some resemblance.

"U-Uncle?" she stammered, for once unable to speak or come up with some witty retort.

"My mother was sister to your grandfather. I met your father a few times growing up, but I wasn't exactly welcome, as my father had been an Earth Wielder and worked on a farm outside the city. I was already long gone by the time you were born," Daryl clarified for her, but Wynnie was too stunned still to comprehend.

"I'm related to Mia?" she asked quietly, pointing to her chest.

Daryl and Clarisse both nodded.

"I think it makes you second cousins," Clarisse answered her.

Wynnie stumbled backwards and Gabriel moved a seat underneath her fall.

"Mia is my cousin?" she repeated slowly, staring around at nothing in particular.

It was a moment or two before Gabriel moved to pull Wynnie from her shock when a sudden ear-splitting cheer rang out. Wynnie leapt from her seat in a single bound and clapped her hands. She turned in the air, white hair spinning around her.

"Mia is family!" she cried out and ran to hug both Daryl and Clarisse. "Where is she? Does she know? Of course, she knows, you would have told my brother and her the moment you saw his shitty little face."

No one had the heart yet to stop her moment of joy.

"Where is that little jerk anyway? Probably counting the ways he can profit off of being related to the Druid, even distantly," she growled. She glanced around the room and then squealed once again. "Oh, I have to tell Jeremy, too."

Gabriel finally decided it was time to tell her. Gently, he reached for her shoulder and she spun with excitement.

"Wynnie, why don't you sit down for a moment. Do you know if Will and Tim are back?" he asked.

"We are!" Wilhelm Corso boomed into the room with arms wide open. "After the day I had back in Elevetia, I must say, I remember why I left with the Elite Guard as soon as I could."

Tim nodded his own agreement silently at Will's sentiment.

"We could hear Wynnie screaming down the hall. What's happened to get her all excited?" Tim asked.

Wynnie spun in her chair, jumping up to tuck her knees in beneath her.

"Mia and I are cousins!" she announced. "Apparently Daryl is a distant Lily."

Tim and Will looked stunned, but Gabriel knew the biggest shock was yet to come.

"Can everyone please sit down for a moment? There's something we need to tell you," he sighed.

Theo shut the door behind Tim. Gabriel hated to be the one to bust this entire bubble, but with a deep breath, he did it. The three Elite Guardsman sitting down went utterly still as Gabriel relayed all that had happened in the last twenty-four hours since they had left. He began with the message with Daryl's finger, all the way until Mia gave herself up.

Wynnie jumped to her feet, anger and fear etched on her brow.

"And where was Jeremy in all of this?" she asked.

"He was back here, getting ready for everyone to arrive from the other kingdoms. Heretia didn't even tell him what we were doing because she didn't want him to stop his work," Gabriel explained.

"Where was Heretia when all of this went down in the desert? What does she have to say about it?" Will interjected gruffly. His arms were crossed, and he was so angry you could barely see his eyes behind his big red head and large scruffy beard.

"She's in the next room. Unconscious," Gabriel motioned to the door.

"She was able to get through the wards Michelo had set up, but he shoved a sword in her shoulder. We had to race back here to save her, and we barely were able to. She still hasn't woken up and we five have been doing the best we can to keep it going until she either does, or we rescue Mia," Gabriel finished with a huff.

Having reinforcements back to help guide this crazy mess of a war was a relief. The weight on his shoulders were starting to already lift.

Without warning, the door flew open and everyone looked up to see the nurse from next door pointing to the hallway. Gabriel was already out of his seat and flying out when she finally found the words.

"Her Majesty is waking up!" she announced.

Everyone scrambled to get to Heretia's room as well.

"Thank the Mother!" Gabriel heard Clarisse through the wall.

How easily the woman had forgiven everything she had thought about the High Queen that was now stirring under the covers before him. It just spoke for the type of loving and trusting heart that she had instilled within her own daughter. The Mother Goddess couldn't have picked two better parents for a Druid, and Gabriel would always be grateful for his time with them. Right then, however, was not the time for memories but to live in the moment. And with a joyous cry, Gabriel reached down to collect the love of his immortal life in his arms as she opened her crystal blue eyes and smiled at him.

Chapter Seven

Theo

Less than half an hour after Heretia had woken up, everyone was settled neatly into her room surrounding the bed. She had been introduced to Mia's parents properly, Jeremy had been summoned, and the other kingdoms had been made aware that she was awake and well. Lotho had sent its regards in the form of a water dolphin that leapt its way down the hall through the floor and did a happy spin in the air at the foot of Heretia's bed.

The gesture had made her giggle, but the joy was short lived.

"Why would she do this to us?" Heretia asked quietly, holding on the Gabriel's arm, and thinking of Mia.

Gabriel had settled himself on the bed next to her and Theo dared a guess that he wasn't leaving anytime soon.

"She thought she was doing the right thing, love. But now it's our job to not only get her back but lead this war without her right now," he explained.

Heretia bit her lip. While she could put on a wonderful front of a powerful and in command High Queen, she was really deep down lonely and worried all the time. She had been pretending for so long that she was in control so that the other kingdoms stayed away from the Second Uprising, that when given the chance to be herself, she was unsure and anxious.

"I have never been able to gain intel on what was going on inside the camp, it's layout, or how many were in there. For all I know, it's a black hole that no one can see in to. Mia even said the Mother Goddess couldn't penetrate it. Michelo's magic is altered and different. What can we possibly do to get to her?" she asked to the crowd.

"Gabriel here reminded me earlier that you were able to do it, Heretia," Theo gave a nod in Gabriel's direction. "We think maybe the magic he has created has a form of blood magic and maybe with that we can at least gain access. Do you remember what type of spell you were performing when you broke through his ward?"

Heretia closed her eyes and thought deeply for a moment. "I was throwing so many out. I was literally just saying whatever came to mind over and over again until something worked. I was so worried, so scared we were never going to see Mia again. I'm not sure which one did the trick, but it might have been *Aperio*, an unveiling spell. You use it on something like a locked door."

"It may be useful to us when we go to retrieve Mia. Can we learn it?" Jeremy offered.

He was standing in a corner of the room with Wynnie next to him. Both were propped up on the wall and arms crossed, but their shoulders were touching. Since they had been reunited only moments before, they constantly found ways to be in physical contact. Theo didn't blame them. He wasn't sure if he was ever going to let Mia out of his sight again once they rescued her.

Wynnie pushed off from the wall and readjusted her stance.

"It's not going to be easy. I've never been a fan of going in completely blind, but I've had to do it once or twice, all with success. Being able to do a Blood magic spell ourselves will allow us to take as few people as possible, which is extremely helpful. It gives room to fly even more under the radar if it's just the Elite Guard going in."

Jeremy stood with a sharp intake of breath to argue, but Wynnie held her hand up.

"No, we're trained for covertness. The Elite Guard does this all the time. While I can admit having an extra set of knowledgeable fighting hands would be useful in a confrontation, right now we need less numbers and more stealth."

Jeremy paused for a moment and then backed down. Wynnie blinked, shocked that he had kneeled to her wishes so quickly. Theo knew that Wynnie had always had to fight for her freedom to make her own choices with her family, and for her Pair to never question her was new.

"So, can you teach it to us?" Will turned back to Heretia who was always watching the dynamic between Jeremy and Wynnie unfold.

"I believe so. It's an extremely basic form of what normal witches already do. Very primitive and simple, it just takes some getting used to the feel of the power it imbues. While a witch can control the heftiness of their elemental magic with just a thought, Blood magic is black and white. The amount of blood you give determines the power that's behind the spell, so you have to learn how much to give without blasting everything to smithereens on accident."

Tim grunted a short laugh. "I think blasting the ward to smithereens is what we want."

But Wynnie shook her head quickly. The white curly hair that Theo now noticed upon looking closer, identically matched Daryl's waved back and forth with the movement. It was a wonder Gabriel and Mia had never put the familial connection together.

"Not exactly. If we want to get Mia out safely, we need to go in as quietly as possible. We need to pick a spot that no one is watching and Michelo won't feel it. Heretia mentioned before that she can feel everything that passes her wards, so he will be able to as well. We will need to go in when someone else is either going in or out, but unseen," she explained.

Gabriel cleared his throat and stood up.

"I guess that immediately includes me in this mission. I'm the only one that can cover us while we sneak in and around. I highly doubt Michelo will sense anything I can put up. He may have destroyed himself creating a new magic, but I am as ancient as time itself and far more powerful when I put my mind to it," he grinned widely, then winked at Heretia who squeezed his hand lovingly.

Will stood and nodded to the Elite Guard and Gabriel.

"Then it's settled. As soon as Heretia can teach us the Blood magic spell effectively, we leave. There will be no reconnaissance save for a way in, we have no opportunity for it. So, we go in with everything we have. Escape plan will be simple, whoever has Mia, get the hell out as fast as you can and don't look back." He stared at everyone in the room. "No matter what."

Clarisse gulped loudly.

"Ez is arriving in about two days?" Heretia asked for clarification.

Jeremy nodded, "That's what the intel says. However, there has been a very odd, yet effective, wind from the East coming West, so it may be sooner. I've got everyone available moving to the Eastern port to meet the Suravian armada and planning to be there no later than the morning. I want them to be there in case they arrive early."

"Then I guess we need to get started on learning the spell," she bit her lip and began to move off of the bed, but Gabriel shoved her back.

"You need to rest, love. It can wait till morning," he insisted.

Heretia firmly shook her head and shoved him away with her little hands. The pure white nightgown scrunched up around her waist as she slid to set her feet firmly on the floor.

"Mia can't wait till morning," she huffed through the struggle.

Gabriel was in shock, but Clarisse and Wynnie were instantly on their feet and helping her up.

"I've been waiting my whole life for her and to make sure that she does her job as well as become the best she can be. If I have to sacrifice myself in the process, then that is what the Mother Goddess wants, and it is what I will do. So, let's get through a little discomfort and exhaustion and get Mia out of there and back where she belongs," Heretia instructed.

The air in the room shifted from worry to determination and excitement.

"Let's get to it then! I'll go get my knives," Wynnie assisted Heretia to her study and then ran off the collect what they would need to practice.

Tim winced at the idea of cutting himself open for this, but even Theo had to admit Heretia was right. Everyone in the room had been placed here for a purpose. They all had something to give, not just Mia who was obviously willing to give everything. Clarisse and Daryl excused themselves to see a healer, as Daryl was growing tired, and neither had eaten yet. Jeremy offered to assist them in getting their basic comforts met.

"Once we eat, I think we should go pay a visit to my nephew and see how Maravette's answer is coming along," Daryl mentioned to his wife.

Wynnie was just returning as they exited the door, and she gave her long lost Uncle a jaunty wave. She also reached up and planted a sweet kiss on her Pair's lips before tossing down her collection onto the table before them. Theo's brows reached his hairline at the sight of how much weaponry she had brought back with her. Knives, swords, throwing stars, tiny boot blades, and some straight edge razors. When she was asked about the level of steel she had offered to use on her own and everyone else's skin, she shrugged her shoulders nonchalantly.

"What? I didn't know if there were rules to this. Can you only do it with a clean blade? Can you only use a knife one time? Does the weapon of choice matter to the magic? I had to cover all the possible bases. It's not every day we get to use Blood magic and I want to get it right," she explained.

Heretia giggled loudly, but then lurched forward clutching her shoulder.

"Owww," she moaned, furrowing her eyebrows together in pain. "Don't make me laugh so much Wynnie, my stitches pull."

Gabriel moved to mother Heretia, but she waved him away.

"I don't think spilling my own blood is a good idea right now due to how much I lost earlier, so I'm just going to have to do this verbally. No show-and-tell for me today," she suggested.

Theo agreed with her and moved to pick up one of Wynnie's sharper knives. He marveled at the craftsmanship for a moment, turning the silver piece over in his hands.

"Where did you get this? I've never seen you use it," he asked, showing it to her when she leaned over to inspect it.

"Oh! That's not mine, that's Mia's. I was just sharpening it for her before we left for the Forest. I hadn't had a chance to get it back to her yet," she said.

Theo instantly recognized the blade as the one Mia had wielded when Wynnie pretended to kidnap her a few weeks ago. It had been an exercise to see how much Mia had learned while the Elite Guard was away on a spy mission to the Ancient Kingdom. Needless to say, she had almost taken Wynnie down in a matter of moments. Theo recalled the feelings that had flooded through him when he had seen how little Mia needed him in that regard. They had discussed his feelings of inadequacy and what his purpose was.

Wise Mia had instructed him to just be there, be her rock when she was breaking and be the one she could talk to and share ideas with. Theo also understood what the Mother Goddess's purpose for him had been: to be the one to go in after her, not ahead of her. Oddly, as he stood there looking over the fantastic specimen of destruction, he was okay with that.

Never once had he ever truly had a problem with a woman leading the charge in battle. In fact, much like today, Wynnie was the one who made quite a few decisions alongside Will. But when it was his own Pair, he had felt like he should hesitate, but he never did. He was willing to follow Mia anywhere, into whatever, and to whatever awaited them on the other side. She had been right, she didn't need a protector, she didn't need a cheerleader, she needed a Pair.

Here he was, learning a whole different form of magic, planning to run into the enemy camp blind, to do just that.

Will went first, with Heretia showing him where to draw the blood offering and how to channel the power.

"You're not just cutting your hand and saying a word," she explained. "You are offering the blood. Take a breath and imagine an exchange of sorts, the blood for power."

Will closed his russet eyes and took in a deep breath. Within moments, a ball of light appeared around his head, making the room brighter.

"Good!" Heretia clapped from her seat. "That was good and simple, but extremely effective when you're in a dark area and need a faint light to see right in front of you. Next time offer less or more depending on how bright you want the light to be. You can even go down to basically a pin prick if you just want to see something for a moment without anyone else being able to see your location. If you want to light up a room, however, you're going to have to give it way more and even squeeze your palm to offer it up. The tighter the initial squeeze, the more you will get and the stronger the magic will be."

Will looked down at his hand and was surprised to see that it was already healed.

"As soon as the magic is accomplished, your body will heal itself. So, make sure you're not trying to do anything extended on a massive scale that would take multiple witches working on it together," Heretia continued.

Tim went next. He wasn't thrilled about cutting his palm, but eventually Heretia talked him through it and he gave it a weak stab. He conjured a see-through illusion of a fox running around in circles at his feet.

That's a good start, but to really make it appear and be a distraction, you will have to offer more. Don't be afraid, it's only momentary and it will automatically heal. I've been doing this a long time, so I'm used to it, but the first few times can be nerve wracking."

Tim looked pale at the idea of doing this multiple times and he had to sit down to start breathing evenly again.

Wynnie jumped in next and sliced her palm open without hesitation. Theo winced at the sight.

"Not so much!" Heretia shouted, and without warning, an explosion shot off inside the room, throwing papers and books everywhere.

The Elite Guard ducked for cover. Gabriel grabbed Heretia and threw her underneath him as gently as he could manage in care for her shoulder.   As everything settled, Wynnie looked around with a wicked grin on her bright face, her eyes dancing with unhinged delight.

"Cool," she whispered and looked down at the now perfectly healed palm. "I can get used to that." She gave Theo a disturbingly conspiratorial wink.

He frowned at her in return, the idea of Wynnie doing that over and over causing him to shiver slightly.

"Well, so that's how you create a huge distraction for a getaway. I really only taught you that spell so you could start with a small smoke screen, but I guess that's a good start. Thank you Wynnie."

Gabriel lifted Heretia cautiously back into her chair and moved to check her wounds again. Everything was still in place, she was just slightly sorer than before.

"Seriously Wynnie?" he shot her a nasty look as he situated the shoulder of Heretia's nightgown back up and covered her with a blanket. Wynnie merely shrugged and looked back down at the collection of blades she had brought along. Theo could see her mind spinning with possibilities. He groaned inwardly, knowing that none of them were ever going to feel at ease again with Wynnie and her certain brand of crazy. Thank the Mother Goddess Jeremy seemed to like it because everyone else was terrified.

"Alright Theo, let's try the unveiling spell," Heretia motioned for a small box that was now the only thing still sitting on her desk. It hadn't moved an inch in all the commotion. "This box holds something incredibly special to me, and important. I have it warded to never be moved or opened by anyone other than me. However, after what I've seen today, I think *Aperio* used with enough offering, could just make it open. Go ahead and try it. You might need a lot for this one, I've got things locked down tight." She pointed and Theo stepped forward to face the box.

With a deep breath, he brought Mia's silver blade to his hand and took in a quick breath. Quickly, he sliced into his palm and made sure it was forceful enough to go deep. Theo immediately squeezed his palm shut to pull out as much blood for the spell as possible and visualized exchanging the blood for power. His veins began tingling and his nerve endings came alive. The feeling of crawling ants took over his arm and he said the spell aloud, thinking of the box opening.

"Aperio," he muttered.

Everything was silent for a moment before a light, almost inaudible click, echoed in the room. Theo's eyes shot open to see the top of the box slightly ajar and waiting for him to reveal what was inside. The tingling in his arm receded and he looked down to see his normal, unmarked hand now smeared with his own blood, before him.

Without thinking, he reached to open the lid. Gabriel moved to stop him, but Heretia held him back.

"Wait, he deserves to see it. He did open it after all," she whispered, not wanting to disturb him.

Inside the box lay two locks of hair. Clearly, they were old and fragile, but there were wrapped together in a single ribbon and next to it, lay a vial of clear liquid.

"What is this?" he asked, not wanting to touch the articles in case they crumbled under his touch.

"That was my only attempt at fulfilling my dream of having a family with Gabriel. It's a lock of his hair and mine from when I was Meloni one thousand years ago," she breathed.

Everyone turned, stunned into silence at Heretia's revelation. She blushed lightly, her porcelain skin pinking under the scrutiny.

"I realized after a few years that we couldn't have children. So, I put our hair aside thinking one day that I might ask the Mother Goddess for help. That day never came however, and I almost forgot about them. It wasn't until I was reborn and looking through my old things that I found the hair again."

Gabriel stooped down and wrapped Heretia's tiny hand into both of his, kissing her knuckles lovingly.

"I'm so sorry, my love," he whispered reverently. Heretia smiled and tucked a string of loose hair behind his ear.

"It's no worry dear. I tried a few times to see if I could make it work, but by that time I only had my Blood magic, my elemental abilities were gone. Had I found this box sooner, however, I still wouldn't have been able to do it. My training as a Life Sorcerer was woeful at best. That vial is the only thing that came close, but without Life magic, I didn't want to risk it. It's been waiting on Mia all these years to see what she can do."

Wynnie made a small sniffle and Theo could have sworn he witnessed her secretly blink back a tear.

"I'm not human, love. It's not going to be possible. There's nothing even the Mother Goddess, least yet Mia, can do about that. I told you all this last time and I thought we got through it," Gabriel said.

Heretia's eyes were shining with her own tears threatening to fall.

"I know," her voice was shaky as she looked down into her lap, wiping at one of her eyes. "But I didn't want to stop looking, just in case. To be the mother of your child would be the greatest accomplishment and joy in both my lives. But it's a fact I accepted long ago. I kept them more as mementos of you and me. I wasn't sure you would find me in this life, and I wanted something of you."

She looked at the box and reached her hand out, begging Theo to bring it to her. He gently lifted the now free box and brought it to her. She kept the lid open while she placed it in her lap.

"I just thought maybe, just maybe, Mia could give it a try when this is all over. Just once, it's all I'd ever ask of her. If it doesn't work, which it won't, I'll be okay with that."

Gabriel shut the box slowly and then gathered Heretia up into his arms. Everyone felt awkward, watching the beautiful exchange of hopes and dreams and the wish that could never be granted.

"I think that's all for right now," Will muttered quietly and moved to the door.

The rest of the group, save for the two who were still holding on to each other, to their hope, left the room shutting the door gently behind them.

CHAPTER EIGHT

MIA

I didn't see anyone else for the rest of the night and was only brought water and a slice of bread the next morning by a Cannibal instead of Judas. I understood why Michelo had allowed another captive to bring me something to eat. He wanted to let me know that even more innocent lives were at stake now and to not try anything funny. I scarfed down the bread and guzzled the water like a ravenous wolf. I would need my strength for the Earth experiment today and I wanted to be ready.

I did regret almost instantly however, after eating the food, that I might be seeing it again after Gregor was done with me. I grounded myself and my Earth magic, rooting it deeply within me so that whatever he brought today wouldn't have a chance at touching it. I even started stretching to loosen my muscles. The memory of how much they had constricted and tightened in pain was all too recent. I didn't want it to hurt as bad today if I could help it. I even attempted some pushups for strength. While I wasn't trying to wear myself out, I also wasn't trying to go weak and act as if all hope was gone.

I still was working under the premise that I was going to find a way out of here, but knowing there were other captives that I was not going to be able to leave behind, including a whole orphanage full of children, that seemed like a long way away. It was a daunting task, but I wasn't going anywhere without them or Judas. I didn't even know where they were located, but I would find a way to get them all out of here with me. I had to figure out where they were held before I attempted an escape. If I had learned anything from Wynnie as she yelled her instructions during our brief training, it was to always have the plan completely laid out. Even if you only had a few bits of information available, if there was a way to learn it, you should. The more knowledge you had going in, the better the chance of success.

Knowing it was more than just my life at stake gave me the heart to continue and keep planning. I wasn't sure I would have tried as hard had I known I was the only one here. The children and Judas, however, had nothing to do with this war, and I wasn't one to stand by and watch innocent people get hurt in something that wasn't their fight.

Finally, at what seemed like noon, the old man came limping in, with a single vial in his hands. It was green, just as promised, and when he uncorked it, the liquid smelled of dank diseased moss. I covered my nose at the rotten smell and backed away.

"Now, now. We don't want a fight like yesterday. I will bring in some back up to hold you down again and force it if I have to," he ordered.

I tightened my lips together and every time he came closer, I kicked or punched out at him. With a fake regretful sigh, Gregor turned and called for my two zombie guards. I struggled in their grasp, but once more they overpowered me. It was even easier today. I was weaker and the effects of the day before were still evident in my limbs.

"Just swallow this and stop fighting, it really does make it easier on everyone," Gregor crooned as he leaned over and poured the nasty smelling and even worse tasting liquid down my throat.

I spluttered against it and tried to spit out as much as possible. It tasted like an animal had died and it felt rotten on my tongue. When Gregor deposited the last drop into my mouth, one of the Cannibals clamped a hand over my nose and mouth to force me to swallow. I felt like some feral dog that had been captured and was being forced to take a pill.

Unfortunately, this medicine was not going to save my life from fleas or heartworms, but very well could kill me by tearing my magic right out of my body. It would then go on to help kill countless others, and I couldn't have that on my conscious. I held my breath for as long as I could to hold the foul-tasting liquid on my tongue. I vomited slightly as my reflexes finally swallowed it down.

I gagged and choked as they released their tight grip on me, throwing me down on my knees. I heaved huge breaths as my lungs screamed for air.

"Now, we wait. I'm hoping you having a Pair with Earth magic makes it that much more potent. If I can't have Fire, which is my first choice for the army, I want the magic I give them to be extremely strong. Earth can do massive amounts of damage if wielded correctly, and I know just the spells to take down that High Castle of Heretia's," he chuckled to himself.

The last thing I saw was a stool being brought in so that Gregor could sit and watch me suffer for the next half hour or so.

Just as I was beginning to think it wasn't going to work at all, the feeling of being ripped apart from the inside began. It didn't go slowly, but erupted with one large rip through my abdomen. I had watched women in labor in videos and in real life, and if I had to describe it, I would say it was along the lines of trying to push twins out at the same time in every direction. There was no ebb and flow to this pain, however. It was one constant tearing sensation that began in my stomach and quickly made its way through every orifice of my being.

As a writhed in unimaginable pain, sparks of light shot through my line of vision, even though my eyes were closed. I could feel something picking away like a knife at multiple points in my body, as if the potion were scraping away at my Earth magic wherever it saw a fray and thought it could grab it. The smell of Theo infiltrated my nose, but was quickly squashed and overwhelmed with the smell of rotting flesh. The little piece of Theo's magic that rested inside my ribs and fluttered when he was near, fled for safety, but found nowhere to go. I reached out and grabbed the piece that was struggling to stay together as the magic began to tear and claw at it.

"No!" I screamed out loud and wrapped my Life magic around the little piece, shoving it deeper and deeper into me, preventing the potions evil intentions from getting to it.

Every time it hit at the wall of Life magic that I had surrounded my piece of Theo with, a burst of yellow energy pounded it back. I fought as hard as I could, still in extreme agony to keep it. For ages I laid there, concentrating on not letting my Earth magic, either my own or Theo's, get taken by force. This was mine and it was precious and nothing else but me was touching it.

Suddenly, my Life magic found a weak point and struck out with full force, blasting the potion with its healing light, and dissolving it away. I felt the last bits and pieces of the horrid concoction wither away and die inside of me, leaving nothing but my own magic behind, untouched, and unchanged. I panted heavily like a wounded dog on the ground, sweat dripping over every inch of my skin and moistening the ground beneath my body.

I faintly heard Gregor scraping to get up from his stool to see what happened.

"What is this?" he asked aloud and his hand came to my face, but I winced away from him and punched out, hitting his bad leg with my fist.

Gregor howled as he dropped to the ground. In excruciating pain, but not wanting to miss my chance, I grabbed both of his ears in my fists and pulled his head down as hard as I could, connecting his nose with my knee. The crack of bone could be heard throughout the tent and the Cannibals came running to the old sickly man's screams for help. I didn't release him, however. I brought my foot up and connected it with his stomach as he laid sideways on the ground in front of me. As I reached out once more to begin pummeling his face with my fists, he was snatched away from me and I was grabbed by my hair.

"What is going on here?!" came Michelo's angry bellow.

I cried out in pain as my scalp was stinging from the yank. Hairs were ripped from their roots and my neck hurt from the movement as well. Michelo dangled me in the air by my hair and then brought me close to his face. I winced at the smell of his nasty breath. Obviously, he had been sleeping when Gregor's shouts had awoken him. Either that, or he didn't know how to use a toothbrush. No matter, it was horrid and in my already exhausted state, I reached up to cover my nose, instead the back of my fist connected with his jaw and I rendered him a weak uppercut.

Michelo barely even flinched, a fly wouldn't have flinched at the hit, and yet he took it as me attacking him and I was punished for it.

"You bitch!" he brought his fist down on my own face and I was sent sprawling back to the ground. My eyes and head swam from the impact and before I could hear another word, I blacked out.

*****

68

Probably hours later, I woke back up with a groan. Instantly, my hand flying to my splitting headache. I attempted to soothe it with magic, but in my exhaustion, I couldn't tap into it enough to do more than create a dull horrid throbbing. I struggled to open my eyes, but when I did, I saw nothing above me but the dark outline of the tent. It was night, the whole day had been wasted being laid out flat by a sucker punch to the face. As far as fistfights go, however, that was my first, and I wasn't dead, so there was that at least. I'd held my own against a weakling old sick man and then had been knocked out with a single blow to the face.

"Wynnie is going to be pissed," I whispered to myself alone inside the dark tent.

There were minimal sounds coming from the outside. Just the occasional shuffle of feet and a noise as if someone were grunting while pulling a heavy object. I suddenly began to chuckle to myself as I thought of how Wynnie would have handled that entire confrontation. She would have Gregor's neck snapped before her knee had hit his nose and Michelo would have been sporting the black eye, not her.

I touched the clearly swollen eye gingerly and then thought better of it as the sting caused me to hiss in extreme pain. I attempted to sit up, regretting that decision immediately, but needed to check over my surroundings. The memory of how close the potion Gregor mixed together had come at removing my Earth magic surfaced. It had felt so close to finding a place to snag at it and pull it out of me. I shivered at the thought. My Life magic saved it however, and even fought back on its own. It had protected itself and the rest of my magic from harm, an idea that hadn't come to mind as something a magic could do.

There was no one waiting on me to wake up. Gregor, Michelo and the Cannibal guards were gone, and I was yet again, alone. I was still heavily shackled to the heavy table. I didn't even attempt to pull at the chains, I knew nothing would happen. I squinted, trying to make out some figures through the shadows across the wall of my tent, but they moved too quickly and silently. I pulled myself up to look over the table and realized, with a huff, that no one had brought me another loaf of bread. My stomach was growling like a lion with hunger and my hands were even beginning to shake from lack of nourishment.

I had been here two whole days at this point, and I hadn't even come close to thinking up a way to escape. I had tried to call out to the Mother Goddess, but remembered that she was unable to see into the camp from her map. I highly doubted she could hear me within its wards as well. I was beginning to lose hope and the daunting task of figuring out a way to escape along with Judas and the children was eating away at my resolve.

I was sitting and contemplating what I could possibly do next when the tent was once again opened and this time, a child walked in holding a tray. Michelo followed the poor shaking girl with a grin on his face. I sucked in a breath, but refused to move, he was holding a knife to her dirty throat and the streaks of dirt coming down her face indicated that she had been crying for some time.

"Good, you're finally up. Figured you would want something to eat since you had missed your noon time meal and dinner as well," he laughed.

I scowled, but still said nothing. I didn't want the little girl hurt because of something I had done or said to anger Michelo further. My black eye was enough reminder of what he was willing to do if something went against his plans.

"I just wanted you to see some of the other prisoners we have here in the camp. This is Maria and she was especially excited to meet you. So much so that she couldn't hold back her tears of joy any longer, isn't that right Maria?" Michelo pressed the blade closer to her skin.

Instinctively, I moved with a handout to stop him, but Michelo yanked the girl closer to himself.

"Now you just cool it, Druid. We wouldn't want Maria to get hurt because I slipped or fell."

I pulled back, locking eyes with the terrified child. I reached out with my Life magic to comfort her, to let her know that she was going to be okay and to stay calm. As it inched closer, due to the sluggishness caused by the wards, I felt Michelo attack the small tendril and choke it.

I cried out in pain and fell to the ground, the squeeze even tightening my throat and heart.

"I've told you before and I guess I have to say it again, no magic," he hissed.

I gasped a hefty breath of air as soon as he released me. My heart was pounding, and I pulled all my magic back deep within me. It was

70

slimy and nasty, the feeling of him touching my magic, and it left me shaken every time.

"Put the food on the table," Michelo instructed Maria, who moved cautiously to lay the tray down without spilling a single drop. "Now, go."

With a jump and a cry of fear, Maria scampered away. I looked after her, terrified of what would happen.

"Eat. I need you strong for tomorrow. Gregor wants to attempt at removing your Life magic. It's the one thing that keeps preventing us from taking the rest. It will do my soldiers no good on the battlefield, but it will help us get the rest from you," he instructed me.

With a shiver, I watched him leave the tent. I waited a moment or two more before pouncing on the scraps of bread and water Maria had left me. I was just about to slam the now empty cup on the table when I noticed a solitary scrap of paper, barely bigger than two fingers, sitting on the tray. It must have been under the cup because I hadn't noticed it before.

I looked around me to make sure no one was watching, and I slowly turned the scrap over revealing a few quickly and badly scrawled words on the piece. I had to lean in close to even see what was so hastily written and snuck into my tent.

He takes it off when he is asleep

I blinked twice in astonishment. Who is he? What is it? And why would I care. I sat back to think through the message clearly when it dawned on me. The only two men in this camp would be either Gregor or Michelo, but Michelo is the greater threat. It had to be referring to something he wears if he takes it off, which means it had to be the Death amulet Michelo had stolen from Heretia.

Whoever had sent this message must be someone that wasn't a Cannibal, could write, and knew enough about Michelo's nighttime routine that it was a known fact that Amulet came off every night. But how would this help me unless I was able to get it while he slept? The only way I could manage that is if I were able to escape completely unseen and have time to sneak in and take it. Michelo losing the Amulet would be a huge win in the war. It was what granted him the ability to fly and touch my magic. Stealing that back would weaken him greatly and give our armies the edge to overtake him.

My mind whirled with the possibility of even granting the Amulet to Heretia so she could wield it for herself as well. It would give her an elemental magic back and make her strong enough to fight as well. My heart swelled and then instantly deflated.

All of this was hinged upon my ability to escape, which was seemingly impossible. Even with it off at night, the moment my escape was alerted, Michelo would snatch the Amulet up and put it on, rendering me useless yet again. I huffed heavily and looked at the message once more. This had to be Judas who sent the message. The children probably couldn't write and from what I had gathered, Judas was kept close to Michelo so that he could use him as a slave.

My eyes were beginning to fall again as I thought heavily on the subject of my escaping but in my last thoughts before sweet sleep overtook me, I ate the note. I didn't need either Gregor or Michelo finding it and punishing Judas for writing it.

Chapter Nine

Theo

Sleep had barely come to Theo as he had tossed and turned in his bed throughout the night. Between thinking of Mia alone in the camp, possibly being hurt, and trying to think of a way to save her, it was just impossible. Finally, he had blinked off for a few measly hours before the sun rose and Will was beating down his door.

"Barracks, now. We've got to start making plans and getting everything together. Jeremy is waiting for us," Will called.

While it felt like his feet were made of lead, Theo was up in moments, dressed, and raced for the barracks to hear what Wynnie might have come up with in the night. Everyone around the table looked as though they hadn't slept much either. Theo could guess it was for the same reasons he had been unable to rest, worry over Mia.

"Alright, Wynnie and I have come up with a semi-helpful plan that may or may not work. More than likely, if we can guess right, it will, but as always there's a chance it won't," Jeremy started, cheery as ever.

Theo grimaced at the level of his booming voice. Tim groaned and hung his even fluffier and out of control hair in his hands.

"Can't we eat first?" he begged.

Will grunted and punched his shoulder with a bit of force. It wasn't enough to knock the smaller man completely over, but it was enough to make him sit up straighter. Gabriel was sauntering in at that time and snickered at the sight. Jeremy nodded toward the man and then relinquished the reigns of discussion to Wynnie.

"I'm going to go and help Heretia with the delegates from the other countries. Hopefully, Maravette has decided to jump in with both feet as everyone else has. There are some logistics we need to work on for right now," Jeremy smiled. He gave Wynnie a quick kiss on her fair forehead and waved everyone else off.

"Well, he seems to be pleased with himself," Gabriel laughed.

He lifted an eyebrow at the only remaining woman in the group. She shot him a nasty glare, catching his sordid meaning, and returned to the map of Purge that she had brought out. It depicted the desert beyond, and in it, she and Jeremy had drawn a rough outline of what the Second Uprising camp looked like.

"Heretia and Gabriel helped me get together a basic idea of what we are looking at going in to. This isn't the amount if intel I usually feel comfortable with, and in essence, we're going in blind. We know that it is a completely mobile camp." She pointed to the center with a single delicate index finger. "Everything is tents and wagons. It seems Michelo has just been building this rough war camp for a few years, but always with the intention of moving around, which he may very well have been doing. Heretia explained that the grounds and water supply from the Cannibals gets infected easily and if Michelo wants to keep himself and Gregor clean of it, they must have constantly been looking for cleaner supplies. We're not sure how they're keeping the Cannibals satisfied, but he must have picked up tricks from Heretia and the city of Purge while he was here."

Will nodded thoughtfully, but Theo just frowned. He hadn't considered any of this when Mia had given herself up. Would she accidentally ingest something that had been poisoned and turn into a Cannibal herself? How was Michelo feeding himself and her to keep them sane? The worry in his gut grew larger for his Pair.

"We've got a good estimated size of the encampment and it is completely in a round shape as Gabriel was able to discover for us last night during a quick fly over," Wynnie continued.

Theo's eyes shot to the man who gave a smirk and a shrug.

"Had to do something after you guys went to bed. The people from the other kingdoms find me," he searched for the right word. "Uncomfortable, it seems. I don't think they like being in the presence of Death itself."

Tim nodded in agreement with that sentiment. "I can understand that. I wasn't sure how to take you at first either." He looked up at the auburn-haired man. "Then you started fighting with Wynnie so easily that I got over it. Maybe that's what we should do. Just stick all the emissaries in a room with you two and let them watch you duke it out."

Wynnie and Gabriel glanced at each other, seemingly considering the thought for a moment before Wynnie shook her head.

"No, that would probably just scare them more and cause Eric to piss his pants," she snorted and then turned back to the map.

"I want to send Gabriel, myself, and one more out tonight to find a pattern and a hole in the wards. I just need one good entrance and I'm fairly sure Gabriel's magic can do the rest. Once we can get in, I don't think it would take us long to find Mia and get her out. We can come up with a signal later that will indicate one of us has her and to retreat."

She motioned to Will who stared at the map for a moment longer. "I'm not the biggest fan of this plan, but it's really the only thing we have right now. I say Gabriel, Wynnie, and Tim go out tonight to find the way in," Will instructed.

Theo's chair screeched across the brick floor with his sudden movement to his feet. "I'm going," he announced, but Will shook his bushy fire red hair.

"No, you and I need to stay here and keep getting ready for the actual battle that is inevitable at this point. The other countries are sure to start sending messages back and I need you to help me communicate with them. As a Prince, you are what they will listen to. Jeremy needs me to help with the war effort and allocating troops appropriately. Lastly, you need to keep working with Heretia on the unveiling Blood magic. Michelo's wards are going to be much more difficult than a simple box, so you need to get ready for that."

Theo deflated, knowing that Will was right, but not wanting to stay behind while Mia needed him too.

"Okay," Wynnie ignored the small confrontation unfolding before her and rolled up the map. "Now that this is all settled, we just need to wait for night fall before we leave."

Will turned to Tim and Theo. "You two go whip up Jeremy's soldiers into shape. With how much he is running, he doesn't want his soldiers and guardsmen falling behind. They need to be ready now more than ever, and he asked for our help in getting them together and prepared."

Tim groaned. Will punched his shoulder again, this time causing Tim to fall completely out of the chair and into the floor.

"No more complaining. These soldiers haven't seen new fighting techniques for over twenty years, not that it is Jeremy's fault by any means," Will quickly recovered under Wynnie's angry glare. She didn't appreciate someone talking ill of her Pair's leadership abilities. "But they need us to update them. Michelo will know what we know, but the Ancient Kingdom is woefully lacking, again not Jeremy's fault."

Will took a step back from Wynnie as he finished. Theo silently unfolded his arms and stalked off towards the barracks, Tim following right behind. There was no arguing with Will on this. Not only was he their Captain, but he was right. Theo had seen the so-called soldiers work and train during some of the days he had been in Purge and while they had the heart, they didn't have the skill. Jeremy had been working off bare bones for years. He had collected a group of strong young men who were still clean from the stain of the Second Uprising, but they were few. The majority of their duties had been guard duty of the castle and of Heretia, so battle was not their strong suit.

Theo walked into the training ring to find five men suiting up in battle gear and swinging swords to loosen their shoulder muscles. Tim came to stand next to him, watching them silently as well.

"I could have sworn there were more than this," he whispered out of the corner of his mouth to Theo, not trying to stir controversy.

"Jeremy sent the majority of what he had to meet Ez at the East port. From what I remember, she should be there tomorrow at some point," Theo responded.

Tim blew out a breath of relief. "Thank the Mother. I was really concerned at what we were working with here. Maybe we can just teach these few guys everything they need and they can pass it on for us and we won't get stuck doing this over and over."

Theo gave a silent nod of agreement and then took a step into the bright sunlight and the training ring. All five men looked up as the two Elite Guardsmen stood before them, arms crossed, and weapons strapped all across their chests and hips.

"Oh shit!" one man muttered.

Theo bit back a snort. They were known all throughout Medeis, but he had never guessed the Elite Guard's stories had reached through the Ancient Kingdom's barrier. The biggest of the five puffed out his chest and stood straighter.

"What do you two want?" he asked darkly.

Theo wasn't sure exactly what these five men knew would be happening today, but from the way the biggest was acting, no one had advised them.

"This should be fun," Tim snickered, and started circling the five to the right while Theo circled to the left.

"It has come to our attention that the soldiers of Purge haven't really had any new training in battle for a few decades. Your Captain has asked the Elite Guard to step up and get you up to date, as it were. While he is off getting the rest of the kingdoms ready, our job is to get you five up to speed as fast as possible so that you can share it later with the rest of your unit when they return," Theo explained.

The five men blinked in confusion and looked to each other and then to the biggest yet again.

"I am their lieutenant and I knew nothing about this. Captain just asked us to be here this morning, ready for more training. He never said anything about you two showing up," he said sourly.

He made another step forward, threatening but useless. Theo raised a dark eyebrow and then smirked.

"Be that as it may, it's what's happening. Now, drop your swords," he instructed.

Not one of the five moved, which didn't surprise Theo in the least.

"I'm pretty sure your Captain wouldn't be pleased to hear that you have disobeyed an order from an Elite Guardsman that he specifically sent to help you," Theo clucked his tongue.

His soldier senses were kicking in. Thoughts of Mia were beginning to ebb away as he assessed his surroundings, took in his opponents, and began to see ways to bring each and every one of them down if need be.

"How do we know that you are the Elite Guard? We knew nothing of you until just recently, and honestly, I haven't been that impressed with what I've seen. You've stepped foot out here once or twice and think you own Purge now? Own this castle? We have spent our entire lives in dedication to the service of our Queen and our Kingdom," the man continued.

Theo was growing bored of the talk and decided to put this soldier in his place. Without a sound, he leapt up into the air. Before anyone could blink, both of his favorite swords were unsheathed and he was coming down with both feet flat into the soldier's chest. Even with the man being twice his size in weight, the force of the impact could be heard and even felt by all around them. As the large man fell to the ground, Theo placed both of his swords over the man's neck and leaned down to meet him face to face. The other four moved to defend their lieutenant, but a quick draw of his bow from Tim had them stopping still.

"I applaud your bravery, Lieutenant. But with bravery, there is always an ounce of stupidity. Do you think for one second, if we were here to do anyone in this High Castle harm, your Queen's wards would have let us through?" Theo hissed.

The man grimaced, realizing that Theo was right. With a grunt, he nodded his head in acceptance. Theo moved to help him up and re-sheathed his swords.

"I am Theodeus Varillian, Elite Guardsman, Prince of the First Throne of Suravia and the Druid's Pair. If you for one moment think that I am not as invested in this war as anyone else, you are wrong. I am probably the most invested, for my Guard, for my kingdom, and for my Pair. Every part of me needs this battle to sway in our favor, and heavily. So, I need you," he pointed to the five men. "To be at your best."

They looked around at each other sheepishly.

"Through no fault of your own, nor even that of Heretia's, you are over two decades behind in training and battle tactics. You have never once had to fight the way you need to. You are fantastic guards and you are physically in peak shape, but war is not your forte." He glanced at Tim who had moved to stand behind him. He had shucked his arrows off to the side somewhere and laid his bow to the side, now donning a short sword at his belt. "It is, however, ours."

Tim moved forward and began speaking. "We will teach you formations and advances that are commonly taught in our two countries. You will need to memorize these so that you can pass it on to your fellow soldiers and began working together as a unit. An army is different than guard duty. You have to work together at every step and be in each other's minds."

The five men began to move closer together, forming a loose chain that Theo and Tim easily divided.

"You must be of one mind and be able to predetermine what the man next to you is thinking as well as read the battlefield for the answers of what to do next. Just hacking away will eventually happen and I'm sure you can do that with ease."

A light chuckle went up among them and a few even nudged each other with knowing winks.

"But that comes only after you have broken through enemy lines and are free to destroy at will," Tim snapped, regaining their attention.

For hours, Theo and Tim seemed to play a game of chess with only knights for pieces, as the five men learned and relearned every formation the two Guardsman could throw at them. At some point, Wynnie joined them, which had led to some grumblings from the five men until she was able to hold formation between Theo and Tim as the soldiers attempted to break it over and over. After a well-placed kick to a jaw on one of them, the grumblings ceased, and she was instantly a fan favorite amongst them.

For a moment during the training, Theo had to walk away to collect himself. He wasn't sure if it was the heat of the sun or the high level of activity in so long, but he was suddenly very lightheaded and needed a moment. As he slurped down a cup of fresh water from a barrel provided under the shade of an awning, he felt his chest tighten. The breath from his body left him and his eyes began to darken at the edges, as if he were about to pass out. He leaned forward to catch himself, but as quickly as it came, it faded away again. He stared down at his hands, slightly shaking from the encounter. It had to just be the heat, he thought to himself, and moved to rejoin the group that was still working tirelessly.

Eventually, Jeremy sauntered his way over. His laughter and delight at seeing the men was obvious.

"You look like a real army!" he threw his arms out and the five soldiers crowded around for handshakes and claps on the back.

Wynnie skipped her way through them and flung her arms around his neck after a hefty leap to plant a loud smacking kiss on his lips. No one was fazed, however, and the training continued, this time with Jeremy on the receiving end of Wynnie's attacks.

He seemed to enjoy it however, Theo noted. Their dynamic was flourishing and not once did Jeremy ever back down from a good fight with his Pair. He never went easy on her and even critiqued her once in a while.

She took it happily and continued fighting with him as the time went on. Theo smiled to himself after shoving one of the younger guards away and lashing out with his sword in a defensive maneuver exercise. In the few years he had known Wynnie, her struggles at being accepted had been her biggest stopping block. Mia had seemed to break down a few barriers with her in the short time they had been friends, but it was Jeremy that was truly lifting her up to rise above. Theo wasn't even sure she considered her family's feelings anymore. She had returned from Maravette ready to work, and not once had she reached for a bottle of alcohol since coming back.

Had Mia caused that type of effect on him as well? He thought this notion over as Jeremy called for a break in the day. It was well beyond noon and even inching on dinner.

"We've got some emissaries to harass for a formal shindig Heretia slapped together in their honor. We've all been requested to attend," Jeremy winked at Wynnie who rolled her eyes.

"That means a dress, doesn't it?" she asked sardonically.

"Only if you think I'll like it," Jeremy replied.

Together they said goodbye to the men and reentered the castle. Jeremy had mentioned that Ez was to land sometime the next day and Theo's spirits were beginning to lift as well, considering he hadn't seen her in so long.

Theo and Tim helped the men clean up and rearrange the weapons nicely, then bid them farewell. The five soldiers seemed exhausted, but thrilled, waving the two Elite Guardsmen back into the castle with calls for more instruction the next day.

"Did Mia change me? Am I better for it?" Theo wondered aloud to himself. He thought over the idea again as he sank into a tub of cold water to relax his aching limbs.

He certainly didn't feel that much different, but considering how uptight and in control he had always been before her, he guess she had. She had taught him to relinquish control, to let her lead him instead of him always protecting her. She had shown him a mother he never thought he could have and had connected with Vanessa easily. Mia had given him love and support with confronting his father. She had given him the room to make mistakes without persecution or berating him, but with understanding and grace.

His heart sank as he considered all that she had done for him, but what had he done for her? He had made her choose between two worlds and she had chosen him. He had left her behind in Lotho when she clearly should have gone with them. Had she met Heretia sooner, this Second Uprising may have already been stopped. He had constantly bombarded her with his own problems and past, but what had he helped her through? Theo closed his eyes with a huff and tried not to think about what Mia was going through right now for him, for her parents, for all of Medeis. She was giving so much up, so much of herself, and what were they doing in return? Asking more and more from her.

A light knock on the door caused Theo to jump from his half sleeping thoughts. Water spilled out on the floor.

"Coming!" he shouted, and reached for a towel, racing to answer the knock.

Dripping with water, he yanked open the door to see Giselda standing there. Her eyes shot wide open at the sight of Theo, half naked in nothing but a towel and panting lightly from the scramble.

"Oh!" she started and then unabashedly trailed his body with her eyes. "I'm so sorry, I didn't know you were busy." The blush creeping up her neck was as red as her hair. Theo placed the door more in front of him and stood behind it.

"Can I help you with something?" he asked, the diplomatic side of him trying to come out, instead of the soldier side that wanted to slam the door in her face with a few well-placed cuss words over being alone in the hallway in front of his door.

"No," she started and after a half a second paused, shook her head, and met his eye. "I was just wondering what you were doing. I know Queen Heretia is holding a big feast tonight to try and woo the Maravette visitors. I was hoping maybe we could sit next to each other. I feel like you understand my position better than anyone else here, being another Heir and all."

Theo's frowned darkened. "Tim is technically an Heir until Tom has a child. Clarisse, a grown woman, is also technically an heir if Mia chooses to forgo her Throne. I'm not sure why I am the one you seek out for company."

His logic smacked her in the face embarrassingly and she was stunned silent.

"Princess, while I feel for your plight back in Elevetia and I swear we are doing everything we can to get your cousin, Prince Judas, back, I am a Paired man. As such, this encounter is inappropriate, and I ask that you not seek me out privately in my rooms. If you wish to speak with me on state or military matters, I am happy to meet with you in either the Library or Queen Heretia's private library with her present," Theo said.

Theo's blood was beginning to boil at the thought of what this slip of a girl was possibly trying to accomplish coming here. The little piece of Mia that rested within him banged against his solid ribs, begging to be let out to give her a piece of its elemental mind.

"I'm sorry," she muttered.

She turned to leave quickly as Theo shut the door and blew out a heavy breath. He had certainly dealt with this type of attention his entire life. He was a Prince, and he knew he was far from hideous, but now that he had a Pair, he had hoped it wouldn't happen anymore. His father always joked that Theo was only as good as his looks and his title, a sentiment that still caused Theo to break things when he thought too hard on it. It was one of the many reasons he had left Suravia as soon as he could. He needed to prove himself as something more than a pretty Prince.

Will had been the first one to give him a fighting chance to show the world that he wasn't just some spoiled rotten diplomatic brat who was just waiting for his father or mother to die so he could be set for life. He had never let Will down for that, and he wasn't going to anytime soon. The only thing in this world that he would choose over Will, was Mia.

He thought back to the time he had practically told her so. In the Safehouse on Lotho after they had found Wynnie stone cold drunk and Mia had stepped in to rescue her from Will's wrath. Will had been pacing furiously in the front room, ready to lash into Mia for butting in, but Mia hadn't been afraid. She had stridden in there, head held high and back straight. She was ready to take on a giant like Will with no fear in her eye. Theo had almost gone to his knees and wept. Instead, he had reminded her that while Will was his Captain, she was his Pair, and all she had to do was say the word and he would take her side.

Tim still didn't let that go. When the two of them were in private, he joked about how Theo had softened when it came to Mia and was "Moonstruck" as he called it.

"She can do nothing wrong in your eyes. That woman could slice your finger off, instruct you to eat it, and all you would do is beg for salt to make it taste better."

Theo didn't like that analogy, but Tim was almost right. Mia was perfection to him. Granted, Theo understood no one was perfect and she had her own problems and faults, like her massive heart that got in the way of just about everything. Or her slight impulsiveness when she felt only she could fix it. But those were strengths to Theo as well. He had truly never admired someone as much as he admired Mia.

The gong for dinner rang out and doors began to open and shut as guests passed by down the hall, light chatter amongst themselves. Theo hurriedly finished dressing and grabbed a ceremonial sword. He chose to bring Mia's silver blade with him so that a piece of her was with him at all times.

He opened the door just in time to see Tim skipping down the hallway with Will not far behind.

"Heard you had a visitor?" Tim smirked as he sauntered up to Theo.

Tim could cut a dashing figure when he tried. Theo noticed as much when he looked him over in his sapphire blue suit, the colors of Lotho.

"Dear Mother, really? I told the girl to go away. Nothing happened!" Theo defended.

Will raised both hands for calm. He was wearing a dark brown suit that looked similar in cut to Tim's, but matched his russet eyes perfectly. He had even combed his beard and braided his long red hair.

"We know, Theo. Don't worry. A maid saw and ran to tell Heretia. Her name is Rebekah, and apparently, she likes Mia for some reason. She wasn't thrilled at what she saw, but Heretia made sure she understood you weren't that type of Pair. Heretia only mentioned it to me in passing, so even she's not worried over it. She just wanted me to know in case someone made a comment," Will explained. He slapped a hand on Theo's shoulder, causing him to buckle slightly.

"I doubt they will. Apparently, the girl is terribly embarrassed and is terrified Heretia or you will say something," Tim snorted from behind the two of them as they walked down. "It's not you or Heretia she needs to worry about anyway."

Theo turned with a raised eyebrow to his friend.

"What are you going to do about it if she says something?" he asked, imagining all the few things Tim had ever confronted a woman about in matters that didn't much concern him.

"Oh, I'm not talking about me. I mean Mia," Tim chuckled as he walked off from Theo, leaving him horrified in the hallway.

"Dear Mother," Theo whispered to himself.

CHAPTER TEN

HERETIA

Considering Heretia had less than a day to throw together a type of party for her first large gathering in the history of her reign, she had given herself some silent congratulations. From the moment the sun had come up, she had this entire evening in the works. Each of the emissaries had received a personal visit from her throughout the day. With the Elite Guard working on rescuing Mia, Jeremy working on getting the war effort together, and Gabriel floating in and around doing a bit of everything, Heretia had taken it upon herself to grab Clarisse and start firming up alliances with the emissaries present.

Word had come that Esmerelda from Suravia was arriving around noon the next day, so there was also that to prepare for. Jeremy had handled most of that by sending all but a handful of guards and soldiers out to greet them.

Clarisse had done gloriously in speaking with each and every member of the guest list. She and Alyssa had hit it off quickly, as did Heretia herself. Mia had recounted a lot of her time in Lotho to Heretia and described the pretty bronze skinned woman before her. Heretia felt the positive energy that exuded not just from Alyssa, but from Thomas as well. Dryan had been a bit of a nuisance. He was here more for the historical significance of the event and was constantly asking Heretia question after question about her Blood magic, her conversations with the Mother Goddess, and most importantly of all to him, her life as Meloni.

Apparently there had been a lot of gaps left in the records about Meloni and what happened after the First Uprising, and he was eager to learn even the weirdest of detail.

"What was your favorite perfume?" he asked excitedly at one point, adjusting the small glasses on his face.

Heretia had held back rolling her eyes in annoyance and shortly answered, "Moon Blossom."

Elevetia was a different story. Giselda had tried to present herself as this all-powerful Princess who was completely in control, but Clarisse ate right through that in mere moments simply by asking her, in the warmest motherly tone available to her, if she was alright.

Giselda had burst into tears and Heretia, from experience, could tell she wasn't acting. The two emissaries with the Princess, Gilroy and Miranda, seemed highly embarrassed by her display of emotion. Heretia had eventually convinced the girl to dismiss herself and let the rest of them discuss what Elevetia was willing to offer the war effort. Clarisse had gone with her, a comforting presence, leaving Heretia to meet with the two remaining adults in the room.

"It is good to finally meet you in person," Miranda began kindly and wisely.

Heretia bowed her blonde head. "Likewise. It's been far too long since the outside world has been safe to enter the Ancient Kingdom. However, as I'm sure Gabriel has explained, I couldn't allow that until I knew there was hope. If the Cannibals here in my city had found a way out, or to hurt others, I would not have been a good Queen to either them or my kingdom." She waved her hand to the window that displayed the ghostly city below. "We don't have much left, but what is there, I have to protect from not only itself, but those who don't yet understand. I am sorry it had to be this way for so long. There is so much I wanted to share with the rest of Medeis, but I just couldn't for the safety of my innocent people who still suffer so much."

Miranda nodded in agreement. Gilroy just grunted from his chair near the window. His short legs barely touched the ground, cutting him a troll-like figure.

"The High Rulers of Elevetia would have understood. They would have rather known the truth than lived in fear for two decades thinking that at any time you were going to swoop in and kill us all," he said sternly.

Miranda turned with a withering glare to Gilroy, but he wasn't fazed.

"No, Miranda. He's right. I made choices, as a Sovereign. Whether we see them as wrong or right now, they were the ones I had to make at the time. I'm sure the High Rulers of Elevetia can understand that sentiment. Sometimes, we have to do what must be done, not what we want to do," Heretia explained.

Gilroy softened at her words, then agreed halfheartedly. After a moment of silence, Miranda reached into her bag and held out a letter addressed to Heretia.

"This is for you. It is from our High Rulers. It lays out exactly what they can send and offer for the effort. All you have to do is reply and it will be on its way."

Heretia nodded appreciatively and then balked at the massive numbers written on the page.

"This must be everything!" she exclaimed in surprise.

Gilroy grunted again. "It is everything, or just near about. We share a land mass with this Second Uprising of Michelo's and should the Ancient Kingdom fall, we're next. We would rather die in battle all together as one Kingdom then let him rule us with his Cannibals."

Heretia fell silent at the man's words. Her heart swelled with pride at the generosity and confidence Elevetia had in her, and in Mia.

"My reply is that the Ancient Kingdom and all of Medeis will forever remember the sacrifice the Kingdom of Elevetia was willing to make when called upon for the greater good of this world. I will inform my Captain immediately and he will make accommodations for your army," Heretia smiled.

Miranda and Gilroy bowed their heads and Heretia bowed hers in return. After some more light chatter and inviting all three of them to dinner that night, Heretia collected Clarisse who seemed extremely thankful for the rescue.

"I know girls that age. I not only was one, but I raised one, and I understand she is under a lot of pressure from her country right now with her cousin missing, but dear Mother!" Clarisse finally let out as they walked down the hallway together. "She is drama!"

Heretia giggled into her hand as they turned down the wing that held the group from Maravette.

"We're going to have to watch that one," Heretia agreed before lifting her hand to knock on Eric Lily's door.

Heretia had not been looking forward to this meeting. Any family of Wynnie's couldn't be good news. Wynnie's history had been somewhat explained to Heretia during their journey to see the Mother Goddess and Heretia was angry to hear how the Lily's treated the beautiful and strong young woman. It had reminded her of the lengths her own mortal father had gone to stunt Heretia's magic and make sure she was useless to anyone and everyone.

Eric himself answered the door with a horridly fake smile plastered on his face.

"Your Majesty!" he greeted then turned to see Clarisse. "Your Highness!"

Heretia frowned slightly. Apparently, the Lily's thought themselves rich enough or too good enough to offer bows to High Rulers of other kingdoms. It made her wonder how they treated their own High Rulers and what she would find when their army showed up to help in the Second Uprising war. If they show up at all, the cowards.

"Mr. Lily, Clarisse was just helping me come around to my guests that I was unable to greet when you first arrived. I've come to offer my welcome and invite you and your two other guests to dinner with me this evening in the Dining Hall. May we come in?" she asked.

It wasn't so much polite, but pointed. This man was in her Castle, under her protection, and he was still standing there in the doorway and not moving aside when she came to greet him. The hairs on the back of her neck bristled with anger.

"Certainly!" Eric jumped, finally catching his error, and stepped aside.

Heretia and Clarisse quickly entered, hoping he didn't change his mind and slam the door in their face.

"I hope the rooms are comfortable. It's been quite a long time since the High Castle was full and my staff was unfortunately put on short notice to ready everything." Heretia looked around to see a spotless and beautifully decorated room. How Rebekah managed it was beyond her. She only had herself and five girls to keep this whole place running and clean when it was just Heretia in residence. Heretia could only imagine what they went through to get the rooms ready. Heretia reminded herself to give them fantastic gifts of thanks when this was all over.

"It will do, I can understand the short notice and made amends for it," Eric said.

Clarisse went still, hovering over a chair that she was about to sit herself in. Luckily, Heretia was facing away from Eric as he said this. Her eyes shot wide open in surprise and she had to count to five before moving another muscle in her face.

"Thank you for that," she finally responded as sickly sweet as she could manage, not that the pompous jerk seating himself into one of her finer chairs cared.

"A dinner you say? I can't imagine that you will be able to come up with anything too formal at such short notice with so little resources. Purge has been cut off from the rest of Medeis for so long," eric mused. He looked out through the tiny window cleaned to perfection that looked directly up at the blue clear sky.

"We have made do with what we have been afforded, Mr. Lily. The Ancient Kingdom isn't completely fallen to the Second Uprising and my agriculture is still flourishing in my further lands and villages," Heretia bit down on her tongue sharply.

Clarisse sensed the tension building and decided to step in.

"We were also wondering if an announcement regarding Maravette joining the war effort could be made? Have the Maravette High Rulers come to their conclusion?" she leaned forward slightly, throwing a brilliantly sweet smile. Eric cleared his throat and twisted around slightly.

"There has been. It seems my sister Wynnie met with my elder sister and had a long discussion with each other. Considering the position, she is placed in as the wife of a High King and a new mother, it seems as though she has found a way to sway the Rulers to act in favor of the war and join its cause. The level of participation is still being discussed, but I should have an answer by dinner," he mumbled, clearly unhappy with the outcome.

Heretia bit back a scoff at the young man's apparent wish to see Medeis fall to the Second Uprising, what else would explain his sluggishness to commit?

"That's wonderful news!" Clarisse clapped her hands together with joy and stood. "Well, we certainly will be excited to tell the others tonight at dinner. If you would excuse us please, Queen Heretia is still taxed from her ailments and I need to see her to her rooms."

It was almost noon and they had done so much already, with tons more to accomplish.

Heretia gave a heavy breath and stood from her chair. She felt fine, but as she looked over to Clarisse for a signal to go, she paused. Clarisse was suddenly very pale, and a sweat was breaking out on her forehead. Eric was already reaching for the doorknob and before he turned back towards them Heretia leaned over and grabbed Clarisses' arm.

"Thank you again for your time and we will see you tonight." The small queen breezed through the door, expertly handling the older woman away from sight. As Eric shut the door behind them with a nod, Heretia leaned Clarisse back against the cool stone wall.

"You're pale. What happened?" she asked quickly and readjusted her grip on Clarisse, wrapping the shaking arm around her neck.

"I feel like I can't breathe," Clarisse whispered and leaned into Heretia for support.

"Let's get you down. Are you okay to make it to my room or do I need to call for someone?" Heretia worried, taking small steps. The fatigue from being imprisoned for so long must be catching up to Clarisse.

Heretia shook her blonde head, kicking herself for exerting her new friend for so long. She could have done all of the greeting alone, but sweet Clarisse had insisted and now she was falling ill from the lack of energy.

"No, just get me there. Quickly, I don't want anyone else to worry," she breathed.

Heretia obeyed and picked up the pace. Eventually they entered Heretia's bed chamber and by the time Clarisse was settled into the bed, she looked immensely better.

"I don't know what that was. I didn't think I was overdoing it, but apparently I was. Maybe it was Eric being an idiot that sped up my heart and made me faint."

Clarisse attempted to reason the episode away. Heretia assented, yet still turned to call for a healer to look her over, they couldn't take any chances with the mother of the Druid. Gabriel came storming in only a moment later, worry etched across his beautiful face.

"What's wrong?" he asked. Heretia frowned at his mood and shrugged.

"Nothing, Clarisse just felt faint for a moment, so I laid her down. Why are you so worried about it?"

He came to sink onto the bed, looking Clarisse over with a worried eye.

"I don't know. I was just walking around, talking to Will about tonight when I just felt horrible. I was dizzy, I was scared, and I felt like my chest was tightening," he explained.

"That's exactly how I felt," Clarisse whispered and looked between the other two.

"What could that possibly mean?" Heretia asked aloud, letting the thoughts hang in the air. Why would Gabriel, the element of Death and Clarisse, a Suravian Princess and the mother of the Druid suddenly feel weak at the same time? Thoughts and connections raced through her mind until one only logical link was left.

"Mia!" she shouted and began scrambling for her balcony. "Something has happened to Mia," Heretia began, but Gabriel pulled her back.

"Let me go, Gabriel. Mia is in trouble. We've got to do something. Her magic must be calling us."

She moved to her massive double windows that looked out over half of the city and half of the desert and flung them open. Racing to the edge of the balcony, she looked out in the direction of the desert, scanning the horizon for any sign of conflict or problems. There was nothing to see. No dust up, no storm, no advancing army of Cannibals. All was quiet save for the grunting and smashing of five soldiers and three Elite Guardsmen battling and training below.

Gabriel assisted Clarisse up from the bed and they joined Heretia on the balcony in quiet reverence.

"Nothing's there," Heretia whispered into the wind and slumped back. Gabriel placed a hand on her shoulder and pulled her against his warm body. "Mia is in trouble."

"My baby," Clarisse fought back the tears that were threatening to spill over. Heretia reached for the weeping mother and gathered her up in a hug.

"We're going to get her back, Clarisse. I promise, whatever it takes. Mia will be back in your arms soon. Gabriel will know if something bad happened to her, so whatever this is, we must trust that she will be okay." Heretia attempted to soothe her.

"My sweet girl," Clarisse wept into Heretia's shoulder.

As Heretia began getting ready to dress for dinner, Rebekah came rushing in, cheeks red with flush.

"Your Majesty! I have to tell you what I saw because you know me, I have to be honest, and honestly, I like the Druid and I don't like what's going on," she rambled.

Heretia blinked a few times at the flustered woman's ramblings. Throwing her hands up for peace, Heretia advanced on her slowly.

"Slow down Rebekah. Tell me what you saw. What about Mia?" she asked cautiously wanting to get a full story and not more broken words and stuttering.

"The Prince was standing at his door, talking to that hussy Princess from Elevetia half-naked!' she hissed the last two words in a whisper, as if anyone could hear them.

Heretia's heart sank. That didn't sound like Theo at all. He was devoted to Mia.

"They were in the hallway?" she asked for clarification, and Rebekah nodded. "Did he invite her in?"

"I didn't see him do that or hear him. I walked off before they could see me. I'm not a sneak!" Rebekah began to defend herself, but Heretia soothed her worries.

"I know you're not, Rebekah. I'm just trying to understand the situation. What did Theo look like? Were they just talking formally or was it something else?" Heretia asked.

Rebekah thought back and then her shoulders dropped.

"It just seemed like they were talking. He had the door half in front of him, but I could tell he wasn't wearing anything on his top half. She was fully dressed in the hallway outside his room," Rebekah explained.

Heretia nodded and said, "I think it was right of you to worry about Mia's Pair. You're a good woman and I'm glad you told me. I don't think there is anything to worry about, but it wasn't wrong to come to me. I'll clarify things with Theo tonight, but I'm sure it was a misunderstanding."

Rebekah nodded obediently and they continued getting ready for the dinner together.

Gabriel really was a showman. Heretia stared in wonder as she surveyed the Dining Hall. The giant table was sized to accommodate every person attending and the arrangement was lovely. Florals fell from every available vase, linens had been cleaned to white perfection, the silver was polished till it shone in the light of the candles floating

92

overhead. The fireplace roared delightfully, and the smell of the food was intoxicating.

"You did wonderfully," she whispered into Gabriel's ear and then settled her lips there with a light peck.

"I learned from you, my love. All those years together before now, it seems I picked up a few things," he smiled.

She giggled lightly as he pinched her cheek. She had to regain her composure quickly, however, as guests were beginning to file in.

"Please take a glass and a seat by the fire. I'd love to get everyone together before dinner first." She motioned for Alyssa and Tom to move towards the other end of the room. Dryan followed behind shortly after, straightening his glasses and smoothing down his little mustache.

"Your Majesty!" he began, and Heretia had to hold back a light groan. "I have researched your last days as the Druid, one thousand years ago, and I found mention to some journals that you kept throughout your life."

Both Gabriel and Heretia stiffened. Who had known about those other than herself and Gabriel? Those had been kept for Mia when she was born, and no one else. How had Dryan found out about them?

"Oh, those silly things? Yes, I kept a journal during that life, but they have to be long gone and forgotten at this point. It's been one thousand years," she quickly laughed away the topic.

Dryan hung his head, his hopes dashed.

"That's too bad. I was thinking maybe when Mia returns, they could possibly be helpful for her." He shrugged his thin shoulders and shuffled off to join his High King.

Heretia instantly felt horrible. He hadn't been trying to bug her at all or learn more about Meloni. He had truly been thinking about Mia. Heretia made note that when Mia returned to ask if it would be okay to let the loyal scholar read through them. Heretia didn't much care anymore.

While they had been her personal feelings, Meloni felt like a different life. She wasn't connected to Meloni anymore than Dryan was at this point. They were Mia's journals now to learn from and take meaning. If Mia was okay with Dryan pouring over them, then Heretia saw no problem either. Feeling more confident in Dryan's intentions led Heretia to view everyone else in a different light as well, that is until Giselda walked in.

"Hussy," Heretia whispered darkly so that no one else could hear her. Heretia had only had a moment earlier in the hallway to let the Captain of the Elite Guard, Wilhelm, know of what Rebekah saw between Theo and Giselda. Will had just snorted and shook his head.

"Same old, same old. We have this problem just about everywhere we go. You would think these young women would figure out that he has never been that interested in romance. Now that he actually has it, even less so. She's a brave one, Giselda. Don't worry, I'll have a talk with her father when he arrives. He and my father were close friends." And with that Will had left to go find Theo himself for the dinner.

Now, as Heretia watched the young princess enter, her blood actually began boiling. While she knew nothing was in the encounter, she was taking it personally for her friend that couldn't be present herself.

Giselda didn't even seem to act any different, still pretending to be some lost and distraught young woman. Heretia ignored her as she greeted Miranda and Gilroy happily. Then, as if on cue, Will, Tim, and Theo walked in. Theo brought up the rear of the trio. Instantly, Theo found Heretia's eyes and made for her without another word to anyone present. Heretia attempted to look away as he approached, but the man was on a mission.

"I need to speak with you," he whispered urgently.

"Not now Theo, we have guests to greet," she responded just as softly with a fake smile plastered on her doll like face.

"I need you to know that nothing is going on with Giselda. She came to my room and I soundly turned her away," Theo continued.

Heretia turned to Gabriel and tapped his arm. "Give us a moment, come find me the moment Eric Lily and his party get here."

Gabriel nodded, giving Theo a side eye that said it all. Heretia steered the distraught Prince back into the hallway from another door and shut the door firmly behind them.

"Heretia, please. You have to believe me in this. I didn't want her there and I don't want you thinking that I'm doing anything while Mia isn't here." Theo jumped right in. Heretia didn't want this conversation to go any further, so she slapped a hand over Theo's mouth.

"No one thinks that of you, Theo. We see Giselda for what she is. While I think she is over dramatic and playing this sole heir thing a little much, she is young and stupid. Much more than you are. Rebekah was just worried, and she did the right thing by telling me, but even I saw it for what it was. Now, get yourself together and act like it didn't happen," she warned.

Theo's shoulders slumped from relief. "Oh, thank the Mother. I was terrified you were all going to hate me and tell Mia something horrible when we got her back. It's bad enough she's not here, but to have some puny Princess banging down my door and making people think I'm being unfaithful to my Pair is worse," he breathed.

Heretia nodded in agreement. "I'll make sure the castle never makes it easy for her to find your room again."

Theo thanked Heretia immensely. Before they turned to head back in, however, Heretia had a thought. "Did you feel something today?" she stopped Theo with a question. He turned, raising an eyebrow at her.

"I know you were busy with my soldiers and working hard out in the sun, but did you feel faint today? Like you were going to fall over at some point?"

Theo's stunned expression told her what she needed to know, but she let him answer anyway.

"Yes, I did. I thought it was just the heat, why?" his eyes narrowed with scrutiny.

"Gabriel and Clarisse, they felt something similar. For Clarisse it was a tightening in her chest that left her breathless and I thought she was going to faint. For Gabriel it was fear and a sudden idea that something was wrong. We think it was Mia," Heretia confessed.

Theo sucked in a sharp breath and fell back a step into the stone wall, attempting to catch himself. "Is she hurt? Was she trying to reach out? Is she?" he let the last horrible question fall away, afraid to ask.

Heretia hurriedly tried to ease his fears. "She's not dead, if that's what you're asking. Gabriel would know and I suspect you would, too. But something was definitely wrong with her magic," she explained quickly.

Theo looked over his shoulder at a large window that faced the desert. "This is horrible, Heretia. I want her home. I need her home." His mouth was set in a firm line and his face was going pale at the thoughts racing through his mind.

"Will, Gabriel, and Wynnie are leaving before the dinner ends to start getting her back. It won't be much longer now. I know she has to be fighting, but as long as she's doing that, there's hope. We will get her back, Theo. I promise," Heretia swore.

Theo didn't immediately turn away from the window. She could practically hear his heart breaking.

"Come on, we have to get back in there. The best thing you and I can do for Mia right now is guarantee the other kingdoms answering her call to arms. As the Druid, she has this right, but while she's gone, we must continue that work." Heretia reached out to touch his arm. Theo jumped slightly, but then nodded in agreement.

"I just can't seem to breathe without her around," he admitted as Heretia moved to open the door.

"I feel the same way," she replied, and together they entered the Dining Hall.

CHAPTER ELEVEN

MIA

Morning was just peeping through the tent flap when I blinked my eyes open. It took me a second to understand why I was asleep on the ground of sand and dirt before I remembered where I was. With a groan, I sat up and rubbed my aching head. I hazarded a guess that my Life magic had been working hard while I slept. My bruised eye was fully open and there was no tenderness left. However, it left me feeling weak and sluggish. I stood and began running through some stretching and fitness exercises, trying to wake up. The strain of Michelo's wards was starting to get to me physically, not just magically. I didn't want to overdo it. I remembered what Michelo had promised about the experiments today, so I didn't push it too far. I would need everything I had to combat the two bastards attempting to steal my Life magic.

Judas was the one to bring me my breakfast this morning. I caught his eye silently as he placed the wooden tray on the table and turned to leave. I didn't want any words to be shared in case he wasn't the one who sent the letter or if someone was listening in. As he turned to exit the tent, he did look back once, made an eye movement to the tray, and then nodded. I nodded in return, letting him know I had received the missive. He didn't even blink as he left the tent, but I knew he was relieved.

I gobbled down the half cup of water and half a slice of bread. They must be trying to wean me off food slowly and starve me to prevent resistance. My hatred towards the men grew darker as my stomach growled, revolting at the tiny amount of food it had received after almost nothing the day before. I placed my hand over my stomach and instantly it calmed, but the attempt left me drained.

Not long after I had cleaned the pathetic excuse for a breakfast, the tent flap opened and Michelo came in, followed by Gregor hobbling along behind him.

"I suggest we don't have a repeat of yesterday," Michelo began darkly and motioned with his head for Gregor to step forward.

I backed away quickly as he pulled out the yellow vial. I began to cry internally. My body reeled at the idea of going through this again and I didn't know if it had any fight left in it.

"Now, be a good little girl and just drink this. It won't take long if you behave," Gregor chided smoothly, as if he were a father talking to an impertinent child.

I clamped my lips shut and backed away as far as the chains would let me. Gregor sighed and turned to Michelo. With a nod of his head, he stepped back and Michelo advanced in three large steps. I couldn't stop of cry of alarm escaping my lips as he dragged me up by my hair and placed his face in mine.

"Drink," he ordered through gritted teeth and reached out behind him for Gregor to hand him the vial.

I shook my head in alarm as it was uncorked, and he brought it to my lips. I shut them even tighter and attempted to swivel away, but Michelo shook me harder and when I accidentally let out a shout of pain, he poured it in. The liquid felt like molten lava burning down my parched throat and I gagged against it, but he had my head twisted back to where I couldn't cough it back up. The pain, this time, didn't wait to start. It was instant and it was excruciating. As Michelo dropped me unceremoniously back onto the sand, I began to scream and writhe in pain.

Wave after wave of stabbing tore through my throat and then my stomach as it settled there, quickly spreading to the rest of me. My magics fought hard to burn it away in my veins, but the fight was too strong. I curled into myself and cried tears of sorrow as each muscle in my body was stretched and contorted to make way for the intruder. My Life magic cowered, attempting to protect itself as the others took over slamming it with fire and ice, but the potion was unaffected this time and kept plowing through me.

As it made its way to my chest, my adrenaline kicked in and my heart began pumping faster and faster. I vomited all over the ground, unable to contain the rush of the natural chemical my body created. I broke out into a sweat and panted heavily. Death magic finally made an appearance, and this time, it didn't stay within my body. With all my might, I forced it to surround the potion that was creeping up and it squeezed tightly, trying to choke it out. Outside of my body, black mist whipped around and encircled me as well, trying to protect me from another physical attack outside.

"Don't touch her!" Michelo shouted from somewhere beyond.

I barely registered the command as the Death magic wrung the dark magic tighter and tighter until finally, it died within me and I took in a sharp, life-giving breath of air. I opened my eyes to blackness, and for a moment panicked that I was blind, but flashes of sunlight escaped through the mist that held me safely within.

"Dammit!" I heard Michelo shout again and something heavy was thrown onto the ground. "Figure this out Gregor! She's fighting everything you throw at her. When one magic doesn't work, the other's flare up. I want something that will get them all at once. Combine everything together and give it to her tomorrow. She can't fight all six at one time."

The room went silent and I was left on the floor, still sobbing at the pain and indignity. The Death magic receded back, disappearing away now that I was safe with a slight kiss to my cheek of comfort. I whimpered at the touch and longed to feel that type of reassurance again, but it was gone. Spent completely in its effort to save its host, it was unable to make another reappearance.

I lay there still, drenched in my own sweat and vomit for another hour, trying to collect myself. I was eventually able to roll over and look up, but everything was still on fire and my limbs refused to move after that round of magical poison.

"Please," I finally whispered to the ceiling of the tent. I was calling to the Mother Goddess, to Theo, to Heretia, and to myself. I wanted someone to hear me on the wind, to hear my call. "Please, save me."

And with that, I blacked out for the rest of the day.

Chapter Twelve

Theo

Relief flooded Theo in the wee hours of the morning when a knock came at his door and Heretia stood there in a simple dressing gown and robe.

"They're back and they have good news," she informed him.

Together they took off for her private study. Hope raced through Theo's heart as he stopped to wake up Daryl and Clarisse. They too ran for the study, on his heels, neither stopping to collect a robe in their haste and nervous excitement.

Wynnie, Gabriel, and Will were standing around a blank map and Tim was staring down as Wynnie began etching out what she could. Jeremy was coming up the other side of the hallway and he beamed a massive smile as he looked to see Wynnie was back and she was safe. He raced to her and they gave each other a brief, relief filled hug at their reunion. Theo's heart sank, wishing it were Mia sitting in the chair next to him so that he could do the same. A part of him had hoped that the good news was that they had seen an opportunity to save Mia, but she still wasn't there.

Wynnie cleared her throat from the public display and turned back to the map.

"We're in a much better place intelligence wise now than we were. The scouting mission was a huge success," she began.

Everyone leaned forward to look down at her map.

"We found a place where the wards are almost nonexistent. I was able to use Blood magic and I poked through it with ease. It didn't even seem to raise alarms, so we snuck in and looked around the outside perimeter for a moment," she continued.

Theo looked up quickly, "Did you see Mia?" he asked, but Wynnie shook her head.

"No, we think she's being held at the dead center, which would be the wisest place. What we did find, however, was Michelo's tent. He has stationed himself somewhat near the front of the encampment so that he can see out towards Purge at any given notice. Gregor's tent isn't far from it and easily recognizable because it is surrounded by the smells of potion making." Wynnie scrunched her pretty nose, remembering the stench that had given her and the other three scouts alarm.

"He's got some nasty stuff going on in there and it didn't all smell natural. He's cooking up more than just the changing potion for the Cannibals," Gabriel added.

Everyone shivered at the thought of what the horrible hunchbacked man could be doing.

Heretia shook her head, "I should have had him killed years ago," she whispered to herself, softly.

Gabriel reached out and rubbed her back comfortingly. Theo gave her a sympathetic look, but he knew even though she had said those words, that was not the woman she was. She would have banished him, sent him away, but she never would have had someone killed.

"So, we have an entry point and we know where to avoid," Wynnie continued, authority dripping throughout her words. "Will and I were able to circumnavigate the entire camp in less than an hour with quick feet, so it's not as large as we once thought. It's still a maze and you can't see more than two movable structures deep, but those Cannibals are practically blind. You can almost walk right up to one and slap them and they don't notice. So really, we only need to avoid Gregor and Michelo and we should be good. It's still a bright idea to play on the safe side and go under Gabriel's blanket of disguise."

Everyone nodded to each other in agreement. After everything they had either witnessed or heard of Michelo, the more cautious they could be, the better this would turn out for them and Mia. Theo's stomach was still in knots at the idea of what he would find when he went in there.

As Wynnie kept making marks of distinct locations she had placed, with Will interjecting points of entry he figured probable, the sun broke over the horizon and Theo suddenly felt nervous.

His heart began to flutter in his chest and his stomach twisted up in knots. The feeling grew worse and more distinct as the sun came up fully and he had to blink back from its glaring rays. He looked over at Gabriel and noticed a slight sweat on the man's head. Clarisses' hand was noticeably shaking. Theo furrowed his brows at the idea that the two of them might be feeling the amount of trepidation as he was.

Suddenly, a slight tightness to his chest constricted over his heart. He was just about to look back at Gabriel again when everyone's attention was jerked away from Wynnie and Clarisse let out an ear-splitting scream.

The older woman launched herself from her chair and fell to the ground, hugging her stomach as if she were in pain. Theo was making a move to help Daryl pick her up from the floor when his own legs were knocked out from under him and the room spun above his head.

"What in the Mother?" he heard Jeremy shout.

Wynnie was on her feet, hovering over the two of them when Gabriel suddenly vomited on the floor.

"What is happening?" Will roared above the cacophony of movement and cries of alarm.

Theo opened his eyes to see Daryl hovering over his wife, clutching at his own chest and struggling to breathe. Chaos erupted as the five unaffected raced to figure out what was going on with the four that were suffering an unknown attack.

"MIA!" Clarisse screamed and pointed a shaking finger towards the double paned window that looked out over the desert beyond.

Wynnie reached out to magically open the doors and Tim scanned the horizon, but again, just like the day before, there was nothing. Theo's vision went dark once more as his magic battled inside of him to stay strong, but his breathing was uneven. Will lifted him up to gently sit him in a chair and then went to examine Daryl and Clarisse. As soon as is started, however, everything vanished, and the three witches caught their first even breath and stopped screaming. Gabriel seemed to recover first, being not human, but he was left visibly shaken.

"Will someone tell me what in the Mother's name just happened?" Jeremy's entire face was dark with worry.

"She's getting weaker," Clarisse finally whispered as she found a way to drape herself over the chair she had fallen from.

"Whatever they're doing is getting stronger. She can barely hang on," Theo added, feeling his magic settle back and the little piece of Mia inside of his heart fluttered and struggled to keep beating.

"It's Mia," Gabriel finally explained to the others who were still confused. "We felt her fighting yesterday against something that Michelo was doing to her magic. It wasn't this bad though. We all just felt horrible for a moment, but this is bad." He looked down at his still shaking hands.

"She's losing the battle," Daryl finished for him.

The entire collection of witches went silent over the thought that the Druid, their Mia, was barely surviving.

"We have to get her out. She can't withstand another day of this. Each time the effects get stronger and each time she's getting weaker. Eventually, whatever their doing is going to work, and she won't make it out alive," Theo finalized.

Wynnie looked to Will, who nodded his assent. "Tonight then, not another day. We go in tonight and no matter what, Mia comes home. This has gone on long enough."

***

Theo still felt weak from his horrible experience in the study earlier. His worry increased tenfold and sleep didn't come easy. Heretia had suggested the four affected rest for a while and then see to helping the invasion for that night. This was, however, impossible for Theo, and eventually he gave up trying to sleep and began wandering the hallways.

Jeremy had reminded everyone that Ez was due to land today and Theo thought maybe he should Transport to the coast and see to helping her there, but then that would exhaust his magic that he needed to find Mia tonight. He felt utterly useless waiting around and went to go find somewhere to be useful. As he roamed the halls, he found himself standing outside of the castle's library.

Hearing movement inside, he opened the door to see who might be researching at this time, or possibly other nefarious activities. He was surprised to find Tim high up on a ladder attempting to reach for a book that apparently sat on one of the more uppermost shelves. Tim jerked slightly as the door opened, and seeing it was only Theo, returned to waving his hand. A small bubble of water appeared and slowly knocked the book into Tim's awaiting reach.

"Hey Theo," he muttered and quickly slid down the ladder rungs.

"What are you doing?" Theo asked him, coming to the table that was laden down with multiple other books and documents that Tim was obviously researching.

"Looking into something. Don't tell anyone you saw me touch one of these books with water, they may just kick me out over that," he grunted and jumped the last few steps of the circular stairs that led to the second story of Heretia's massive library.

"I can see that, but what exactly?" Theo probed, turning over a few volumes to check out their titles. "Legends of Medeis? Tim, is this really a time to be looking into children's stories?" He tossed the book back and watched as Tim settled back over another stack of book on the other end of the table.

"I'm not reading them for pleasure, Theo. I had an idea. We've been talking about the war over and over, but everyone has seemed to forget that Michelo controls the Wild Beasts, except for Nandina, who you killed, Cetus, which Mia got rid of, and Aqrabuamelu, who we killed. However, we've forgotten that he has been searching for the Phoenix as well and possibly intends to resurrect those three. If he had all of the six Wild Beasts at his disposal, it wouldn't matter if we rescued Mia. We're done for."

Theo's heart sank in horror. Tim was right. Everyone had forgotten this fact and no one had made moves to discover how to stop it.

"You're looking for a way to get Tailong and Antamba back from him. Couldn't we just use the Mother Goddess' blood on them as the others?" Theo inquired.

Tim shook his shaggy head. "How in Medeis would we be able to get two Wild Beasts to drink that potion? No, there's no getting them back. They will have to be killed just like the others. What I'm looking for is the Phoenix. If we can assure that Michelo can't get to Phoenix, we stand a chance. Armies can take down two Wild Beasts, but we can't take down five and their forever regenerator."

He flipped through a few more dusty pages in the clearly forgotten book.

"Have you made any headway in finding it?" Theo came to peer over his friends' shoulder, glancing at the titles all dealing with legends, stories and early forgotten Medeis history.

"No! What Mia reported seems to be true. The Phoenix has never been seen and even less spoken of. In all of these books, I've found only two references to Phoenix and both are just legends. The Mother Goddess has hidden Phoenix away carefully since the dawn of time," Tim slammed the book shut and groaned heavily.

"That's a good thing though. If we can't figure out where Phoenix is with this massive library, Michelo has no way either." Theo moved to the side and sat down next to the disgusted Tim.

"Oh, the same man who happened to find an amulet that only one being in all of Medeis knew about? He somehow found Gabriel's amulet and Heretia didn't even know about it. Who's to say he didn't scour through every single library in Medeis. This is only one receptacle of information, there are four other kingdoms worth of books. Maybe he found something elsewhere and we just have no idea about it. For all we know, he's hunting Phoenix now and we're toast," Tim lamented.

Theo's eyes fell, staring at the floor and unable to think through the only emotion of fear. This was just getting worse by the minute. Having the Druid, while of utmost importance to Theo, seemed to be trivial if they couldn't win the war against Michelo.

"I don't know Tim. Maybe Heretia might know something. She and the Mother Goddess spoke in her past life as Meloni as well, she may have an idea," Theo offered, but Tim shook his head.

"I've already asked. Her response was the same. She wasn't even aware that Life had created a Wild Beast either."

Theo started searching through his mind for more answers.

"And before you ask, Gabriel is useless too in that department. He remembers Phoenix being created, but he hasn't seen or heard of it since. The Mother Goddess never spoke to him about it either." Tim banged his fist on the table.

"Getting Mia back means nothing, Theo," he growled. "It means nothing if we can't keep Phoenix away from the Second Uprising."

Theo scowled at his friend's words. "It doesn't mean nothing, Tim. It means a great deal, not only to the war effort, but to me."

Tim shifted his demeanor and met Theo's eyes, filling them with apology.

"I know, I'm sorry. I didn't mean it that way. I know you need her back, we all do. I just can't see a way to winning this without Phoenix," he whispered, trying to find hope in the darkness.

"We will, Mia will find a way. We've just got to let her take charge and be the Druid. We just need to be the friends we were meant to be. Mia will defeat them. I know she will," Theo responded.

Tim didn't move for a moment as the silence descended over the two men. Finally, Tim spoke the words Theo hadn't wanted to think about for since learning of the Second Uprising.

"I just don't want her to kill herself trying."

****

Tim had left the library not long after, silence still heavy, leaving Theo to mull over his dark thoughts. Tim was right, Mia would do whatever she needed to end this once and for all. Her heart was too big and she still, even after everything they had been through, thought she wasn't important enough to save. This was made evident when she gave herself up as hostage and now, here she was, being tortured in ways Theo couldn't understand but he could certainly feel. And if that was just what he was getting as blow back, Mother only knew how horrible it really was for her on the other end of the connection.

Not wanting to sit around any longer, and still feeling useless, Theo left the library without another word and made for the Throne Room. Heretia and Gabriel would be in there by now, possibly gathering more information from the other kingdoms about when their armies would be arriving. He clenched his jaw tightly when he heard the slithery voice of Eric Lily floating from the door leading to the side entrance. Theo couldn't quite make out what he was saying, but as he reached for the door handle and opened it, he was almost forced backwards against the stone wall with the blow of Wynnie's anger as she reacted to whatever her nasty older brother had uttered.

"YOU SLIMY TWO FACE BASTARD!" Wynnie screeched.

Theo was only just regaining his footing when he witnessed her launching off a chair for her brother's throat. With a speed and deftness that only Wynnie could manage, she leapt over it in one bound, wrapped her tiny but strong hands around his thin throat, and they both went tumbling backwards in a fit of screams and spitting rage.

Gabriel and Jeremy leapt from their seats and hurried to stop the tiny beast from disemboweling her brother. Heretia was gripping the arms of her own throne with white knuckles. She was also trying to control her own fury and doing a much better job than Wynnie it seemed.

"You snake!' Wynnie shouted. "You pathetic coward! You rat shithead!" Every time she threw a well-placed curse, she slung his head around in her grip and squeezed harder. "I should have killed you when we were children!"

Her pretty face was turning purple with seething anger. Jeremy finally got close enough to grab her arms and, pinning them behind her, hauled his Pair off her brother. She went spitting, kicking, and screaming like a feral cat thrashing about, clawing for release. Theo stood there in the doorway, too shocked and frankly too amused to try and stop anything.

"Wynnie!" Jeremy firmly chastised, but he wasn't shouting by any means. He too wasn't thrilled with the young man laboring for breath on the floor before them. A moment of silence descended, and Theo figured it was time to make his presence known. It would have been rude otherwise.

"Bad time?" he called out. Every head whipped around as he shut the door behind him and took a few steps in. "I mean, I'm all for family squabbles. My father and I have had our share but if it's too personal, I can come back."

His delight at seeing Wynnie so angry, and Eric getting his butt kicked, was too much and a sly grin spread across his face.

"No, it's not a bad time. Mr. Lily just shared with us some upsetting news," Heretia managed to say, but Theo could see she was still holding back her own fury.

Theo cocked a curious eyebrow and was about to ask Eric exactly what he had said to cause Wynnie to go off, but the certain woman in question informed him herself.

"The bastard only asked for three squadrons of soldiers from Maravette!" she kicked out again at her brother, but Jeremy still had the wild cat firmly in his grip.

Theo's stomach dropped out.

"What?" he thundered, taking two steps towards Eric, who was just scrambling to his feet. Gabriel stepped in front of Theo and shook his head.

"He reported that the Second Uprising wasn't as important as I told the High Rulers and they need not send more than that. Basically, he told them that it was an internal squabble between High Ruler and her people and if they wanted to save face, they should send that little, but nothing more," Wynnie finished, then jerked her arms out of Jeremy's grip, flinging her hair out of her face, shooting an angry glare at Eric.

She didn't move again on her brother, but Theo did.

"Why, you little," he began, and Gabriel had no time to stop him.

Faster than anyone could see, Theo darted around the magic of Death and called on a stone to come flying out of the wall and slam into Eric. The impact threw him backwards, and Eric went flying through the air into a pillar where he was heavily pinned from the attack. Theo heard the air rush out of his lungs, but he didn't stop there. With Eric locked into place, Theo unsheathed Mia's knife and went running at him, ready to slice his throat open. Wynnie took this move as her second chance and darted across the room as well.

"Enough!" Gabriel shouted.

Theo felt warmth wrap around him, pinning his arms to his sides and causing his feet to leave the ground. He looked to see black smoke clinging to his body and squeezing him tight. Wynnie gave a cry of anger and he saw that she, too, was being held back by the Death magic. Theo thrashed and struggled with Eric barely two steps from him.

"Put her down!" Jeremy roared and threw a fist at Gabriel's head. His own fist found itself wrapped in the black mist of Death magic, unable to move another inch from where it hung.

"I said," Gabriel began, hissing through gritted teeth. "That is enough."

The mist moved and Theo felt himself pulled away from the young man cowering against the pillar, protecting his face. Wynnie continued to struggle and spit fire but she too was pulled back and sat into a seat.

"Now, we can either all lose control of ourselves, or we can figure out what to do next," Gabriel began. Theo's head snapped to the auburn-haired man and the small blonde woman who was now standing at her throne.

"Gabriel's right. Killing Eric won't help us with Maravette. It may even make things worse." Jeremy's hand was released from its prison and he came to stand next to Wynnie, who was still soundly bound by the black mist. Theo, however, was also released once he was settled neatly into another chair.

"Since when did Gabriel become the voice of reason?" Theo barked angrily, sheathing Mia's knife at his waist. Gabriel's face held no laughter this time, no joke was thrown out in response.

"As Death I have seen my fair share of war. I have witnessed kingdoms rise and fall, I have seen the folly of men destroy entire nations over a simple act of vengeance. I may be hasty in plans of escape or rescue, I may not always think things through to completion, but I do know war. The Ancient Kingdom needs Maravette, without it, everything is lost. We need Maravette's money and riches, supplies, and access to more. We don't know how long this war will go on and men only last until they are cut down."

Theo hung his head. He hated that Gabriel was right.

"Mia needs Maravette. If she can't have it soldiers, which Mr. Lily here has seen to apparently, we will ask for its support in other ways," Heretia spoke.

She came around the table, placing a calming hand on Wynnie's shoulder before moving to stand before the still cowering man. "I'm not sure what your goal was in all of this, but I will make one thing clear, Eric."

Gabriel came to stand behind her, and Theo swallowed in fear when he saw the black mist still creeping from his being. It swirled menacingly, reaching out to almost touch Eric, and then moving back. It grew to block out the sunlight and cast a shadow over him. Heretia rose up to her full height and even Theo paled at the image they created. A Queen of an Ancient Kingdom, brilliant silver crown atop her head. She hid secrets for decades, held onto power, and protected an entire kingdom single handedly. Gabriel, Death incarnate, every inch of him oozing power and darkness. His eyes had turned from their normal pale yellow to two shining iridescent golden orbs as he wielded his nature for all to see, the outline of feathers grew from behind him.

Theo's jaw fell, stunned. Gabriel had wings! As they came into full view, he wondered over their glory. They shone with a glimmer of night sky and starlight but were as dark as the deepest reaches of the ocean.

110

Heretia's own blue eyes came alive with a snap of lightning and brimstone, as blue fire danced in her pupils. They were intimidating and rightly so. Heretia with her Blood magic that could break even the mightiest of elemental spells and Gabriel with his raw untapped source that no single witch could control in its entirety. Only a Druid could hope to do half of what Gabriel could blink into existence if he wanted. Together they were a fright for even the strongest of willed men. Eric practically pissed himself in the full presence of Death and his Queen.

"We may not can end you over this, but we won't forget either. Maravette has been given a warning. Send your pittance of an army, but don't ever ask the Ancient Kingdom or the Druid for anything after today. This slight, that I highly imagine was all your own doing, will go unforgiven until the end of your days. The House of Lily, save for Wynnie and her issue and Daryl Wardman and his issue, will be banished from this kingdom after this war," she warned.

Eric swallowed hard and Theo could swear he saw a wet spot gathering between the man's legs.

"Go," Gabriel hissed between his gritted teeth.

No one needed to tell Eric Lily twice. With a squeal, he flew from the room.

Gabriel linked his arm into Heretia's and escorted her slowly, and without speaking, to her Throne. Theo had no words for what he had just witnessed. He had seen Mia lose control of her power, the night before she gave herself up and he thought that was terrifying. Her eyes had been the color of molten gold and shone with just as much fury as could be found in Gabriel's eyes as well. Heretia had chosen to calm down and the glimmer of quicksilver had left her, leaving just the pleasant sky-blue Theo had always known.

Wynnie had stopped in her throes of anger, in awe of the power Heretia had just wielded. Jeremy didn't seem too surprised.

Finally, Theo collected himself enough and straightened his jacket.

"Remind me never to piss you two off," he muttered.

Gabriel threw him a dark scowl and looked about to say something when the doors to the Throne Room flew wide open. Everyone turned in surprise to see midnight black hair and blazing green eyes strut into the room confidently.

"Where's the party?" Esmerelda called, a brilliant smile plastered onto her face and her arms open wide.

"Ez!" Wynnie and Theo shouted at the same time. Theo bounded from his seat and ran to wrap the curvy woman up in his arms. Wynnie struggled for a moment against the Death mist before Gabriel noticed his mistake and released her. She too flew into Ez's arms with a grin and held her tight.

"I thought I'd never make it! Remind me to never travel by sea again. I couldn't handle one more minute with some of those men and I Transported straight here." She made an exaggerated wave of her hand over her face. "To say I'm exhausted is an understatement."

She looked around her two friends at those still standing on the dais. The feelings of dark power and authority had still not settled completely in the room and Ez instantly recognized it. Her smile fell from its spot and she searched the room with her eyes quickly.

"Umm, where is Mia and who are those scary looking individuals?" she pointed secretively from behind her hand at Gabriel and Heretia.

Theo's excitement thudded like a stone to the floor as he remembered that Ez wouldn't know what had happened in the last three days.

"We've got a lot to talk about," he began and waved her to join them all.

Chapter Thirteen

Esmerelda

To say that Ez was stunned to learn of what Mia had done, what Michelo had done, and the state of the war effort was barely scratching the surface. Even Tim's presence did not calm her. Theo had called for Tim to join them and the brilliant man had come running to greet her. With a big sweeping hug and a chaste kiss to the cheek, he had set her back down and the story had continued.

Ez squeezed Tim's hand tightly as she heard more and more bad news being thrown at her in all directions. She did quietly thank the Mother Goddess that all this had happened just as she set sail, or Ogden would have been able to prevent the entire armada from leaving port. Harold, Prince Bertie's only son, would be arriving shortly and he wouldn't find any of this appealing either.

"So, she's gone?" Ez finally whispered, feeling the heat in her cheeks rising, a sure sign that tears threatened to fall. "And she's being tortured Mother only knows how?" Her voice caught at the mere idea of her friend in pain. So much pain, apparently, that those connected magically to her were suffering the effects at times as well.

Tim nodded his head, silent. Her sweet Tim always knew what she needed and always knew when to give her space.

"But you're getting her back, right? Tonight, you said?" she asked.

Theo's lips went thin.

"Yes, Ez. We're going to get her. I feel confident I have enough intel to get her out and back to us safely," Wynnie leaned forward and offered the comfort with conviction.

The blonde man she had just met placed a large hand on Wynnie's shoulder. Ez had probably been just as stunned to find out that Wyndetta Lily, of all people, had a Pair and he was truly a god among men. His size, stature, and good looks were swoon worthy, but it was his confident attitude while still being humble that she knew attracted Wynnie to him.

Ez was happy for her, truly. Thinking of those types of feelings had her looking to Tim again. There was an attraction there, always had been, but every time they got close to admitting anything for each other, one or the other had halted the process and backed off. Ez wasn't sure if it was her own heart that faltered, or his, but she knew that one day, maybe soon, she was going to have to push past it and admit her feelings for him. Even now, just having him near was all she needed to hear this horrible news.

"Okay, well I guess there's nothing we can do about that until you guys return tonight with Mia in tow. I'm going to say it now for everyone to hear, I am her healer. No one else touches her but me." She pointed a warning finger at the Elite Guard that had gathered. Will had been sent to the Castle gates to welcome any other soldiers that decided to Transport into Purge and get them settled. He had clear instructions from Heretia to bring General Harold and Admiral Rawlings straight to them as soon as they arrived.

"Speaking of arriving, I'm going to see to helping Will with whatever he may need. Your Majesty?" Jeremy turned to his Queen who had calmed down immensely.

Heretia stood from her throne and floated down the steps of the dais to join her Captain.

"We will see you all for dinner tonight," Heretia called over her petite shoulder as the two of them left the Throne Room.

Gabriel and Wynnie watched them go warily, but turned back to getting Ez acquainted with the news.

"Gabriel, huh?" Ez turned her attention to the Death magic in human form. The auburn-haired man with the yellow eyes raised a quizzical eyebrow in response. "I'm not really sure how to feel about you yet. You've been a thorn in my side my entire life. I've been trying to heal, to bring comfort and relief. However, Death has felt the need, on unnecessary occasions, to steal patients of mine from me. While I know it's not my place to question the Mother Goddess, I have to say

I never thought I would have to meet my adversary face to face." She crossed her arms in front of her ample bosom.

Gabriel seemed stunned by this turn in conversation and then, suddenly, burst out into raucous laughter.

"Oh, I like her!" he finally belted out and held his hand out to Ez, who gave a small coy smile in return.

"Adversary? Really Ez?" Theo moaned and hid his face in his hands.

Ez rolled her eyes at her friend. He always took things way to serious and was constantly embarrassed by her dark humor and inability to keep her mouth shut. Tim, who at first has sucked in a breath, then let out a small chuckle of his own.

"My dear woman, I am not an adversary. I don't kill people. You should know good and well I just assist them in their passing. I have nothing to do with who lives and who dies. That is all the Mother Goddess's wish," Gabriel wiped away a tear. "But I like your spirit. There are not many bold enough to say those things and know they will live through it on sheer force of will. I think you and I will be great friends," he winked.

Wynnie groaned outwardly and flung herself back in her chair. "Yeah, just don't follow him on any adventures. Half of why we're in this mess is his fault." She threw a lazy hand in Gabriel's direction.

"Hey now! I have some wonderful plans. They led you all here, didn't they? I say that was first class planning on my part." He brushed off an invisible fleck of dust from his suit jacket.

"You had no idea who Heretia even was!" Theo jerked his head up and snapped.

Gabriel just made a dismissive noise. "Still got us all here."

There was a small cacophony of the three Elite Guardsmen bantering back and forth on Gabriel's bad ideas before Ez finally help up a hand.

"While I enjoy this rigorous discussion on Death actually being impulsive and reckless," Gabriel shot her a frown. "That still doesn't get us anywhere on what we do next. Now, I got my letter from Mia asking for Moondates and I've brought them."

Everyone turned in confusion to her.

"Moondates? Why did you bring Moondates?" Tim asked.

Ez looked around them, obviously she knew something they didn't.

"For the potion for Mia. She made mentioned that she had a specific potion she had to create to make an ocean of water, but she needed Moondates and lots of them. I figured it had to do with the desert." She shrugged, then reached to pull out the letter Mia had sent her by Transport messenger and had reached her less than a day before the armada was due to leave for Purge's shore.

"Why would Mia want to create an ocean in the desert?" Tim asked and reached for the letter, but it explained nothing more than the need for the fruit.

Ez looked to Wynnie who shrugged, at a loss for words and ideas herself. Theo was up and pacing the floor, thinking through the puzzle Mia had left for them.

"Turning a few droplets into an ocean. What would she need a lot of water for?" Gabriel started naming off spells that included tsunamis, hurricanes and other water related natural disasters. Tim interjected with a few ideas of his own before finally Theo gasped and stopped pacing.

"It's not for the war," he muttered. Everyone turned to him. "It's for the cure. It's to turn the Mother Goddess' few droplets of blood into more than enough to cure every Cannibal in Michelo's army and those infected in Purge."

Silence fell as everyone ingested how much planning Mia had put into her surrender. Even with giving herself up, she hadn't left them helpless. She had given them an opportunity to create an even bigger army from those who had long been infected and give them even more hope.

"How many people are Cannibals within the city of Purge?" Ez finally asked. Gabriel thought for a moment.

"From what Heretia has told me, it's upwards of five thousand. This city is much more crowded than it looks. When the early water supplies were tainted, it spread far and wide. She collected every last one within these walls to contain them," Gabriel mused.

Wynnie's jaw dropped. "Five thousand? How many men would be able to fight in all of that?"

Gabriel shrugged at her question. "Heretia and Jeremy probably have an old census here somewhere that would give us a rough idea. You think half are men, at least half of that is sword wielding age, so not many. But what use will they be? They will be too weak from years of starvation from real sustenance."

Ez shook her head in response. "But they can be helpful to me, to the Life wielders and healers. They can help manage tasks within the camps and keep things running and clean. They can be useful, just not strong."

Tim beamed at her, and her heart tugged at his smile. The way he looked at her now was breathtaking, maybe it was time they finally talked about the future. Theo looked reinvigorated.

"We have to tell Heretia. We need to get those Moondates within the city first so Ez and the others working on the potion can create it. We need the people of Purge cured quickly."

Gabriel nodded, and without another word, took off flying in the direction Jeremy had escorted Heretia.

"Well, I'm exhausted. Where will I be sleeping?" Ez looked around at her friends and waited. Tim finally stood and held out his hand.

"Can we talk for a moment, in private?" Tim asked.

Ez looked to Wynnie, stunned. The small blonde woman shrugged her shoulders in a nonchalant response. Theo also offered nothing of an answer. Finally, she simply took Tim's hand and allowed him to lead her away. He led her down a long hallway out of a side entrance she hadn't noticed before. When he had checked to see if they were completely alone, he turned and kissed both of her knuckles.

"Esmerelda," he started slowly. Ez sucked in a hesitant breath. What was going on?

"I don't want to wait until after the war, because there might not be an after the war for me," he continued. Her heart began to beat wildly in her ample chest, a war drum sounding out a rhythm of anticipation. "I only ask this, not because I'm afraid for the future, but because I should have asked a long time ago. Probably only about two days after I met you. I know we're not at home, and I know your mother will probably freak out, but that's okay. I can handle whatever she throws at me for even asking this. But, if you'll have me?"

"YES!" Ez blurted out before Tim could finish his sentence. Shocked at herself, she clapped her hands over her mouth, but the excitement still overflowed. She squealed behind her hand and began bouncing with joy.

"Can you at least let me ask?" Tim's eyes twinkled with glee. Vigorously, Ez nodded her dark head.

"Esmerelda, will you marry me?" he tried again. This time Ez remained only slightly calmer, took in a deep breath, and removed her hand from her mouth.

"Yes, Timothy Unda. Yes, I will marry you," he replied.

They both couldn't contain their joy any longer. With a cry of relief, they both met with a large kiss and wrapped together in a massive hug.

"When?" Ez finally pulled away long enough to ask the one-word question.

"Tonight, Heretia can do it. We can get married right now and announce it to everyone at dinner. There won't be much time. The Elite Guard is leaving to rescue Mia as soon as the sun sets," Tim explained.

Ez nodded and together, they both hurried off to go find Heretia at the gates of the castle.

*****

Tim only asked his nephew, Tom, to be there for him. Ez asked Theo to be her representative. Together the five of them recited all the blessings within the walls of Heretia's private chapel and the Mother Goddess accepted their offering. The flowers and spiced smoke turned white as soon as Tim and Ez finished their spells of binding. With a whoop of joy, Tom gathered Tim up in a massive bear grip and swung him around.

"When this is over, we're going to have an official reception in Lotho. The whole country will be happy to have something to celebrate," he announced, punching Tim in the shoulder. Theo gave Ez a chaste kiss on the cheek.

"Congratulations," he smiled and then, with the smile still plastered widely on his face he added, "I'm not telling your mother for you."

Ez waved her hand sarcastically and blew a raspberry. "Like I care what she thinks about this. I'll send her a letter by a ship, nice and slow, to let her know and that will be it."

Everyone chuckled at the image of Felicity opening that letter and falling off her Throne in surprise.

118

CHAPTER FOURTEEN

THEO

Theo was finishing tying up the last part of his jacket when a knock sounded. He tensed for a moment and sent a silent prayer up to the Mother Goddess that it wasn't the Elevetian Princess again. He already wasn't ready for what would happen when Mia found out, adding a second appearance would only add fuel to the flames.

"Who is it?" he called out carefully, refusing to answer until the reply came.

"It's Will!" The large man's voice came quietly from the opposite side of the wooden door. With a sigh of relief, Theo opened it up and moved to let Will inside. "I wanted to let you know that we will be leaving two hours after sunset. Considering how long it will take to get to where Wynnie wants us to enter from, I want us leaving early."

Theo snapped to attention.

"I also wanted to make sure you were prepared for this, Theo. I know Mia is your Pair, but no one knows the state she is in. This may not be easy, and I don't need you going all Pair psycho on me when we do find her,"

Theo stiffened, trying not to imagine how horrible Mia may look. He nodded is assent without words.

"I mean it, Theo. No storming off to kill Michelo, no making unnecessary moves. The moment someone finds her, we're all out of there. No questions, no side missions, nothing. In, grab her, out," Will said.

Theo opened his mouth to respond, but Will shot a finger up to stop him.

"I mean it," he warned one last time. Not wanting to upset his Captain and friend, Theo relinquished his argument and agreed.

"Yes sir," he finally agreed.

"Good, now. I hear that Tim is married." He crossed his arms and raised a single dark red eyebrow. Theo shrugged his shoulders with a boyish grin.

"Don't ask me. Ez just grabbed me and told me to follow her. What can I say? I do as I'm told," Theo laughed.

Will shook his head with a look of humorous defeat.

"When have you ever done as told, Theo?" he inquired.

Theo chucked a pillow at the man.

"Plenty of times! I've been a great Guardsman for years. When have I ever given you trouble?" he asked as the two of them began to exit the room and head to dinner.

"Only every single time something doesn't go perfectly to your plan!" Will fired back, but with a laugh they made their way down to the Dining Room. They must have taken longer than expected to arrive because as they entered a massive congratulatory cheer went up.

Their eyes scanned the room to see people floating towards the newlywed couple with felicitations and handshakes. The room was exponentially more crowded with the entire Suravian army's higher ups joining them. The other kingdoms had a few more representatives present as well.

Lotho's High King Ludwig was now there, as well as High Queen Odette. The former looking simply disgusted and the latter giggling with joy at the idea of Tim being married.

Elevetia has sent a few generals and Giselda's father has joined them as well. Apparently, word of her behavior and lack of control on her weepy emotions had gotten back to him, and he had immediately Transported in to handle the damage control.

Wynnie had also been surprised to see her sister, Georgianna, and her husband, the High King of the Third Throne of Maravette, merely an hour before dinner. Wynnie had sent a message to her sister telling her what Eric had done and immediately the wrong had been righted; Georgianna had seen to it herself.

Theo noted the relationship between the sisters, while still cool, was not tense or forced as it had been in years past. Maybe Georgianna having children of her own had shown her how horrible the Lily's behavior had been and she was trying to make amends. Eric sat back pouting as the two sisters raced to hug Ez together.

Everyone began chatting amiably and it seemed as if no one in sight even cared that they were all gathered in the High Castle of what they had once thought was "The Mad Queen of Purge." Theo's pride swelled, thinking to himself that this was all Mia's doing. It was her name that had spread far and wide to get their attention. Her actions had caused them to rethink their past, and her cry for help that had spurred them into movement. This was all for her, and tonight, they would get her back.

Heretia seemed so at ease with all of the people now crowding her home as well. She flitted from group to group, making small talk, introducing herself, and putting others new to her presence at ease. She seemed in her element and was happy to finally be doing what she was always meant to do. Theo reminded himself that she had led such a lonely life this time around, but she would have remembered what it felt like to be Meloni. In charge, powerful, and a diplomat. That's what she seemed to be right now, a woman trying to help everyone find common ground and work together for the sake of all of their kingdoms.

Slowly but surely, any form of tension when it came to Heretia, and Gabriel for that matter, eased away, and High Rulers along with their generals and soldiers opened up to her about the coming war. Some had questions, others concerns, and still others bright new ideas they could employ to defeat Michelo and the Second Uprising. Ever the tactician, Heretia would quickly either allay fears, answer any doubts, and direct certain persons to those who would best suit their form of inquiry.

Suravian nobles and generals stopped to hail Theo down and attempt to talk battle with him. Harold even waved and nodded once, but he knew all too well how annoying being bombarded could be, so he left that special kind of hell to the rest he had brought along. Theo even caught a glimpse of Captain, now Admiral Rawlings, smiling and shaking Tim's hand.

Theo was finally able to wade through the crowd, just before the dinner began, and capture Heretia's attention. It was really Gabriel who had seen him first and he, looking for any excuse to get away from the barrage of questions about who he was, happily jogged over to greet him.

"Are you ready for tonight?" he beamed a toothy white grin. He looked like a child talking about his favorite pet rock. It was if he was more excited to join in a covert mission under the cover of darkness to rescue a possibly extremely foolhardy and wayward Druid than spend one more second in the massive throngs of those who wished to question his very existence.

"What? Don't like mingling with only the most rich and powerful in all of Medeis?" Theo waved his hand out to signal the throngs that were beginning to seat themselves comfortably around the table.

"Me? No! I love this stuff," Gabriel gave everyone a sidelong glance. "I just find my talents better used elsewhere."

"What talents? Causing chaos wherever you go?" Theo jested and both men moved to be seated as well.

"Laugh sir, but sometimes chaos is what is needed to shake things up a bit. What comes out after could possibly be even better than it was before," he winked.

Theo snorted through his nose. Gabriel had grown on him. The wit and the constant jesting wasn't so bad after all. He had also come to appreciate the eons worth of wisdom that Gabriel would spit out every now and then. Theo was glad, deep down, that Gabriel was joining them tonight.

The large party seemed to go on forever, and Theo was quickly becoming bored. It was beginning to feel as if he were back home in Suravia, forced into yet another boring dinner with yet some more boring nobles that needed to be dealt with a light hand. After so many, "Yes, thank you" and "The weather is certainly nice," he was beyond bored. Everyone seems to say the same thing. Eventually, the dinner finished and Heretia stood to address the crowd.

"Ladies and Gentlemen! I want to thank you, once again, for a wonderful evening. But it's time to work. Generals and High Rulers are asked to follow Captain Jeremy to the barracks so you may begin directing your soldiers on where to camp for the time being. Captain Jeremy has come up with his working plan and will also be updating each and every one of you on the status of the Second Uprising and what we know collectively."

Jeremy rose and nodded, leading the way for almost seventy-five percent of the party out of the doors and away from the Dining Room.

"Everyone else, if you would please adjourn to the library for after dinner drinks," Heretia clapped her hands and two footmen arrived, shepherding the rest away. Only the Elite Guard, Gabriel, Esmerelda, and Alyssa stayed.

"Girls, you two are with me. We have what we need now to free the people of Purge out from under the Cannibalism and we are doing so tonight. I've had my scholars putting the finishing touches on the potion Mia left us and I think we should start handing it out immediately."

Ez and Alyssa both nodded quickly and moved to follow the Queen from the room as well. Ez squeezed Tim's hand one last time as Heretia kissed Gabriel.

"We will see you when you return with the Druid," Heretia finished and then left the room in a flourish. Tim smiled after his new wife as she herself ran off to help in the effort to save the city.

"Well, I think that's our cue guys. Let's go suit up," Will announced. He rose and the other four followed dutifully.

No one was present to watch them go as the Elite Guard and Gabriel took off by horse into the night. They were going to ride to just within sight of the encampment and then disembark, taking the rest of the way by foot. It was wholly dark, and the moon was nowhere to be seen as they quickly ran up to the point Wynnie had chosen for entrance. There was no forestry or object to block their view from the wide-open desert, which didn't sit well with Theo.

"We're getting close," Wynnie said with a quiet tone in her voice. It was pointless to whisper, as there wasn't a single person within sight, but the covertness of the operation still led to a lowering of voices.

"Just show me where and let's get in there," Theo responded, wanting this over with as quickly as possible and Mia back in his arms.

"Patience, young Prince. We're here to win the battle and the war," Gabriel chided from behind him. Theo rolled his green eyes in response.

"Right here," Wynnie finally pointed. With a nod Theo removed Mia's silver blade and, remembering to cut deep, sliced his palm open. With a massive squeeze he reached out and recited the Blood magic incantation he had been practicing over and over again for two days.

"*Aperio.*"

A spark ignited in the air before him and with a bubbling squelch, the weak point in the wards brightened and then fizzled away. The hole grew to the size of a mid-sized man, certainly big enough for four of them to walk through, but it caused Will to duck his head.

"Okay, step one completed," Gabriel brushed off his jacket from the dust that had settled there during the ride and the run. "My turn now." He finished and in a blink of an eye a warmth settled over Theo, causing him to jump ever so slightly from the sensation. For a brief second, he dreamed up that they had been caught, but the warmth was slightly familiar and, looking down, noticed that he was slightly hazy. It was just like when Mia had cast the Death magic over him, and everyone had been invisible.

"You're free to search now. No one will see you, the only thing I can possibly think will counteract that would be Michelo's amulet, but he would have to think to use it and find you first," Gabriel declared.

Will nodded his head and looked to his soldiers.

"That front tent it Michelo, next to it is Gregor. Let's enter from this western point here and go straight for the middle. As we go deeper, we will split up to span a wider area. If you find her, just get out. Gabriel will be waiting on the edge of the encampment and when he sees you, he will fly into the air and do one circle. That will be the signal to leave. So be looking up every now and then, don't get too focused and miss the signal," Will instructed.

Everyone nodded and turned to head towards the Second Uprising encampment. As they neared, Wynnie tapped Will on the shoulder and pointed to the group of tents.

"Doesn't it seem a little less inhabited than it did the other night?" she pointed out. Will scanned the line and looked for signs of movement. Tim grunted in agreement.

"Something doesn't feel right, Captain. She's right. They may be waiting on us," Theo scoffed at him.

"How would they know we are here? Michelo may just have them doing other tasks to get ready for war and they are on the other side of the set up," Will hoped. He looked between his soldiers and levied the options. "Even if something is going on, we are under Death's invisibility magic. They can't see us. If something is about to happen, we have all the more reason to get Mia out now than ever. Let's keep with the plan and move forward, just be even more cautious."

He had already made his mind up. Wynnie grimaced at the idea and Tim cleared his throat. Theo wasn't understanding the hesitation from the two of them, did they not want Mia back?

"Ready?" Gabriel called from behind in a husky whisper, clearly irritated at the delay.

"Yes," Theo replied, and with a big breath, set foot inside the perimeter.

Chapter Fifteen

Mia

I was awoken by the sound of heavy feet scraping over and over again outside my prison tent. I blinked back the sleep from my eyes and wiped the sand from my face as I searched, pointlessly, for the reason for the noise. No one came in my tent, so I was curious as to why it seemed so hurried. Generally, the Cannibals were slow moving and useless but now they seemed excited and filled with purpose.

Was Michelo about to make a move on Purge? My heart quickened with anxiety and I rose to stand, stepping as close as I could to the entrance in hopes I could catch a glimpse of what was happening. I was just about to peer through an opening when the tent was flung open and Michelo shoved Judas straight into me. I cried out in alarm, as did the young man who was so unceremoniously tossed in my direction.

"Good, you're up. Get those chains off of her and let's get going. We don't want to miss the excitement for the night," Michelo barked orders to Judas, who hurried to take the key that Michelo was holding out.

"Excitement? What's going on?" I asked before Judas could begin to unshackle me.

"You'll see," Michelo smiled at me, the evil thing it was, and said no more.

Judas' hands shook as he worked the chains free and the raw skin that had sat beneath them screamed with relief as the cool desert air touched them for the first time in almost four days. I whimpered as the sharpness of the pain set in. But my delight at being free of the bonds was short lived. With a shout, Judas was shoved to the side and Michelo immediately wrapped a thick cord around my hands, pulling them together in front of my person and setting it tight.

I hissed from the pain of the rough rope gnawing at my sore and exposed skin and flinched away from it.

"Just to make sure you don't get any funny ideas of how this is all going to play out," Michelo cackled, and with a yank of the rope, he pulled me forward. He reached for Judas' chains as well and moved him along beside me. "Hurry now, we don't want to miss out."

My body began to shake with fearful anticipation. Whatever Michelo was excited about must mean I wasn't going to like this. I glanced towards Judas who also seemed worried. As soon as our eyes met, I attempted to raise a questioning eyebrow, but he just shook his head. Whatever this was, he didn't know either.

"You won't be staying long. Either of you. I just wanted you to see how much power I really do wield and to remind you not to try me again."

I shivered at the thought of what this could all be. After a few minutes of stumbling and walking behind Michelo, I finally looked up to see a massive fire in the back of the encampment. I quelled a shocked gasp at the amount of people standing around it waiting. Possibly waiting for Michelo. The Cannibals parted without a thought as Michelo paraded us through the crowd. No one spoke, no one even whispered. They all just stood there mindless and waiting. I felt as if a thousand pair of eyes were on me, but when Michelo finally stopped us right before the fire and turned us to take in the crowd, my stomach sank.

There were way more than a thousand Cannibals before us, possibly upwards of five thousand. Where did all these people sleep? Where did they all go during the day? I imagined them either sleeping on the sand every night, exposed to the elements in their horrible state, or never sleeping at all possibly.

Judas, however, was unmoved by the number of Cannibals as I was. Why would he be? He had gotten to see the entire encampment firsthand this whole time while I had been shackled away.

"Witches!" Michelo began with a booming voice amplified by magic. The Cannibals straightened up to listen. "You have waited long enough to see what I have brought for you and tonight you will enjoy!

We move on the city of Purge in two days' time, then once that falls, we move on to the rest of Medeis!" he called out.

The Cannibals gave a weak cheer, possibly at Michelo's magical command.

"To prepare, you must be strong! So tonight, I give you sustenance!"

My throat went dry. Sustenance? Food?

My eyes darted first to Michelo's back and then to Judas. His face was now filled with horror and a sweat broke out on his forehead. The heat of the fire was immense, but with how pale his skin looked, it wasn't from that.

"My gifts to you!" he waved his hand and a knife was presented to him. I took a wobbling step back away from the weapon, but the rope kept me close.

"No!" I shouted and began to pull away. Judas also began to thrash about when two sets of hands clamped down on our shoulders and we were forced to our knees. We were going to be sacrificed and eaten by the Cannibals!

My heart pounded in my chest as I yanked back and forth, attempting to get the hands off me.

"Let's begin!" Michelo announced and he moved to my left, leaving Judas and I untouched. I halted in my attempt to escape and looked over to figure out where he was moving. What I saw made me want to vomit on myself in horror.

There, just on the other side of the raging bonfire, were the orphans Michelo had spoken of. About one hundred of them were corralled together, tears flowing down their poor dirty cheeks and quivering in fear. As Michelo approached, the older ones began to scream and run, grabbing smaller children with them, but they were no match.

"NO!" I screamed. Adrenaline kicked in and I shoved the Cannibal from behind me away and scrambled to my feet. Calling on the Air, I lifted myself up and began to run for Michelo. I was going to snatch the knife away and shove it into his back.

"Druid!" Judas called from behind as he too found a way to overtake his captor and join me in my mad dash to save the children.

I ran full force with my hands out to snatch the blade away, but Michelo was much more nourished and immensely stronger than I without magic, and he simply sidestepped me, sticking his foot out to trip me up.

I fell face first into the sand, my cheek finding itself burned with a rash from the impact. I grunted, but quickly moved to pick myself back up. I gathered what little magic I could and flung a ball of fire at him, but it was pathetic and weak. I called on Air to knock him over as I rose again for another run for it. I looked to see Judas being wrestled back to the ground by three Cannibals.

"No, please don't!" he was screaming as he hit the ground. I winced as the sound of a bone cracking reached my ears.

The children continued to scream in horror. I turned my head to see a Cannibal grab one little boy from the group, dragging him forward.

"Don't touch him!" I kicked out, causing the Cannibal to slightly lose his balance, but it was no good. He only righted himself, with the blank stare in his eyes, and continued dragging the small boy towards Michelo. I attempted to shove Michelo once more, but he just lashed out and beat me down into the ground with a single back hand to the face. My head went dizzy and my eyes almost blacked out from the impact.

"Enough!" he shouted and kicked me in the ribs. I wheezed from the attack and curled in on myself. Michelo held his hand out for the boy to be placed there and I struggled to right myself again.

"Please!" I cried out, reaching for the boy. "Don't! Take me instead. Take me and let the children go. I have the power that you want, not them. They have almost none at this age and are useless to you. Please, take me instead!" I begged, searching for any type of change in Michelo's mind.

Judas joined in, "And me! I am a Fire Sorcerer. Isn't that the type of magic you wanted most? I'm a Prince of Elevetia and therefore much more useful to your army than these children."

Michelo just chuckled in response.

"You two would barely feed ten of my soldiers. These children will feed almost all of them. Any type of sustenance for them is better than nothing," he drawled and lifted the child, the little boy, into the air by his hair.

"No!" Judas and I both screamed as the blade came down sharply across the tiny throat and the scream was shut off.

130

I turned away in horror, retching all over my already destroyed clothing. Judas too emptied his stomach and clutched at his chest.

The Cannibals shouted in joy as the body of the small boy, practically a baby, was tossed into their midst. I began to sob uncontrollably and crawled to a place in front of the children.

"Stop, please no!" I cried over and over as the children screamed into my ears and wailed with fear. I reached for the girl closest to me and she moved to run into my arms, but again, another child was snatched up away from me. She kicked and screamed, drug her nails over the Cannibals hands, and even succeeded in getting the Cannibal to almost drop her.

"Take the Druid and the Prince away! They have learned their lesson enough!"

I kicked and fought to be let go, eventually being bodily tossed over a Cannibals shoulder as the children pleaded through their tears for me to come back. They reached for me and I for them. Judas had to be completely knocked out to move him. My soul broke as the babies disappeared from my sight, but their screaming continued.

I continued my fight to go back to them, but I was useless. Judas was still unconscious as the Cannibals selected to remove us finally broke from the crowd and the sounds died down. My soul shattered. I couldn't let this happen. I couldn't just not do something. I closed my eyes to pray to the Mother Goddess, hoping she could hear me when a heavy thud rang out right next to my ear and the Cannibal carrying me crumpled to the ground.

I gasped as I fell to the sand, but no impact came. Two strong arms caught me and pulled me close to a warm and earthly scented body. I hauled off and punched out at my newest assailant, connecting my clenched fist with Theo's nose.

"Oh Mother!" I cried out in shock and completely fell out of his grasp in surprise. I heard Judas groan and looked to see Wynnie standing over the body of the other Cannibal.

"Who is this?" she asked and pointed to the Elevetian Prince.

"Wynnie! Theo!" I cried in joy and reached to hug Theo tight around the neck. My tears turned to those of relief, but the emergency of the current events was still heavy on my mind. In my joy, my heart began to skip beats within my chest, and I felt a small flutter of my Earth magic rise to greet its Pair. I let out a small whimper of relief as

Theo pulled me close. As soon as he began inhaling the scent of my hair my eyes snapped open, we didn't have time for this!

"We have to hurry! We have to save them!" I called out as Wynnie reached to cut my binds. Theo was searching me over, and with how thin his lips were set, I could sense that he wasn't happy with what he saw.

"Save who?" came Tim's voice, from behind another tent. I turned to face him.

"The children! Michelo is sacrificing children that he stole from an orphanage. He's letting his army eat them. We have to hurry!"

Gabriel and Will suddenly appeared alongside our group.

"Children?" Theo repeated and spun me to look at him.

"Yes! He captured them days ago. Judas and I tried to stop them, but we couldn't."

"Judas?" Wynnie parroted. I rolled my eyes, sick of the delay.

"Yes! That's Judas! He is an Elevetian Prince and we have to get the children!" I whirled on my Pair and grabbed him by the front of his leathers. "There are babies in there Theo! We have to get them! They are just babies!"

Everyone's mouth firmed in anger as their heads turned to the noise coming from the bonfire.

"Is Michelo wearing the Amulet?" Gabriel finally spoke.

I thought back over and over in my mind.

"No," came Judas' voice from the ground as he moaned and rolled over. "He took it off earlier for a bath and I hid it. I was terrified he would punish me for losing it, but he didn't even seem to care when Gregor came in all excited saying he had figured out how to steal the Druid's magic finally and they took off. This sacrifice must be because they know how to do it now."

My heart leapt as Judas produced the black Amulet.

Gabriel snatched it up and wrapped it around his neck.

"Lucky for us," he commented and tucked it under his own leathers.

"The children!" I reminded them all again.

"Right, how many are there?" Will asked, finally speaking up.

"At least a hundred to start, but he's killing them one by one. We have to save them," I shouted.

"Gabriel can create a distraction for a moment with a fly over, while Tim magics an illusion, something that will get their attention.

132

Wynnie can then make a bomb go off behind the illusion to give it effect and scare them into running, or at least create confusion. Then we can all snatch the kids and run," Will concocted a hairbrained scheme.

I nodded, about to take off when Theo's arm shot out and pulled me back.

"How are we supposed to get them all out?" he asked, actually thinking clearly.

"With this amulet and Mia, I may can even lift them as one unit and we can get the hell out with them," Gabriel responded. He began to move forward towards the bonfire, and I followed.

"Gabriel I can't! I'm useless right now. The wards have sucked me dry," I called out after him.

"Theo, can you get rid of the wards?" Will asked from behind me as everyone started running into action.

"I'm going to need help. Maybe we can just blast one section nearest to us and open it up enough for Mia to regain her magic," he responded.

I blinked, stunned. "How can you get through his wards, in fact how did you get through them tonight?"

"We all learned Blood magic from Heretia," Wynnie called as she headed off with Tim in the opposite direction of Theo.

Everyone was falling into place quickly. Will stayed by my side for physical backup and to help hold back any Cannibals who might follow us. We circled to the side of the fire that Theo had run off in, ducking behind tents as we went. My heart was racing, this was it. I was getting out with the children and Judas, who was being unceremoniously drug by Wynnie with her.

"It's not pretty. Be ready," I whispered to Will, shivering at the image that I had witnessed only moments before.

"Don't worry Mia, we'll get them out," he promised. He rested a heavy and calming hand on my shoulder. With adrenaline racing, we edged closer to the children as they continued to scream and sob. I couldn't let them see me just yet, I didn't want them giving us away. My heart ached as we waited the few moments for Gabriel to fly over and get the Cannibals and Michelo attention. They were so scared, and I could already see that a number were missing from the group.

With a crack of lightening, a massive cloud of black billowed from behind the Cannibals and the two men still standing before the fire halted in their reverie. A small girl was able to snatch away from their grasp and scramble back into her friends trembling arms.

"YOU DARE DESTROY THE CREATION OF THE MOTHER GODDESS!" Gabriel roared from the skies.

A massive shockwave went off from behind the dense black cover and the sounds of hundreds of feet could be heard, chain mail and all. My eyes grew with wonder as the outline of soldiers, all armed to teeth began to materialize behind Gabriel.

"Michelo, you have gone too far! There is no one left to have mercy on you! Death you have caused and Death you will answer to!" Gabriel proclaimed from on high. While it might have been for shock and awe, Gabriel was angry, and no one could deny that. Even from his place in the sky, I could see the molten gold shining within his eyes.

Will and I watched the scene unfold, just waiting for Theo to blow a hole in the wards large enough that my magic could come back. We waited only a moment longer before I felt it, flooding like a river through a canyon after a storm. It was strong and it was full. He must have created a sizeable hole because, like a breath of fresh air in your lungs, my magic filled my soul. Within seconds, I felt my strength return. Michelo, Gregor and the Cannibals were in mayhem, but Gabriel held his place. He wouldn't move until he knew Wynnie, Tim, and Judas were gone from their hiding spot and it was all up to he and I to get the kids out.

I hauled myself up, making sure I was still blocked by the tent and waited, breathing evenly, and forcing my emotions to settle, I needed everything for this.

"We've been breached! Soldiers! To arms!" Michelo shouted above the noise of thunder and armor clanking. Cannibals began moving in all directions, every back turned to the children. Four of the Cannibals started the process of corralling the orphans, but I couldn't waste time on that. I conjured a wind and sent it towards Gabriel, my message clear upon it.

"Now!" I shouted. I watched as he heard it and in unison, we gathered our strength and created a bubble around them. Michelo and Gregor had already taken off in another direction, away from the illusion of an army. This was our only chance. As silently as possible, Will knocked down two of the Cannibals closest to us still guarding the children and grabbed two up in his arms that had been too far away.

134

"Shoot," I muttered and saw that while Gabriel had grabbed his half, I had missed about ten total.

"Follow me!" Will barked at the remaining eight. An older girl grabbed up two smaller children and one older boy grabbed two more. Together they took off running while Gabriel and I began to move our collected children together. I lifted them higher from the ground and rose with them myself. As I scanned the horizon for Theo, I saw Wynnie, Tim, and Judas running toward us completely out of breath.

"Sorry, had to take a long way!" Tim called out. I pointed to the remaining kids running on foot. Tim grabbed the two from the boy, Wynnie grabbed the two from the girl, and Judas scooped up the last two who couldn't keep up.

Will shot off in a direction that I only hoped he knew was correct and I followed. Gabriel, however, continued to hover in his place as a distraction, directing his ball of children after me with a mere thought. I forgot at times how powerful he really was.

A sweat broke out on my forehead as I concentrated harder on holding my magic together. It may have been back, but I was still weak. I was beginning to pant, and the strain was starting to set in when I finally saw Theo ahead of me in the darkness.

"There!" Wynnie called out to spur the running older children on and faster they went.

"Hold on!" I called out to the rest. Thankfully, they remained still. I had worried briefly about the kids getting hurt during the flight to safety, but they apparently realized what was happening and were quietly seated.

I looked back one last time to see Gabriel coating the entire encampment in black mist and then flying off to join us. We didn't wait for him, as there was no time. It would only be a moment before Michelo and Gregor figured out it was all an illusion and headed straight for us.

"Wynnie!" I directed from above. She looked up at me in response.

"Send a message to Heretia and Jeremy for whatever army they can muster to head our way. We're going to be followed and we will need them to help us get the kids back."

Wynnie laughed out loud.

"Already done, Druid! Sent it the moment Theo broke through the ward that we were going to need help. They should already be riding out. Jeremy says hello, by the way!" she called back, and I let out a snort of laughter. Only Wynnie could find a humorous moment in an extremely dangerous situation.

CHAPTER SIXTEEN

Despite my exhaustion, I directed everyone to keep moving for the next hour. Will led the ground crew towards the horses and the few children they had charge of. They galloped away quickly on horseback. With our heavy burden and my weakened state, Gabriel and I were forced to remain at a slower pace. I came next to him in the air, the bubbled children before us, and began to ask each one how they were. Most of the children refused to speak. They were still in a state of shock, but those with their wits still about them were able to mumble that they were hungry and scared.

Gabriel was still angry as we flew in relative silence, save for the sniffles and small cries from the younger of the crowd we raced to safety. His eyes still shone brightly and the power radiating from his body was immense. I flew closer to him, hoping maybe to soak in some of his Death essence and restore my waning magic.

"I'm not going to hold out much longer, Gabriel," I finally admitted, forcing myself to steady mine and the children's flight again.

"Just a bit further, Mia. I can see some of the torches off in the distance. Heretia and Jeremy will be waiting on us," he coaxed.

I turned my head back, unable to make out the light of the Second Uprising behind us.

"Do you think they will follow?" I asked aloud, worried that even though I was free as were the children, this wasn't the end of the night.

"I can only hope that idiot does," Gabriel replied darkly. I felt his anger and wish for revenge but hoped for myself that Michelo didn't follow. It would be suicide to leave in the dark after us, but the man was crazy in his own right, and after tonight, I wasn't sure what he would do.

Finally, when I was almost positive that Michelo wasn't coming, I verbally relented my fight against the strain and lowered the children to the ground, as well as myself. Gabriel followed suit, drawing weapons, and stayed to the back.

As the children regained their footing and started to stand, I walked around each of them, touching them lightly to assess any damage. As far as I could tell, without pushing myself too far, everyone was just slightly malnourished, but no worse for wear. I counted sixty-eight in our charge and with the other ten with the rest of the Elite Guard, which meant we had lost twenty-two precious souls to Michelo's twisted obsession.

My eyes filled with tears. I was thrilled to have this vast number among me, but knowing that I couldn't rescue the others would haunt me forever. I knew there was nothing more I could have done, but I knew I was feeling the loss Meloni did all those years ago. Never again would those twenty-two babies have a chance at life and happiness.

I heard horses hooves galloping in the distance and I looked up, my heart beginning to hammer against my chest with fear. From the direction of Purge came a team of horses, tens of them, all with wagons behind them. I breathed a sigh of relief and hurried to the front of the frightened pack.

"It's okay. It's the soldiers to come take us home. It's safe, I'll talk to them. You guys just stay here and stay calm," I soothed as cries of alarm went up amongst them.

Little girls and boys shivered against my best attempts and clung to each other. I felt a small hand tug at my dress and I spun to Maria, the little girl Michelo had brought to me one night, looking up at me.

"Maria!" I exclaimed and reached to scoop her up.

"Druid!" she called back and buried her head into my neck as she strangled me with her arms. I let the tears flow freely and began to sob onto her tiny dark and dirty head. I knelt down, finally letting my strength give out. As I did, the children circled around me and began to cling to whatever part of me they could reach and they began to cry as well.

It was relief, it was fear, it was sorrow that we all felt. I stayed there, just feeling their warm little bodies encircle me as we waited for the soldiers to close the distance.

"Thank you," Maria finally whispered through her cries. "Thank you for not leaving us."

I blurted out a half-hearted laugh and pulled her back in.

"I would never leave any of you. This will never happen again. You all are safe now, you're with me, and I'm not letting you go, I promise," I called out.

The other children joined in with more thanks and others wishes to be safe. I petted each head I could reach and kissed every forehead near my face that I could.

Gabriel stood watch over our little scene as we waited. It didn't take long for the soldiers to reach us, and as they did, I heard Theo's voice cry out to me.

"Mia!" he called, unable to find me amongst the bodies of children that wrapped around me.

"Theo!" I replied and attempted to stand. The children moved to let me by, but it was no use. My legs finally gave out and I stumbled back to the sand. Maria and two other older boys grabbed at me and attempted to help me rise, but I was too heavy for their malnourished arms as well.

I looked up as the soldiers cast balls of light into the air and Theo was already racing towards me.

"Mia!" Theo called again and knelt to pick me up.

"I can't move. I'm so tired Theo. I couldn't fly anymore," I explained weakly but he shook his head to silence me.

"No, love. You did great. Everyone did great. We're here now and we are going back. You're safe and so are the kids," he crooned and began to walk away with me cradled in his arms. The children raced after us.

"Wait," I called out to stop him. "Maria." I reached down with one arm and immediately little Maria was there, grabbing on and not letting go. "She stays with me," I instructed.

Theo blinked at me in shock and the looked to the dark-haired little dirty girl with the massive watery blue eyes. He hesitated for a moment, and then gave a single nod in agreement. Slowly, he escorted me and my newest friend to a sturdy single horse and loaded us together. I held Maria in my arms while Theo sat behind us to steady me, as I was still too weak to hold myself and a child up.

Gabriel began splitting children up and herding them into the wagons as quickly and efficiently as possible. Soldiers dropped from their horses and formed assembly lines to pass the children quickly into the awaiting modes of transportation. All the while, everyone kept a wary eye out in the direction of the Second Uprising for any movement whatsoever. The air was tense and we worked as fast as possible, wanting to get back to safety and under cover.

"I'm so tired, Theo," I finally whispered, leaning my head back against his chest. Theo kissed my forehead and my heart fluttered to life.

"Let's go, love. Gabriel has this under control. No one is going to hurt them ever again and you need rest. Ez is waiting for you back in Purge and has demanded that she is your one and only healer."

I gave a barely visible smile. "As it should be," I muttered and fell into a light snooze, careful not to completely fall asleep and loos my grip on Maria who was also barely hanging on to consciousness as well.

The ride back was uneventful, but the greeting at the gates of Purge was enough chaos to make up for it. Hundreds upon hundreds of adults, soldiers, witches, generals, and dignitaries were already there with blankets, water, food, and instruction. Jeremy had ridden out a few hundred yards to instruct us on what was going to happen.

"Heretia has rearranged the entire castle for the children to have their own wing. She, Ez, and Alyssa were about halfway through administering the cure to the city when the message from Wynnie came in. Everything has stopped for the time being on that front and the children are the first priority," he reported. "Dormitories have been created and everyone has thrown in on getting the rooms ready. We prepared for about one hundred."

My eyes dropped to the now sleeping Maria.

"It's only seventy-eight," I admitted in a defeated whisper. Jeremy caught my meaning and lowered his own head.

"That sick bastard," he muttered darkly through his teeth, eyeing the horizon.

Theo squeezed my middle for reassurance, but the loss was still too fresh for me to find comfort in it.

"The cure will resume tomorrow with the help of the armies that have assembled. Purge will be free of the Cannibals by tomorrow evening. All thanks to you, Mia." I looked up at Jeremy's words, but my eyes went right through him.

"I didn't do it. I just found a simple potion I thought would work. Ez, Heretia, and Alyssa apparently did it," I countered.

Jeremy shook his head and with a serious gaze told me, "No, this was all you. Gathering everyone. Calling the Rulers and the armies to battle. Finding and bringing back the cure and realizing the right potion we needed for it. They may have done the labor, but it has all been because of you. Hell!" he waved an arm out at the sight of the first few children being lowered from wagons by loving adults with waiting arms and food. "Even this was all you. We didn't even know they were there. You saved them. You are a hero, Druid."

His words had no effect on me, even as he bowed his head in reverence. The forefront concern I was wrestling with was the twenty-two lives gone forever. Jeremy felt my silence as well as heard it and looked to Theo for help. I felt him shake his head from behind me. With a heavy sigh, Jeremy directed his horse away from us just as I heard voices from the crowd call my name.

"Princess! Mia!" It was the sweetest and most known voice known to me since childhood.

"Amelia!" came it's Pair.

My head snapped to attention and my eyes franticly scanned the crowds for the owners of those voices.

"Mama!" I shouted in response, with Maria stirring in my arms.

"Daddy?" I called again and began to squirm.

Theo found a place to safely bring the horse to a stop and reached to pluck Maria from my grasp. I struggled to throw my leg over and the horse and fall to the ground, but Theo held me back.

"Mia!" my mother's voice called out again. I was still searching and struggling when my eyes found my father's tall white fluffy head bouncing through the crowd and my mother running out in front of him. As soon as our eyes met, I launched myself from the horses' seat. Theo barely held on to my tattered dress to break my fall and I took off.

"Mama! Dad!" I called again and with open arms I collapsed into their embrace.

"Oh, my baby!" my mother cried and strangled me into her.

I didn't care if I couldn't breathe right then. All that mattered was that I had my parents back and we were together. Mom burst into uncontrolled sobs and wept tears of joy into my ear as dad held us both and stroked my head over and over.

"My baby!" Mom whispered again and then looked up to check me over. "I am so sorry!" she began with a loud cry. "This is all our fault. We should never have left, we should have told you the truth about who you were. We should never have held you back and taken you away from here. We are so sorry."

Dad pulled her close and kissed her cheek.

"No, mom. It's okay. I get why you did what you did. But we're here now and we're together again. We're safe and we are together," I reassured her. Dad wrapped me in his own hug with one strong arm.

"Thank the Mother Goddess you are safe. We were so terrified what would happen to you. Your mother and I are never going to forgive ourselves for this," he promised me.

I shook my head as I felt Theo approach, Maria in his arms. I looked back to them and instantly, Maria reached for me. I took her onto my hip and held her close.

"We're safe now. All of us. And soon, Purge and the rest of Medeis will be, too," I promised in return. Maria beamed happily at me and threw her tiny arms around my neck.

"Who is this?" my mother asked quietly and looked over the small child she had never met before.

"This is Maria. She bravely brought me food one day and we're kind of a team now. Aren't we Maria?" I asked. Maria nodded and gave a gaping tooth grin. Mom giggled and reached up to grab Maria's hand.

"Hi Maria, I'm Clarisse and this is Daryl. Do you want something to eat?" she asked in her most motherly tone. We all began walking back toward the Castle together, the five of us. Theo never took his hand off my waist, guiding and supporting me. Mom and Dad flanked our sides. Maria seemed enchanted by the size of the Castle and a little afraid of the soldiers and the other adults.

"Theo, where is Ez? I'm ready to lay down for a while," I muttered. Two seconds didn't go by before we were whisked away into the Castle doors and a giant cheer went up. I winced at the noise and clutched the now trembling girl tightly in surprise.

"The Druid has returned!'

Another massive cheer went up. What seemed like hundreds of people stood around the courtyard leading to the back gates, all helping children, directing traffic, and moving supplies.

"Three cheers for the Druid!"

Three massive hurrahs erupted into the sky. Heretia was in front of us only a second later.

"Let's get you to bed. Ez is waiting for you. Hello?" Heretia stopped and looked at Maria curiously. "Do you need me to take this one to the children's dormitory?" she offered her hands, but Maria shied away.

"No, Maria stays with me," I responded, and Heretia graciously nodded, lowering her hands. As we began to turn another cry went up.

"The Druid rescued the missing Prince!" a man cried from the gate and flung his arms out to present a battered and exhausted Judas. Another massive cry of jubilation went up and what I guessed was the people from Elevetia swarmed in on him. A young red headed girl in the front threw her arms open wide and grinned widely.

"I guess that solves Giselda's problem," Heretia muttered under her breath.

I noted a hint of sarcasm, but decided to ask about it later. I looked to Theo to see if he had anything to add, but he only grew slightly nervous and his eyes darted back to me and then away quickly. I was too tired to think on it anymore and let Heretia escort me and my little group back to somewhere I could lay down and eat.

Ez had everything at full blast when I stepped through the door.

"Mia!" she cried with joy. "Clear the way! Everyone! I want that bath finished in the next two minutes. Where are those clean linens I asked for? Who moved my healer kit?" She continued to bark orders to the two or three assistance she seemed to have scrounged together for my arrival.

My eyes were barely open as Theo assisted me onto the bed and curled myself around Maria who snuggled deeper next to me.

Ez immediately began to work, looking me over as gently as possible, shooing everyone but the necessary people out, and removing dirty garments from my body.

"Who's the kid?" she whispered behind her hand badly to Theo. Theo shook his head.

"Her name is Maria and don't even try to take her away from Mia right now. It won't end well," he responded.

I cracked my eyes open as Ez lifted parts of my body to finish looking me over.

"A few marks and bruises. Nothing is broken. Her magic is weak though, and I mean very weak. It's a miracle she got the kids out the way she did. I want her on a strict regimen of my herb concoctions and poultices for the bruises for a few days. No magic from you, Mia."

I didn't have the energy to even nod my head. It wasn't like I wanted to do anything but sleep.

"Maria is perfectly fine other than malnourished and dehydrated. They need a bath and good rest with a large meal in a few hours," Ez continued.

Instantly, my parents and Theo went to work lifting and moving Maria and I around to bathe us. I continued to cling to the girl throughout the bath and the redressing. Ez shoved a warm tea into my hands and a tiny mug into Maria's.

"Drink all of that and then lay down. Don't get up until I say so. Once I'm done with you here, I have to go look after the other kids. I've got healers doing triage and the worst cases are waiting on me."

She straightened and turned to Theo, handing him a satchel. "Put this on her bruises while she drinks. They should be mostly gone by tomorrow night, but I don't want them to linger. If anything changes at all," she raised a perfect eyebrow at me. "I mean at all, call me and I'll be right here."

My parents thanked Ez as they shut the door behind her. Maria and I drank down our teas quickly. It was the most sustenance we'd had in days and it tasted so good. I had never enjoyed a tea like this in my life.

"Theo, why don't you let me do the bruises," my mother offered quietly. Theo pulled the satchel away.

"Why?" he asked cautiously.

"Because I don't want you to get upset seeing them up close like that. I don't think you're in a state of mind to look at them right now." My mother reached her hand back out. Theo's countenance darkened even more. I darted my eyes between them.

"Do as she says, Theo. Why don't you bathe in the other room and then come back and sleep with us? You're tired and dirty, too," I mediated.

Theo wasn't happy with this idea, but seeing that both his Pair and her mother were against him, my father just led him away and out the door with some distracting conversation about how women needed only other women at certain times.

Mom gingerly came to sit on the bed with Maria and I and I lifted the sleeves of my nightgown to expose the green and purple bruises on my wrists.

"My poor baby," she began to whimper, her eyes filling with tears.

"Now mom, you sent Theo out for this exact reason. Don't make me do it myself and send you away, too," I warned gently.

Mom nodded immediately and wiped away the single tear that threatened to fall.

"You're right. I'm sorry. Let's get this done," she whispered. She reached into the pouch and dug out a fistful of handmade poultice from Ez and began her work. My wrists, biceps, ankles, knees, and throat were the worst. There was only a dot of bruising left around my eye due to my own willpower and magic.

"I'm not one to do harm. You know your father and I are peaceful people," she said. My mother began to muse as she collected the bag and headed to the door, depositing it on my side table. "But after what that man has done, I can't promise that given the chance," she began and reached for the door to leave. "That I wouldn't run him through the belly with my own sword and pluck out his eyes with a dagger."

With a flick of her wrist the lights were extinguished, and I was left to awe after her words in the darkness.

CHAPTER SEVENTEEN

To say finding yourself in a place you had never expected to see again was disconcerting, to say the least. To find yourself in that unexpected place and being awoken by the screams of a small child caught in the fit of a nightmare was an altogether different feeling. I was so deep in my own sleep next to Theo that I never felt Maria begin to thrash around on the bed next to me. I was holding her tiny hand, but my mind was too far away again. It had been Theo to stir first, and just as he was about to wake me, Maria let loose an ear-splitting scream.

Heart pounding, I scrambled from my place and threw my hands around, trying to find the location of the frightful disturbance, only to find my arms and legs being wildly kicked by Maria. I leapt into action, not fully aware of where I was yet in the darkened room. For a moment, I thought we were back in Michelo's camp. I needed to silence her in case Michelo heard us. She wasn't supposed to be in my tent, and I didn't remember for a moment how she got there, but I had to make it stop.

"Maria!" I called out and pulled the child into my chest, letting the weight of my own body hold her down and still her wild movements. "Maria, stop. I'm here."

Maria began to slow, and her eyes shot open, darting around the room. I looked up as well and saw Theo racing around to Maria's other side. He snapped his finger and the torches came on with a low light, so as not to blind everyone. In my still half dreaming state, I looked for any sign that Michelo heard and then shook my head.

"We're not there anymore. We are back in Purge, we are safe in my bedroom," I reminded myself. I repeated them soothingly in Maria's ear as she was beginning to lightly cry small tears into my chest.

As I hugged her closer, Theo hovered over us, unsure what to do for a moment.

"Water," I suggested quietly to him. I could see that he was out of his element, unsure of his footing now and how to handle this type of trauma. He nodded at my gentle direction and raced to the side table where Maria's mug had been left earlier and he filled it. Quickly, he handed it over to us and I took it from him.

"Drink this. Sit up and drink this down. It was just a bad dream," I coaxed. Maria nodded and took the cup in her hands, slurping down two good gulps before handing it back.

"Do you want to try sleeping again? Or are you ready to get up?" I asked her carefully.

While I had seen the events of the night before, I wasn't aware of what exactly had happened to the children Michelo had taken hostage before then. I wasn't even completely sure how long they had been there.

"I'm ready to get up. I want to go check on my friends. They may be scared, too," she muttered from behind her fingers.

I nodded, and together we dressed and followed Theo to the newly set-up children's dormitories. As we approached, I heard noises of children and adults walking around, whispering and seemingly already up and getting ready for the day. Seemed as though there were others that couldn't sleep either, and even with the sun barely peeking out over the horizon, the day was going to go ahead and start. An elderly woman dressed in dark attire sat in a chair at the entrance to the hallway.

"Why do you have a child out of their rooms? Where did you find her?" the woman hopped up from her guarding place and came racing with arms out towards Maria. Maria pulled back behind me and cowered.

"Maria stays with me. She hasn't left my side since last night. Who are you?" I asked cautiously. Theo took a looming step from behind me to come in closer.

"I am their new Matron. Her Majesty Queen Heretia sent for me last night from the closest village and charged me with getting this wing in order and keeping everyone safe. My name is Hera. Who exactly are you, and why do you have this child?"

I slackened my stiff back. She was only doing her job, and for that I was grateful.

"Oh! Hello, Hera. Thank you so much for coming at a moment's notice. I'm sure Heretia wouldn't have called for you if she didn't trust you implicitly. My name is Amelia and I," I paused for a second.

"This is the Druid that rescued the children," Theo finished for me, noticing my hesitancy.

I was still slightly uncomfortable throwing my weight about when I thought a gentler hand was needed. Theo, however, did not. Hera's eyes went wide and her back stiffened.

"The Druid?" she asked, and I nodded. She looked stunned between the three of us before finally bowing her head. "I'm sorry, Druid. I didn't know. Please forgive me. What can I do for you?" She wasn't simpering or groveling. This type of woman even when shocked still held airs of importance and dignity about her.

"Maria woke up badly and then wanted to check on her friends. I think she needs to see them and then she needs to eat. Am I allowed to drop her off with you for a while so I can check on developments elsewhere?" I asked kindly.

Maria's head shot up and her eyes looked frantic.

"I want you to stay with me!" she began to whine.

I knelt down next to her.

"I have adult work to do for a bit. Why don't you go with Matron Hera for a few hours? Eat, rest up, check on your friends, and let everyone know that it's going to be okay. Make them feel as safe as you've made me feel. Can you do that? Can you be as brave as you were back in the camp?" I asked her gently.

Maria's eyes darted between me and Hera for a moment before nodding.

"That's a good girl. Maria, you said your name was? What are your friend's names? I've got everyone accounted for and set up in rooms so I can help you find them," Hera smiled. She held her hand out, and together the old woman and young girl walked down the hall chatting away.

I watched her go warily. For some reason I was growing overly attached to this little girl that I had only met once. Maybe it was a form of trauma attachment that would end up being unhealthy, but I wasn't ready to face that yet. With a big breath to steady myself, I turned back to Theo and fell into a huge hug.

"Are you ready to eat something?" he asked me, and I nodded my head silently against his chest.

"I need food and I need answers," I responded.

Theo began reciting all that had happened since I was gone in the briefest of terms, letting me know who had shown up and what preparations were being made. My heart began to flutter with anxiety at the thought of all the people he had mentioned. I voiced my concern and Theo paused in our walk. He could see the worry written on my face and I'm sure I still didn't look fully recovered from my ordeal in the desert.

"Heretia has started removing most of the new arrivals into the city as the water is purified with Water Sorcery and Cannibals are cured. There are hundreds of homes that have been abandoned for two decades that they are magically renovating and moving into for the time being. The Castle was getting too crowded, so only the Rulers are staying," Theo tried to allay my fears.

I nodded, but five rulers each from four kingdoms and their families was still more people than I was willing to deal with right now. I was still weak from malnourishment and my magic was strained along with it.

"Is it possible to eat in our rooms and have Heretia and my parents come to us?" I suddenly asked, not wanting to face all these people in my current state.

Theo looked ahead at the doors at the end of the hallway that held the Dining Room and then, after thinking for a moment, nodded, and led me back to my room. Rebekah, Heretia's favorite maid, was there cleaning up when we entered. With a little start, she jumped and rushed to stand up.

"Druid, I was just getting your room in order while you were at breakfast," she apologized, but I shook my head.

"Don't worry about it, please, Rebekah. I don't think I'm ready to take everyone on right now. Can I have two plates sent up here so I can rest?" I asked, as Theo settled me back into bed.

Rebekah curtsied in response. "Of course, Druid. I will have that done immediately and bring it myself."

I closed my eyes and leaned back. "Can you let Her Majesty know, too? I want to see her so badly," I called after the spritely woman. Rebekah curtsied again.

"Absolutely, I'll go now. I know she has been so worried about you. We all have, Druid. We are so glad your back here and safe." She flicked her eyes over at Theo, who didn't notice as his back was turned to her. I caught the second-long glance and furrowed my brow, but she left before I could see what it meant.

"Thank you," I muttered, as Theo propped me back up with pillows.

"Whatever you need, love," he replied, and settled in next to me.

I leaned into my Pair and inhaled deeply. Just being near him again was helping settle my nerves and my magic fluttered again.

"Thank you for coming to get me," I whispered.

Theo shifted in his seat and looked down at me. When our eyes met, I saw the flash of sparkling green color dance across his worried face.

"I will always come get you, Mia. I may not can stop you, but I can always save you."

I gave a small smile at his words and leaned further back. It wasn't long before Rebekah came floating back in with a tray of two steaming plates with Heretia and Gabriel hot on her heels.

"You're up?!" Heretia shouted and floated in brightly.

I sat up slightly to accept a hug from her and the plate was settled gently on my lap.

"I was worried you would sleep most of the day, but it would have been understandable. Ez told me other than a little bruised and malnourished, you were going to be okay."

I began to eat my meal ingloriously in front of them. The taste of the eggs, even without salt and pepper, was like luxury on my tongue.

"Rebekah!" Heretia suddenly chastised and turned on her maid. "Esmerelda said specifically to not feed her this much and no hard-chewing food for at least another day. Only soft food." Heretia reached to take my plate away and remove the ham chunk that was set there, but I swatted her hand with my fork lightly.

"Don't you dare," I warned lightly. "I'll deal with Ez if she says something."

Heretia just shook her head and made a scoffing noise. "Don't blame me when she tosses you out of the window. That woman has stormed through this castle and whipped my entire new infirmary in to shape, along with completely organizing the Curing of the city. She's unstoppable and now with her husband at her side, she's."

Heretia's lament was cut off by the sounds of me choking on the piece of meat I had just insisted I eat. Everyone flew up to their feet. I coughed it up and took in three deep gasps of air.

151

"I knew you couldn't eat that!" Heretia shouted and reached to take it.

I grabbed her wrist as I still took in one last breath.

"Her husband?!" I asked, still in shock from her words. It wasn't the meat that had made me choke but in my shock I had inhaled it instead.

"Did you just say, her husband?" I asked again. Theo pursed his lips and looked away conspicuously. "What husband?" I asked into the now silent room.

I heard the door click shut lightly as Rebekah exited.

"Oh, uh," Theo began and scuffed his foot. "Ez and Tim got married."

"What?" I shouted, unable to contain my surprise.

"It all happened so fast. She got here yesterday afternoon, and a few hours after she got in, she grabbed me and made me a witness to their marriage. Heretia performed it," he answered hurriedly.

"Ez and Tim?" I asked, still not fully comprehending this idea. I had known there was something between them since I had met the couple, but never in my wildest dreams did I imagine I would be gone for barely four days and would come back to them married.

"Yes, dear," Heretia sat back down on the bed and covered her hand with mine.

I glanced between the three of them. Gabriel was in the corner grinning wildly. This was his favorite type of chaos.

"I just, I don't know what to say. Where is she?" I asked Theo, who shrugged. He looked to Gabriel who finally righted himself into a standing position.

"She's back out there in the streets administering the Cure," he answered me.

"I guess I need to congratulate her later," I sighed. I leaned back, suddenly not hungry.

"Is this really so upsetting?" Heretia inquired, but I shook my head.

"No! Not upsetting at all, just shocking. What else has happened in the time I was gone?" I asked.

Heretia and Gabriel launched into a full-scale rendition of what happened every day. From Heretia's recovery, which she looked amazing now if still a tad stiff, to the dignitaries arriving, Elevetia admitting Judas was gone, and then the problems with Maravette. I bristled at this bit, but Theo assured me Wynnie had handled it completely and the entire kingdom was soundly on board.

"Remind me to slap him if he ever wants anything from me," I mumbled darkly.

Theo smiled, knowing that would never happen but the words made me feel better. Thinking of violence like that reminded me of my mother's words as she left me last night and I shivered remembering the coldness in the threat.

"Where are my parents?" I finally asked as the tale ended.

"Rebekah will find them for us and let them know you're awake. They have been a great help with Maravette," Heretia answered me and then shot an eye to Theo.

It was the third glance I had seen that made me unnerved and I had just about had it.

"Oh, for Mother's sake, what is it? Don't coddle me, just tell me what you want to say," I blurted out in frustration.

"Well, he's been a big help with Maravette because it turns out that, and Mia don't get angry at him for this, but he's related to the Lily's," she explained.

This made my breath stop. My mind whirled with the idea that my dad was a Lily and all feeling went numb. After a long tense moment, I finally spoke, "I would like to see them now."

As the words drifted out of my mouth, my mother burst through the door, sunshine radiating from her smile. She ran toward me with her arms outstretched. My feelings about my father's heritage immediately escaped me as she wrapped me up in a hug and cradled my head closer to her chest.

"Oh, my baby!" she cried, tears of joy fell from her eyes as we rocked back and forth for a moment, finally getting to feel each other again properly.

My Earth magic danced and sang, doing small flips all around in my chest. It had never been free of its constraints around my parents and, for the first time in its life, was able to reach out and feel my mother's magic as well. Her own magic responded in kind and rushed to meet mine halfway. Her magic felt like a dew kissed lawn on a cool spring morning. It was like balm to my soul and I breathed easier having met it for the first time. Theo stood near me and I guess his own magic noticed the bond. It was squirming slightly with what felt like jealousy. I glanced at him and he shifted his weight from one foot to the other, attempting to restrain it. I gave him a glance and he nodded in return. He was fine, but having been away from me under such circumstances, his magic was only within its right to feel that way.

My father followed in after my mother and wrapped his arms around us as well, just as he had the night before. His magic felt like solid stone, a mountain unmovable and unyielding. I grounded myself in it and steadied my nerves. Tears were abounding and even Heretia let out a small sniffle as Gabriel threw an arm across her shoulders for comfort.

I finally pulled away from my parents and leaned back to see them. My eyes immediately darted to my father's hand where a small pinky finger was now missing on the left. My anger bristled at the thought of why he was now marred forever, and the feelings of hate returned. Hate for his situation, for my own torment, for the children lost forever, for what Michelo was doing to the Cannibals back at his ramshackle encampment he called an army. I turned my eyes away from it, feeling the sting of frustration on my cheek.

"How are you feeling?" my mother finally asked, stroking my hair.

"Weak, tired, but I'm okay. I just need to eat and rest and I'll be ready to take on whatever the Mother Goddess throws at me," I said. I attempted a brilliantly convincing smile, but it didn't work.

"Princess, you just rest as long as you need to. We've got everything under control with the other High Rulers. They saw the state of those children last night, and you for that matter. They won't be upset if you take a few days to yourself," My father counseled sweetly, but I shook my head.

"I'm afraid we don't have a few days. Michelo is angry now. Angry he lost me, lost his chance at taking my magic, lost Judas as a bargaining chip, and the children as a sacrifice to his monsters," I argued.

"Take your magic?" Gabriel echoed and moved closer to the end of my bed.

"What do you mean, take your magic?" Theo sat down heavily to also edge closer.

"It's what he had planned for me. Apparently, Gregor has been concocting potions he thought could strip a witch of their elemental magic and bequeath it onto another witch. Preferably his Cannibals. They're so weak right now, they can't do anything. He wanted to give them all a powerful magic so he could wield it on the battlefield," I explained.

154

Everyone looked to Gabriel for answers.

"Is that what we were feeling?" Theo asked him. Heretia placed a hand on her lover's shoulder.

"Is something like that even possible?" she whispered in fear. Gabriel hung his head, stunned into silence and then with a great sigh, lifted himself to his full height.

"To answer Theo, yes that must have been what we were feeling," Gabriel nodded.

I looked between the five of them, worried. "Feeling? What did you feel?" I asked.

Theo took one of my weak and trembling hands as Gabriel explained. "While you were gone. Theo, myself, and your parents were randomly attacked, but in the magical unseen style. Weak, nausea, fainting, and pain. We had an idea that he was torturing you, but no idea how."

I blanched at this statement. I hadn't saved any of them from pain with giving myself up after all. I had just made it worse and gave Michelo an avenue to weaken them along with me. I felt sick to my stomach. How much had they endured? As much as I did?

"It would only last a few moments and then be gone. We weren't sure if it was a by-blow of what Michelo was doing, or if you were calling out to us. As soon as we realized it was our connection to you, we acted even faster," Theo said.

"But why were you four effected? I was so far away and shrouded by the wards. How could you feel it?" I asked.

Heretia shook her head. "They all have a connection to you either magically or physically. Your parents through blood, Gabriel through magic, and Theo being your Pair. No one else felt it but them."

I blinked in shock. Had I known it was hurting them, too, I wouldn't have been able to make it. But I had fought hard through it all thinking I was the only one suffering.

"To answer Heretia's question. I don't think it is. Magic is part of you, woven into your very being. My siblings gave their physical bodies up and integrated themselves into witches very existence. The magic can't exist without them, and witches can't exist without magic. It's as a part of your bodies as your eyes, ears, and mouth. Whatever Gregor is attempting can't possibly work. It would end up killing the witch, and with it, the magic he was trying to take," Gabriel explained.

Everyone mulled this over for a few silent moments before I finally spoke.

"Then we need to end this before he tries again. If he can't have me, he will start with whoever is available. Enough people are going to die at his and Michelo's hands. This war just got even more serious," I snarled. I moved the covers from my lap and twisted my body.

My mother jumped up, hands in front of her. "What do you think you're doing?"

"My job," I responded and slipped my feet into the slippers awaiting them on the floor.

CHAPTER EIGHTEEN

I could hear the murmur of people talking and whispers on the other side of the door from where I stood, waiting to enter the Throne Room. I had called a meeting of the High Rulers but now the nerves were starting to creep in as we waited for them to assemble. Theo stood at my side as I took in a deep breath, then a shiver snaked its way down my spine.

"Are you ready for this?" he asked me gently, covering my hand with his own that I had rested upon his arm. I swallowed and nodded.

"Considering this is my first major appearance as the Druid and not some simple witch or even a Princess, I guess so. I'm not sure how to act or what they expect of me. How do I even address them? Am I above them, or below them?" I began to prattle.

Theo gently squeezed my fingers to silence me.

"Love, it's fine. But yes, you are above them, and I promise you, they're not the biggest fans of it. Just go in there and say what needs to be said. Let them come to realize that the Mother Goddess chose you for a reason. It's not yours to actively prove. You're the Druid and they are not. Just act like you know this," he winked.

My heart swelled a little at his confidence in me, but I wish I had his bravado when it came to facing hordes of possibly angry, highly likely jealous, and for sure terrified Kings and Queens.

Heretia came up behind us, righting a small circlet on top of her head and then straightening her back. Gabriel smoothed out his jacket and flicked an imaginary piece of dust off of it. He also sported a circlet that matched Heretia's. I swooned slightly at the sight of them. They were just too precious sometimes.

"Okay," Heretia finally huffed and looked towards me. "Jeremy says everyone is there, so I'm going to head in. Just come in whenever you are ready." As she began to walk past me, I had the sudden urge to reach out and grab her. Heretia paused as I did just that and looked down at our joined hands.

"I don't know if I've said this Heretia, but thank you," I began. She was clearly confused at my outburst, so I took a breath and continued on. "Thank you for holding it together till I got here. Thank you for being patient. Thank you for not losing your soul to the madness. And thank you for giving up your home to this war. You will be repaid ten-fold when this is over, I mean it."

Gabriel looked to Heretia to see her reaction. Finally, Heretia let a bright grin break out on her face in contrast to the single tear that threatened to fall.

"Oh, Amelia," she choked and moved to pull me into a tight hug. "You are already repaying me. In ways you could never know. You brought Gabriel back to me, you're saving my people, and the children of my kingdom. You've cleared my name to the rest of Medeis, and now, you're going to end this once and for all." She pushed me back to arm's length and rested her hand lovingly on my cheek. "I never did any of this for payment, but if you must give something. Know that you already have."

I nodded silently and then released her.

"Ready?" she turned to Gabriel who held his arm out for her. As they walked away from us, Gabriel turned back and nodded his head once, a gesture that I took as a thank you for my own sacrifices and actions as well.

"You really are an amazing woman. Let's just go show these braggarts that, too." Theo chucked my chin lightly with his finger and together we walked into the den of lions.

The murmuring I had heard just moments before was more of a low roar that rang in my ears as soon as the door was opened. I straightened my back and trained my sights on Heretia standing on the dais, waiting for me. The sounds of over a dozen chairs moving back, scratched at my nerves, but I refused to wince. In silence, we made our way up the steps to the thrones Heretia had brought for us.

"This was one of the Thrones I had in my later years as Meloni. The High Rulers won't recognize it, but we'll make sure they remember," Heretia had mentioned to me in passing as everyone had dressed for the audience.

My throat gave an involuntary small swallow as I looked at the piece of ancient craftsmanship. There were symbols etched over the head representing each magic, and swirls and loops carved expertly into the arms and legs. It was really beautiful in its own way, but frightening as well.

Theo guided me to stand before it and paused before turning to face the Rulers below.

"Diplomacy is about grandeur and effect. Give them the show they have been waiting to see when it comes to a Druid," he counseled.

Taking this to heart, I scanned the room with an attempt at an imperious eye, making them wait to sit. After about three full seconds, I slowly sat down and waited as everyone placed themselves back comfortably. Every eye in the room turned and every ear leaned in to hear my first commanding words as the Druid. I still looked horrible, felt horrible, too, but the clock was ticking against us.

"Your Royal Majesties!" I began, using Air to amplify my voice. No reactions, so I guess I hadn't started off badly. "As you have been made aware, we are at a very precarious state in our world, and we have no time to waste. You are all aware of what is happening beyond the walls of this Castle and what we are up against. I, myself, have also fallen victim to the monster known as Michelo Unda, formerly of the Kingdom of Lotho."

I saw all the Lotho Rulers flinch lightly at the reference, but I couldn't care right then. Pride be damned, this was war.

"We are fighting a curse found from ancient times, reborn and reconstructed to take this entire world out once and for all."

A few people shifted in their chairs uncomfortably.

"The people of Purge are already being freed of this curse as we speak. Princes Esmerelda of Suravia is distributing the potion granted to us by the Mother Goddess, herself, to all those afflicted."

A young, fiery, blonde man stood up from one of the groups suddenly.

"Why can't we just give this potion to those in Michelo's camp as well? It would seem easier to taint their water supply with the cure than it would be to fight them," he called out.

Whispers could be heard in the room, but I just raised my hand for silence.

"Excellent question, Your Majesty," I began. "We can't cure them. The one who administers the original changing potion must be dead. The potion attaches the Cannibal to the person like a puppet to puppeteer. As long as Michelo is alive, no one in the Second Uprising camp can be saved. Those in the kingdom of Purge were changed long ago and their puppeteer is dead."

This answer didn't placate the young Ruler, but it did make him sit back down.

"As I was saying, Purge will be free of the curse in a matter of hours, but we have a long road ahead. No one from this city, save for Queen Heretia's current army, can fight with us. She has sent word across her kingdom to those regions unaffected for help, but they are farmers, not warriors. While vital in keeping armies fed and clean, they are useless in battle. This war is up to you and your kingdoms to finish."

Queen Felicity, Esmerelda's mother, and a Ruler of Suravia, stood this time. "How is this our problem?" she sneered and then pointed at Heretia. "She is the one who couldn't take care of it. It's her fault this happened."

One or two heads nodded in agreement.

"The Second Uprising began in its infancy long before Heretia was Queen, by her father and the other Rulers of the Ancient Kingdom. She was just a child and therefore unable to stop them. You know as well as anyone else that once changed, there is no stopping it. Once the water supply is tainted, there is nothing you can do. It's spreads far and wide," I explained. I leaned forward in my chair to steady myself. "Queen Heretia has dedicated her life to containing this Second Uprising, but she is just one woman and had no aid from her neighbors of fellow High Rulers. I guess the question really comes down to: Why did no one reach out to her first?"

They all fell silent.

"Instead of sitting back and hating the Ancient Kingdom, there were many chances given to each one of you to reach out in her early years and offer assistance. But that is beside the point at this moment." I changed the subject. I didn't want to get into a bad-mouthing match of Heretia.

"We need to take care of the present, and presently, we are at war. I spent almost four days in the Second Uprising camp. I endured torture and starvation and I gained valuable information. What I saw

160

there was beyond reprehensible, and we need to act fast. Michelo Unda and Gregor are working on developing potions meant to take a witch's magic away from them and give it to one of their empty vessel soldiers."

Noises of shock and dismay went up at once. They were obviously not prepared for this piece of information.

"It is horrible, and it is brutal for a witch to endure the pain the potion causes during the attempt. Luckily, or unluckily for me, after many failed and painful attempts, I believe it cannot be done. However, those two are not going to stop killing trying to obtain this ability that only the Mother Goddess can wield. I propose that we act fast and we act now. Michelo is angry and his Second Uprising is in a state of confusion since my escape, and that of the children he was planning on using as Cannibal sacrifices."

Heads shook, eyes lowered, and others even gave small gasps behind their hands. If the lives of the orphans didn't spur these people, nothing else would.

"But there is more and far dangerous obstacles we must face. We must prepare ourselves for more than a battle with Cannibals." I took in a breath, ready to drop the final blow that even I still didn't have a plan on. "Michelo has the Wild Beasts under his control."

Chaos erupted. Kings and Queens stood, screeched, and shouted their anger and surprise. Someone from Elevetia stood and boomed above the others.

"It's true! Our own Prince Judas, who the Druid rescued from captivity as well, debriefed us last night. Michelo has Tailong, the Wild Beast of Fire."

The man sat back down quietly as more protests erupted. This wasn't effective, so I used a more forceful Air charm to lift my voice higher.

"Enough!" I called out, quieting the crowd of twenty below me. I reached for Theo's hand to steady my nerves. "We know Michelo has Tailong and Antamba. Nandina, Cetus, and Aqrabuamelu are dead, but we think they might not be for long. Michelo is still searching for the sixth and final Wild Beast, Phoenix. We understand he still has not found it, but if he can, with it he can raise the three dead Wild Beasts and he will be unstoppable. Phoenix won't even have to fight. It would just keep raising them over and over until we are defeated."

Everyone was silent now, which was just as scary as it had been when they were shouting and arguing. I could practically hear the defeat from half of the room and the minds of the other half whirring violently to come up with a solution.

"Do we know where Phoenix is?" Uncle Michael finally spoke up and it lifted my heart to see him sitting, happy and healthy, in the crowd.

"We do not, no one does. Not even Gabriel knows. We have searched and tried, but not only is Phoenix not in our history books, but the Mother Goddess did not mention it to me when I spoke with her in the Forest," I relayed.

"Well, that just means if we can't find Phoenix, Michelo can't either. So, let's just plan for war with two Wild Beasts and end it now," a Queen from Elevetia announced wisely.

Most of Lotho, Suravia, and Elevetia nodded in agreement. Maravette stayed more wary, but I could see the determination in their eyes. Whatever Wynnie had said to rile them to arms, worked enough for what we needed.

"Excellent. We need to act fast. Captain Jeremy and I, along with Queen Heretia, will be meeting with your Generals in an hour after you have given them the news." I waved my hand to signal Jeremy to step forward and bow just in case they hadn't met him yet.

I looked back at the crowd of terrified Rulers, people stirred to action at the idea of losing not only their place, but their people and their own lives.

"We will fight, and we will win," I began and stood from my chair. "We have the Mother Goddess' blessing, not just in our cause, but in me. She will not abandon us, she will not desert us, and neither will I. I was sent for this purpose, and while I may not have been raised here in Medeis, it is now my home. My family is here," I stared down the Rulers from Maravette with a knowing eye. Only one man met the gaze and bravely nodded his acknowledgement. I assumed, rightly, that he was the husband of Wynnie's sister, my second cousin as I had learned.

"My Pair is here," I reached for Theo's hand, and he instinctively took it, standing to his full height next to me. "My friends are here." I looked to my left where the Elite Guard and Gabriel were placed. "And my people are here. I will fight with every last breath in my body till I see it safe. Yes, there will be casualties, yes there will be destruction, but this world and its witches have grown complacent and separate.

We are no longer Five Kingdoms, we are Medeis. We will take back what is ours, fight for our survival, and ensure that our children have a future to look froward to."

I stared each one of the Rulers down. First the Rulers from Maravette, then to Lotho, and as I crossed over Thomas, he suddenly stood and began thumping his chest with a fist. I paused, staring in surprise at him, but he never broke eye contact with me. Out of the corner of my vision, Uncle Michael stood and mirrored the action, adding to the eerie sound of a heart beating. I took in a quick breath as Vanessa and the rest of Elevetia stood collectively, thumping their chest to the unknown rhythm. One by one, each Ruler stood and joined in the chant of fists and flesh.

I stood, stunned by the gesture and unsure what to do. Theo moved to bend and whisper something in my ear but at the same moment, my heart realized what I had to do. I took my right hand and began thumping it in the same way on my chest. Beating it in time to the same rhythm that was playing out before me. As those seated on the dais with me joined in, I picked up the speed.

Faster we called out with our flesh, faster we heard with our hearts and faster we sent the call to each other. We sent a promise of our swords, our magic, and our lives to each other. As it came to an overwhelming head, the noise growing in my ears. We came to a sudden stop as one.

While the movement was gone, our magic had created the sound within the space, and it still bounced from the walls, ceilings, and rafters. It rang out inside the halls of the castle, and into the streets of the city below.

The message was clear. We were coming, and we were one.

CHAPTER NINETEEN

The meeting with the generals was much more exhausting than I had anticipated, and my presence was almost unnecessary. I knew nothing of war and battles and tactics, and it showed. For the most part, I sat and listened to the grown men and women arguing and debating, back and forth over and over again. Finally, when Jeremy had given me a look of exasperation, I called it quits for the moment and asked that everyone take the information that had already been discussed and to begin preparations.

Some had mumbled and groaned, mentioning we hadn't planned enough, or one kingdom was holding us back more than the others, but I ignored them. What we had was a good start and I wanted to see Ez's progress with the city.

Back in Heretia's library, we all assembled to do just that. Everyone had changed clothes to go out and walk on foot and the Elite Guard were strapped with various light weapons just in case there were problems. Ez entered shortly after we gathered, and I wrapped her in a huge hug.

"I think you still need rest, Mia. It's really hot out there and you haven't fully recovered." Ez voiced her worry one more time since I had mentioned the outing earlier.

I waved her away and smiled, "I'm fine Ez. This is much more important. Besides, I rested enough in the war council meeting doing absolutely nothing. I feel great!"

She raised a manicured eyebrow at me one more time while looking me over and then shook her head. "Alright, but after this you begin resting until tomorrow. Your body is healing itself at a good rate, so I guess I shouldn't worry too much. It's just been so long since anyone has been around Life Sorcerer's, I guess we forgot how fast you guys heal." She tucked her dark hair behind an ear and I caught sight of a pretty silver band on her wedding finger.

"By the way, congratulations again on you and Tim. I'm really happy for you guys." I squeezed her shoulder one last time before moving out of the door.

"Thank you. It was sudden, but we're happy. I think deep down I always knew Tim and I would end up together, but neither of us was ready to admit it yet. It's weird when you meet the person you're meant to be with at a younger age. It feels like maybe there is some life left to live on your own, but when push comes to shove, all you ever want is them. So why deny it any longer? Why stop yourself from having the person you want the most all the time? I just wish we had admitted it sooner, honestly." She spoke frankly as we walked down the hall.

Tim came up to join us and took his new bride's hand in his. I smiled to myself, watching them be so in love and happy.

"You guys are amazing," I said out loud. Ez blushed ever so slightly, but then quickly returned her focus on the task ahead.

"The people of Purge are fully free of the Cannibalism. The potion worked like a charm and made plenty for not only the city, but anyone left afterwards from the Second Uprising. But I'm going to warn you, it's not pretty. They are weak and most are confused. Some of them don't remember much from before and others are outraged at what has happened."

I nodded at her words. Straightening my back, we left the Castle and walked down into the city. We passed the first few rows of homes that from the outside seemed abandoned, but I had been told were being currently occupied by visiting dignitaries for the time being. Ez led us straight to a huge meeting hall type building and opened the door.

"We have five of these set up all around the city. It was the best place to keep them all until they regained their motor function and memories. You ready?" she asked me, the noise already filtering from the open doorway. Sobs, murmurs, and low voices met my ears along with a smell of dirt and sickness. I swallowed hard and then nodded.

Once inside I waited for my eyes to adjust from the bright sun to the darkness of the room.

"We have to keep it dimly lit. With their newfound consciousness, we discovered that the bright sun was hurting their eyes and the people

166

were struggling to cope. I've got aides and healers that have been brought from every kingdom working around the clock to get them comfortable and up on their feet. The kitchen is not only for cooking, but for mixing together herbs and other potions to help with the recovery." She motioned to the open area near the back where five Life wielders were busy working over hot flames and pots.

I took in the room around me and felt my hand flutter to my chest.

"It's worse than I thought," I whispered, and leaned in closer to Theo for support. Dozens of women and men leaned against the walls, laid out on the floors, and struggled to move.

"Every muscle in their body is beyond weak. They've been physically moving for twenty years under the latent power of the Cannibalism, but in reality, they were pushed beyond their boundaries. Heretia has done well at keeping them alive, but the magic had fought off as much as it could, and when they were returned to normal, they were left weak." Ez explained, her voice full of pity.

I knelt down beside one sleeping woman and placed my hand on her head.

Instantly I felt my Life magic leap out and begin the process of healing her, but it was so much and so unexpected, that I cried out from the feeling. The woman instantly snapped her eyes open and sat up, scrambling to get away from me. She whimpered in fear and cowered away.

"No, no!" I called and lifted my hands up to stop her.

"Get away from me!' she begged.

"It's okay. I'm not here to hurt you, I'm here to help. My name is Mia, and I was just checking on you to make sure you were okay," I soothed.

The woman relaxed slightly and looked to the healers eyeing me warily.

"Like the Life wielders?" she asked me, still cautious.

"Yes, exactly like the Life wielders. No one is going to hurt you. What is your name?" I asked her, coming to sit on the floor instead of crouching down.

"I," she stammered and then hung her head. "I don't remember. I do know it was my grandmother's name, but I can't recall it. All I remember is going to the market when I was seventeen to collect food for dinner, and the next thing I knew, I was here. I don't remember anything anymore. They told me I had been sick for over twenty years.

They told me I was now forty years old!" Her eyes began to well up, tears threatening to fall fast down her face. "I'm forty! My whole life is gone. I can't find my family. I don't remember where I live, and I can't do anything. I never got to have children, or my own house or anything. My life is ruined." Her weeping broke my heart and I scooted closer, wrapping her in my arms.

"I know, dear. I know this is going to be hard. I know what it feels like to think everything is gone, that you have nothing left. To be somewhere strange with no idea what to do or how to function. But we're going to get you through this. I promise." I rocked her gently for a moment. I choked my magic down to a single trickle and let it flow into her, relaxing her body and settling her emotions. Her pain lashed out at me, and I bore it silently. It hadn't crossed my mind what life would be like for those who had been unwittingly afflicted all those years ago. Waking up to a new body, a new age, and missing the vast majority of their life was terrible. What about those who had been children?

My heart broke for her, for all of them. I looked up at Theo and I saw the pain he was feeling for them. He turned and began to do what he could as well. Wynnie, Tim, and Will followed suit. They abandoned their roles as protectors and Guard to become caretakers and healers themselves. Ez was busy directing Life Wielders and assisting other newly cured to food, water, and warmth. Heretia was at another corner asking and taking notes about families, those the cured could remember, and beginning the process of reuniting those whom she could.

I felt a twinge of anger at the stubborn Rulers from some of the other kingdoms who were still unsure if they wanted to be a part of this war. If they could see what I was seeing, they would change their minds. I vowed to require each one of them to come out here and see this, help, and heal with the people. I needed them to see how horrible the Second Uprising could be and what it would leave in its wake if we didn't win this fight.

Eventually, the woman slowed her tears and pulled back to look up at me.

"Thank you, Mia," she whispered and wiped her face with a dirty hand. "I think I'm hungry now. I'm going to go ask the Life Wielders for something to eat."

168

I nodded, watching her rise and walk away. Ez helped me back up and we both waited as the rest of the Elite Guard looked over other individuals and brought them comfort with other magical means.

"That's the case for almost everyone here. They have lost their life to this. Years forever stolen that they will never get back. Some of the youngest are only just now in their early twenties, but they remember nothing as they were only babies or small children. They won't be ready for families or jobs or anything anytime soon. Most can't even read. There is no one left in the city younger then twenty-three," Ez explained.

My heart ached as I walked around meeting others and dropping nuggets of healing on them all. Any advantage at peace I could give them, I would. This war was going to need them, and they had the greatest reason to want to see it end.

We spent the rest of the day going to all four other meeting halls where people were collected. A few had already felt good enough to begin looking for a home to stay in, and I had Ez direct other witches from the armies to help get them set up. This city needed a shock back to life and I wanted to make sure it got it.

"Don't burn too much energy, just get them started. Conjure up beds, functioning bathrooms, and kitchens with maybe somewhere nice to sit. If a family can be found and put together, let's get that happening, too. The more stability we can give them, the better," I instructed.

Witches of all kingdoms went off in all directions to do their jobs rebuilding the city of Purge. I also had a messenger draft together an official summons of the Rulers of each kingdom to get out here and help. I was determined they were going to get their hands dirty in this. If they wanted to push back, then they would deal with me later that night.

Heretia herself was able to track down a man who claimed to be the father of a young girl that had only been one at the time they were lost to Cannibalism. Through some deduction and dedication, she found the daughter still alive and extremely confused. However, the young woman briefly recognized her father's now aged face, and together they found a new home and began working on their new life.

"Juliette, that is her name," he told us, as we settled them down into a nice apartment above a shop front. The father had told us he remembered finishing an apprenticeship in paints and dyes. "I'll keep looking for her mother, but at least I found my baby girl."

His smile was withered and drawn, but the joy was beginning to drown out the sadness deep within his eyes. Juliette could barely speak, having never had to as an adult, but her face showed love as they closed the door behind them.

The sun was setting over the horizon and I knew it was about time to get back to the Castle. Heretia didn't want to leave her people yet, neither did I for that matter, but we needed rest. I had spent a lot of magic today, even if it was just in little bits, and I needed to eat and lie down. I also wanted to go collect Marie and see how her day was before dinner.

Walking up to the hall the orphans were being housed was a totally different experience this time around. Where there had been quiet and the feeling of gloom this morning, now it was a cacophony of laughter, squeals, giggles, and small children flying in every direction. Heretia had directed the castle to create for them their own Dining Hall and the entire stone room was alive and constantly moving. The matron, Hera, was amongst a certain large group directing a craft of puppets, while others were already putting on shows and laughing at the antics their characters were portraying. I smiled at the image and quickly scanned the room for my little friend whom I had missed during the day.

"The Druid is back!" I heard a shout from one corner and instantly all eyes flew to me.

Hera looked up from her own work and a smile tugged at the corner of her mouth as screams of delight echoed. The children came racing to hug me, grab my hands, and just be near as I was taken down by a mob of little people. Their untapped and unbounded energy was a lift to my burdened heart as I collapsed under their weight. Theo let loose a hearty laugh as he watched me struggle to stay upright.

"Hi guys!" I shouted back over and over as each one greeted me with hugs and smiles.

"Druid!" one particular voice rang out and my head shot around to find Maria who had shouted for me.

"Maria!" I called back, and eventually she waded through her friends to also jump on me with her arms wrapped around my neck.

"We've had so much fun today! Matron Hera has taken us to the garden in turns, we've eaten all we wanted, we've sang songs together,

170

and now we're making puppets to put on a show for everyone!" she squealed, and I couldn't help but smile.

"That sounds wonderful! I know that was fun for everyone," I responded. I finally reached my hand out for Theo to help me up and I felt myself lifted from the pile of small bodies that kept me restrained.

"Alright children! Back to your crafts! The Druid is busy right now, but she is going to love your puppet plays when you're through with them. Practice makes perfect, so run along," Hera clapped her hands for attention. Attendants came and herded the children away to their stations and their fun continued. Only Maria stayed with me, holding my hand.

"Maria and her friends have had a wonderful day," Hera began informing me.

"I don't think I, Heretia, nor even this kingdom can thank you enough for what you're doing. The people put in charge of city planning have already begun getting them a house ready to accommodate every single one of them and we hope they will be done soon. It would be really an immense honor to everyone if you would stay on as their matron, Hera. You've done a great job helping them in only one day," I offered.

I heard the door open and Heretia glided in right behind us.

"Your Majesty," Hera bowed at the neck.

"Mia is right, Hera. We would love it if you would take on the permanent position of the children's matron. I know it's a lot of them right now, but there are a lot of people out there newly cured who have lost family, loved ones, and the chance to have children, so I'm sure they won't be staying long. These young ones might be just the ticket in the right homes for this city to heal." Heretia took Hera's hand, pleading with her. Hera bowed her head.

"I not only say this because you are my Queen, but because I find I love these children, so yes. I feel the need to stay with them," Hera agreed.

Heretia and I beamed, and I left them to continue talking about the plans for the inner-city orphanage. Maria followed Theo and I out of the room, skipping the whole way.

"You don't want to stay with your friends?" I asked her as the door closed behind us and the noise died down considerably.

"Nope, I'll see them tomorrow. I'm not scared they will go away anymore."

My heart sank at her words, understanding what she meant.

"No, they're not Maria. You're right. They're not going anywhere anymore. They're safe now."

CHAPTER TWENTY

Maria regaled Theo and I with more detailed events of the day as we rested before dinner. Ez wafted in at one point to check on me, causing a stir with her bustling and routine. I asked if the High Rulers had begun helping in the city as well and Ez firmed her lips in response.

"A few immediately left and went out, asking how to help. Others, however, feigned that it wasn't their place and sent servants and other witches instead."

I frowned heavily.

"I want a list of who is refusing to help," I responded.

As soon as my friend had satisfied herself with my recovery and determined that I was as well as I was going to be, she left to carry out the task I had set to her. I was determined to make sure these High Rulers understood what was at stake here and the only way I knew how, was to have them face it. Even Ogden, who I had only caught a glimpse of earlier, wouldn't turn a blind eye to the people of Purge.

Eventually, my mother floated into the room and immediately swooped down on Maria, showering her with love and attention.

"Where is dad?" I asked her, noticing he didn't follow.

"He's helping with the city. A lot of older stone structures were falling apart, so he insisted on helping restore them. He will be here for dinner. I've been working with Alyssa on reinvigorating the gardens around the city so that the new residents can have small patches of land to cultivate and use for grocery items."

My heart swelled with pride at my parents being so thoughtful. Theo's mother even stopped by to see me and gave me a hug bigger than I thought possible of her.

"I'm so happy you are okay," she whispered, and I felt her tremble slightly under my touch.

"I'm glad to see you, too, Vanessa," I responded.

I was thankful, however that her husband did not accompany her. Theo was still in a state of heightened anxiety and his father's presence would do nothing for him.

"Michael is right behind me," Vanessa mentioned and I turned to look at my mother.

"I've already seen him, dear. I met him as he came in the first night he was here," she reassured me.

I blew out a breath of relief. Knowing my uncle and my mother, however, there was no real cause for alarm. They were just alike in their boundless capacity for love and forgiveness. My uncle didn't even knock, he just came barging in with two servants following behind, laden with boxes.

"Mia!" he shouted and clapped his hands together. I reached up to accept his hug, and what a hug it was! He squeezed and rocked me back and forth, never wanting to let go. "Let me preface this fortuitus reunification with gifts!" He waved his arms to the servants who toppled forward under the weight of the packages.

"Gifts?" mom and I exclaimed.

"Yes! Gifts! My sister is back, and my niece is safe. What better way to celebrate than with gifts and a party?" he asked, and began handing us each box after box. He even threw a small package towards Theo who caught it deftly.

"You really do know how to spoil a girl, huh, Uncle Michael?" I teased and pulled Maria onto my lap.

"Hello? Who is this?" he reached out and tweaked Maria's nose, causing her to giggle and blush.

"This is Maria, she was my friend in the," I stopped talking, unable to voice what had happened to us yet unnecessarily. The room went silent for only a brief moment before Michael sprang into action.

"Then I'm glad I brought this!" he reached down and grabbed a smaller box. In it, upon a velvet cushion, sat two pretty silver bracelets.

"I had worried they were too small for Amelia's wrist, but something told me to grab them anyway. I guess it was the Mother Goddess herself making sure I got you, little Maria, something, too."

Maria's eye widened in surprise and wonder as she slipped them on her tiny wrist. They were slightly big for her, but she would be able to wear them for years to come.

"Thank you!" she cried out and leapt to wrap her arms around Michael's neck. Everyone laughed and even Vanessa seemed to be taken with my small friend.

Eventually, it was almost time for dinner, and Maria was asking to eat with her friends. I sent a message to Hera to come pick her up and an assistant was there almost instantly to bustle Maria away. With a hearty hug to everyone present, Maria skipped off, new bracelets clinking on her wrist.

Theo came to settle down next to me as we all sat back to relax once more.

"She's precious," Vanessa whispered as she waited for the door to close behind the bright little girl.

"I don't know why I'm so attached to her. I only saw her once while I was there before the night we escaped. But she trusted me to save them, and now I can't seem to completely let her go. I know she needs to be with the other orphans, readjusting and beginning her new life, but I keep wanting to see her smiling face. It's my reminder that I got them out, if not all, most," I responded, looking down at my hands in embarrassment. My mother reached over to me and squeezed my hands still.

"It's okay, Mia. You, Judas, and those children survived something horrible together. Judas has even been asking after you. I think he is also dealing with a lot."

I nodded and made a mental note to see him tonight during the dinner and check in on him.

"Is everything ready for the war? I'm not sure what exactly to call this whole mess, honestly," I asked.

Michael gave a grim smile. "It is war, Mia. The worst kind, too. It's not just a war for money, land, or title. This is a war for humanity and the survival of every witch in Medeis. While some High Rulers might not want to face what is going on in Purge, they understand it enough to fight for it. This whole day has been nothing but war councils and preparations." He stretched his back and sighed. "I have to hand it to that Captain of Heretia's. He's really coming through on this one. I don't think I've ever seen a man so in his element commanding this many troops all at once and more to come."

Vanessa and my mother nodded in agreement. Another knock came at the door and Heretia entered with Gabriel. "I was worried you had worn yourself out." She nodded to me and greeted Vanessa and Michael appropriately. Gabriel, however, grinned and nodded his head. I rolled my eyes.

"I'm okay now. Ez even thinks I'm good to go. Being a Druid has its perks," I added jokingly.

Gabriel laughed, and then sat down on the foot of the bed. As he did, I noticed the chain around his neck that had been there since the night of my rescue. In all of this, I had almost forgotten that now having the amulet changed the game in our favor.

"Still wearing the amulet, I see?" I pointed my thoughts out to the Death element who then reached down to pulled it out.

"Yeah, the more I have this thing around me, the more I realize how stupid I was for making it in the first place," he huffed and twisted it back and forth, examining it over once more. "It was a stroke of luck that Judas had the thing at the right time. I never expected seeing this thing again till Michelo was dead, but here it is."

Heretia made a face of disgust at the object.

"We should destroy it, it does no one any good and will always be a liability in the wrong hands," she suggested.

I watched as Gabriel tucked it back into his shirt.

"We will go into that after this is over. Can't hurt to have it on our side for a short time, and then we will get rid of it," he countered.

I didn't completely agree with him, but I did see his point a little. Heretia wasn't convinced, but said no more.

"Just make sure you know where it is at all times until we are through this," I directed, pointing to the spot on his chest where it rested. Gabriel nodded and began to stand.

"I think we've got a grand feast planned for tonight, your Royal Majesties and Highnesses!" he clapped his hands and his fast burst open with a toothy grin. Everyone began to stir at his declaration and began to part ways. Before he left, watching Heretia take Vanessa's arms and listen to Michael tell a story, Gabriel pulled me back and pressed something heavy into my palm.

"You need to keep it," he whispered. I looked down to see the Death amulet placed there, warm still from the heat of Gabriel's body and heavy with importance and danger.

176

"No! You made it, it's yours to hold on to," I began to hand it back before Theo turned back around from talking to my mother.

"That's what I need people to think, but really, it was made for a druid. I have no use of this thing at all, but when the time comes, you will be the one who needs it," he whispered.

I hesitated again, but Gabriel just kept talking. "I've worn it just enough so that people will think I have it and I want it to stay that way. Take it and keep it on you at all times. Don't let it out of your sight, and when the battle starts, I want you to rip away with it. It's stronger than I remember, so just unleash and give them hell."

I looked down once more at the weighty object and then slowly donned it, tucking it away under my blouse. I felt the magic within it stir slightly in response to my nearness, but it went quiet after just a moment.

"You don't have to say anything or do anything. It reacts just like your Druid magic does. You simply think and it will do," Gabriel finished as Theo came sauntering back over to us.

"See you guys in an hour. Don't be late!" Gabriel waved us away as he jogged after Heretia, who was now laughing at something my uncle had told her.

"Did Gabriel need something?" Theo asked as we shut the door behind us.

"Insurance," I responded.

****

Dinner was certainly grand. Heretia had yet again managed to outdo herself and the room was glorious. Every inch of it was covered in the regalia of all the kingdoms. Every single one was represented somewhere in either the colors, the décor on the table, or the walls around us. Food from every kingdom was also presented, and the servants that had been brought in were even helping out dressed in their finest.

Ogden was the first person I saw as I entered later that night. Heretia had sent a lovely white concoction that had been lined with dark brown fur of some kind. The white was a brocade, heavy and comfortable. It made me feel secure, all tight and snug inside of it. She had sent Theo the matching suit, white of the same brocade pattern and lined with dark brown piping along the seams.

"You two look comfortable here," Ogden started as he neared us, glass of wine in his hand. Theo's mood darkened at his father's entrance.

"We are among friends, Your Majesty. Why wouldn't we be?" I asked formally, summoning my own glass of wine to hand.

"I mean in this whole saga. This war," he corrected and took a deep sip of his wine. "I've seen what's going on. I've seen the organization. I watched you two earlier today in the Throne Room and since then, I must say," he began and took in a breath between his teeth. "I'm impressed."

The air was sucked right out of my lungs at his words. Did he just compliment Theo? I looked up at my Pair who also seemed just as surprised as I was.

"Impressed by what exactly?" Theo pressed his father further. He must be thinking that there was some sort of back handed remark coming.

"With what you've done here so far. I mean, you've been able to collect all five kingdoms somehow under only one roof. Rallied their entire armies and began a war campaign. All of this in less time than it takes to plan one of those stupid holiday parades Felicity loves so much." He finished with a small sneer at the idea of a parade, taking another sip of his wine and glancing in Felicity's direction.

She was, as usual, adorned with more jewelry than necessary and laughing hysterically at something that was clearly not that funny. I turned back from examining the other Royal Queen to see my Pair still floored at the idea that his father was proud of something.

"It was all Mia, father. She accomplished this, not me," he corrected.

Ogden shook his head. "Yes and no. I agree they came because Mia sent the letters, but you both have done this."

Finally, having enough of the awkwardness, I stepped in.

"Thank you, Ogden. That is very kind of you. We want to thank you as well for coming as you promised. This whole effort would have been for nothing if Suravia wasn't invested as well. I can only hope that if we survive this war, all of Medeis can continue to work together in this way for the greater good."

Ogden eyed me a little skeptically and then nodded his head, leaving us to ourselves.

"Well, that was," I began but Theo cut off my sentence. "Suspicious," he finished.

"Oh, Theo. Don't read into it too much. Take it for what it is, a compliment. We need his help right now and if he's going to offer it not only willingly, but with good faith, then we need to accept it." I steered him away to the table as a gong rang out across the room. Heretia held her hand out to me and motioned to the head chair.

I gave her a confused glance, but she just shook her head and motioned again. I, without another word, sat at the head of her table while everyone was seated down the massive length of it. High Kings and Queens, along with spouses, were all present. The heads of war were off preparing and arranging, practicing, and polishing while the heads of state prepared in another way. Dinner was served grandly, and I had to marvel at the organization that had occurred in such a short time. I had never eaten so well in my life, but I enjoyed every morsel. My appetite, as well as my energy, were back, and I ate every last piece of whatever was presented to me.

Chatter happened lightly throughout the entirety of the meal, and I chimed in on a few conversations here and there. The Elite Guard had been sprinkled throughout the table as buffer zones. Will looked slightly put out, as did Wynnie. Both clearly wanted to be elsewhere, and I could take a large guess as to where that was. Tim was quiet but beaming next to his new bride. Ez was chattering away to anyone who would listen about the progress down in the city. Theo expertly played the ever-diligent diplomat, throwing out jokes, laughing brightly, and mentioning past funny anecdotal stories that he shared with the other Rulers around him.

I had never realized how much he knew about the other kingdoms and their Rulers, the lands, the wealth, and the bonds that connected each one until now. My heart swelled with pride as the understanding of why the Mother Goddess had chosen him for me came home. He was my bridge to this world in a way that no one else could be. His charisma, when he wanted it to show, was bright and appealing. His education was vast and his ability to float seamlessly between opinions and conversation was like quicksilver in its fluidity.

No one else could have been a better pick for a Druid who had never even heard of Medeis until a few short months ago. I sent up one last thankful prayer to the Mother Goddess for Theo and then returned to my dessert.

We were just finishing the final course when I felt my magic twitch deep in my chest. With it, the amulet grew warm, and I reached for it, confused. Gabriel sat up, watching my movement. His attention was quickly followed by Heretia's who sat up and looked around as well. Gabriel and I made eye contact and nodded slightly. I too, nodded back. We were both feeling something. A warning perhaps?

I felt my magic and senses heighten as I intentionally scanned the room in silence, knowing my eyes must have been glowing gold at the effort it took to see others more closely than I had before. No one seemed bothered as the three of us were. Finally, I sat back and waited as Heretia got up and came to stand behind my chair. I leaned back to hear her whisper.

"Something is coming close to my wards. It's testing the edges, like a mist or a fog," she informed me. I strained to hold back the fear in my face.

"Take Gabriel and go see what it might be. It may be Michelo, it may be Gregor," I instructed.

Heretia nodded her head, and without a word, Gabriel also rose and left the table silently. The action and decision were so quick that very few noticed it. I plastered a smile on my face.

"The after-dinner drinks haven't arrived; they are going to check on them now. Such good hosts!" I lied through my grin for those that had witnessed the hushed exchange. No need to cause a panic just yet. A minute ticked by. Theo took my hand in his. I looked up to see him standing behind my chair as well.

"What's wrong?" I heard him whisper against my wrist.

I gave him a grim look and pointed to my chest, the spot where my magic rested, as did the piece of him. Theo went quiet for a moment and then nodded. He knew what I was trying to say.

"I think it's time I do the rounds and go check on our friends to see how they are holding up?" he suggested, eyeing the rest of the Elite Guard.

"Sounds good," I squeaked out, magic now starting to do flips. I continued to survey the table, not one person other than myself seemed ill at ease. Finally, I could take it no more.

"Excuse me," I asked of the two or three Rulers still left within earshot of me as I made my way to the door of the room. Enough alcohol had been applied that no one seemed to care that ever so slowly, important figures were beginning to disappear from next to them. When I finally made it to the hallway, the amulet was very warm against my skin and I was beginning to sweat from the restlessness inside of me. Theo and Wynnie were waiting for me just outside the door, descending down as soon as it was shut.

"What is going on? Theo said something was wrong with you." Wynnie blurted out. I frowned.

"Nothing is wrong with me, per say." I threw a small glare my Pair's way. "Something is coming. Heretia felt it testing the wards. Gabriel and I both responded to it and felt it, too. Whatever it is bothering my magic and I needed to get out of there for a moment."

We began to make our way to Heretia's office, where I figured we would find her when Gabriel called out.

"The balcony!" he shouted to us.

With a quick turn of my heel, I raced for the balcony off the back of the castle that overlooked the desert. My heart sunk. It most certainly was Michelo that was causing this. My fears roared to life. We weren't ready, the children were still in the castle, and the people of Purge weren't recovered. We needed more time.

The doors were already thrown open wide, the light gauzy curtains blowing in their breeze.

"Heretia? What is it?" I called out as we came through into the cool dry night. Heretia stood at the edge of the balcony, slightly leaned forward, squinting hard to peer out into the night.

"I can't tell yet. It's still just testing. Poking and prodding. I've already reinforced what I can in all directions. I cast a new net over the city," she informed me as I came to stand next to her. A bowl sat precariously on the railing, filled at the bottom with blood. She held an ornate knife in her other hand.

"Is it that serious?" I asked, thinking of how that must have drained her.

She nodded silently and scanned the horizon once more. "I believe so."

We waited, the Elite Guard staying silent behind us and Gabriel hovering above and just beyond the edge of the balcony.

"Wait," he finally muttered and then stopped.

"There!" Tim called out and with a jerk, pointed a finger slightly to our left. Gabriel was already flying off towards it.

"Don't leave the perimeter!" Heretia called after him in warning. I watched, hesitantly, as the object grew closer. It certainly was flying under its own volition and at first that seemed slightly odd to me when a realization dawned with damning speed. Nothing in this world could fly except Gabriel and me. Nothing, except the Wild Beast.

"Gabriel, stop!" I shouted out after him as the thought finished in my head. Theo pulled me back as I attempted to jump from the balcony myself. With a thundering boom that shook the entire city and forced everyone around me to their knees, the Magical Beast of Fire, Tailong, slammed its entire body weight into the side of the blood magic barrier.

Screams could be heard throughout the city and within the walls of the castle. I heard cracking of foundational stones and worried Tailong had brought the city down in one hit.

Panting in shock, I stared awestruck as the scaled beast, with its shimmering armor of reds, yellows, oranges, and whites, reared back to attack again. Even from where I stood, I could see that it's eyes blazed golden, almost as if in anger but there was no real life in them, not anymore. Tailong was under Michelo's direction, and this was the warning shot. The announcement of the war.

Michelo had finally revealed what we had worried ourselves sick over, the kidnapping of the Wild Beasts and the harnessing of their power. Horror struck me dumb as Tailong threw itself once more into the invisible barrier Heretia had constructed, staring Gabriel down as it did so. Dozens of footsteps came pounding up behind us as the High Rulers, having heard the attacks and certainly felt them, joined us to see our first shot across the bow.

"Is that?" one woman called out.

"Tailong!"

"What the Druid said is true! He does have the Wild Beasts, we're doomed!"

As we each gazed up at the massive size and power of the Dragon before us, I couldn't help but to feel the same.

CHAPTER TWENTY-ONE

Tailong's battering of the wards lasted for another half hour, just enough time to make me worried, but not long enough for an actual assault to begin. As we stood watching Tailong fling itself into the ward time after time, soldiers from every kingdom below began to congregate and form a perimeter around the castle facing the desert. Generals sent messengers to Rulers in case of word, but I held them off.

"Do nothing!" I commanded with a shout over the growing roar of whispers and worries. "That is still a Wild Beast, Michelo won't be stupid enough to lose it in such a petty way. This is just meant to scare us. Nothing more."

I turned back to judge again for myself that I must be right. If Tailong broke through those wards now, it would most certainly die, but at what cost to us? We were still so unprepared, unequipped, and scattered about. Our armies were only half ready and in place, we hadn't even collected all we needed to begin the campaign. The master smiths hadn't finished outfitting the newest recruits from across the kingdoms, supplies were still pouring in. We hadn't even set up temporary base operations in the desert.

I thought back to all the plans that had been made earlier with the Generals in the War Council and realized that we had spent way too much time talking and nowhere near enough time doing. I had let those men and women bicker too much, spout off unnecessary statistics, and discuss way too many theories that now seemed stupid and irrelevant. Finally, just as my nerves were about to fray, Tailong turned away, circled the city twice in a matter of a few minutes and darted off back to the left of the city far off into the desert.

It seemed as if the entire city held its breath as we waited for Tailong to disappear before letting go a collective sigh, but not one of relief. It was anticipation, it was dread, and it was most certainly fear that come flooding towards me in waves. Emotions ran high, creating a swamp worth of magic that I had to block out. With effort, I slammed down a mental wall to erase the burden that was beginning to weigh on me. If I didn't shut everyone out, I would go mad.

"Druid?"

I looked behind me to see a Queen from Elevetia, red wild hair and brilliant green eyes shining with fear. I let her in. She was screaming on the inside, every inch of her was trembling. There was more, fear for her family back home in Elevetia, fear for her people, her soldiers, and her own life. Uncertainty swam around as a slimy eel in her veins but as she and I looked each other, another emotion began to creep in. One stronger than the others, small but mightier by far. I reached deeper to discover this feeling that was beginning to calm her raging horror.

It was hope. I furrowed my brow, trying to think of what could possibly be giving her hope. I looked to the horizon, no one was approaching, nothing was coming. I looked around our vicinity, but no one moved, no one had arrived to make her feel this way. No comforting husband or child to ease her fears. Then, as I looked back to meet her gaze, the answer hit me. It was me.

I made her feel hope. In her moment of terror, knowing I was on their side gave her that little bit to keep her from falling to her knees and breaking apart. Even with the knowledge that we may not make it through this war, after witnessing the proof that the Wild Beasts were against us, she still had hope.

"Yes?" I answered her.

Eyes slowly began to turn and all face me. The flaming Queen stepped forward with her hands out. I reached to meet her as she grasp mine tightly.

"What next?" she whispered.

I had this moment, this one moment to make her, make them all, feel safe. I couldn't waste it. I glanced around once more and straightened my shoulders.

"We prepare for war," I replied.

The Queen's mouth set firmly, as did her resolve. With a nod, every single High Ruler turned and left the balcony, including the red headed Queen. In silence, the Elite Guard and I found ourselves alone. Heretia had left as well to begin her preparations with Jeremy. Gabriel had found his way back to the balcony, floating down silently but keeping post at the railing. His eyes trained on the horizon that Tailong had darted off towards.

"I guess it's finally time," he spoke to no one in particular.

"If that wasn't a warning, I don't know what is," Will agreed, hefting his sword belt higher on his hips.

Tim characteristically remained quiet as he and Theo exchanged a glance. Wynnie sighed and stepped towards me, hands on her hips.

"Are you ready for this, Mia? I mean, I know we are, but what about you?" she asked, shooting me a concerned glance.

"I don't have a choice, Wynnie. I think this conflict was always my destiny, my purpose. If you would have asked me a few months ago if I thought this would ever happen to me, I would have laughed you off. Now," I turned to grasp the balcony edge. "Now, it feels like this was always coming for me. I don't feel as scared as I would have, in fact, I'm madder than anything else," I admitted to her.

Wynnie paused and then nodded her head, understanding. "Then get mad, Mia. We're going to need it."

No one slept that night. The armies began to move out to the desert to begin the camp set up, directed expertly by Jeremy and the assisting Generals. By dawn, a second massive city of tents had been erected facing the direction of the vast empty desert beyond. It spanned the length of the castle and jutted out inwards close to a mile. I found myself in the largest set up tent just after the sun broke the horizon looking at a map of the desert and a list of the units brought by each kingdom. It had been placed directly in the center of the encampment but not quiet on the front row. However, I did have an excellent clear view shot to the desert beyond with its rolling sands and emptiness.

"In total, we have upwards of thirty-five thousand soldiers at our command with another seven thousand in support personnel. Life wielders for healers and varying other witches who are also smiths, attendants, and messengers. It's been cobbled together, but it is what we have," the General from Maravette reported after handing me the list.

"It will be enough, General. It is the best Medeis has to offer, and it will be plenty," I answered and put it aside.

"How goes the recovery in the city, Ez?" I asked as a greeting to my friend who was pushing aside the tent.

"As well as can be expected," she huffed, sweat beading on her forehead. It was unreasonably hot this morning. "Those who can are offering to help and we're putting them slowly to work. Mostly keeping water clean and making sure it's handed out constantly."

"Good, I want everyone at their best. The citizens of Purge have a long way to go, but even that is important, and their work is vital," I nodded appreciatively.

The General from Maravette bowed his head to the two of us and quietly left the tent. Ez let out an exasperated huff and flopped down on the chair across from me.

"This heat is brutal. Even with the citizens of Purge working around the clock, there is going to be heat exhaustion. We need to cool it down out here," she said.

I looked up and raised an eyebrow.

"Can the Air Sorcerer's help?" I asked, running through what I knew of their magic.

"Yes, I wanted to make sure you were okay with it first. I'll get them right on it." And with that, she breezed out of the tent, leaving me alone for a few moments. I looked over the map again and sighed. As I went over in my head all of the numbers that had been thrown at me, a creeping feeling of anxiety snuck into my chest. We were ready for war, real war. I had never seen war in my life. I had seen death, I had seen accidents and blood and trauma, but never war. Even the soldiers surrounding my tent and this camp were nervous wrecks. I let my guard down for a moment and attempted to calm the fears of those nearest the tent, mostly to give myself some peace. It wasn't enough.

I was immediately inundated with fear, anxiety, and most of all, sadness. I very quickly rebuilt my emotional wall and leaned forward, breathing deeply from the strain.

"Druid!" I heard a shout from just beyond my tent, and I rose to follow the sounds of feet running towards the alarm. The sun blinded me momentarily as I pushed back the flap and followed the noise of the crowd.

"Mia!" I heard Theo call from behind and I turned to find him jogging up, sword slapping his thigh.

"What's happening?" I asked, the noise level rising drastically by the second.

186

"Michelo's army. They've been spotted moving into position."

I swallowed hard as I took my Pair's hand and pulled him closer to my side.

"Already?" I whispered, fear creeping into my voice. Theo set his lips firm and nodded.

"It seems the warning was decently fair enough," he voiced, and together we made our way through the ever-thickening crowds to see for ourselves.

I approached just as a few of the Generals who had been surrounding the encampment all day bustled up as well, concern hardened on their faces.

"This is it, Druid," one muttered next to me.

I steeled myself and looked out to see the clouds of dust being kicked up under the feet of the Cannibal army. With a hard swallow, I glanced at Heretia and Gabriel, both watching the scene unfold before us as I had been.

"Let's get everyone in position. I want to be ready in case this isn't just Michelo setting up camp closer, but actually getting ready to attack," I instructed.

The generals nodded and ran off to begin corralling their own forces. Soldiers were already suiting up all around us, no one was taking any chances. I stood there for a long moment, just watching as the ever-present feeling of doom weighed down on me. Finally, I turned to Theo.

"What do I do now?" I asked, desperate for guidance. I wasn't ready for this. I probably never would be.

"Get ready to lead, my love. That is all we can do now. The Elite Guard and I will keep watch and signal you if anything changes at all. If they advance, or if they halt," he spoke.

With a last hug and a kiss, I left my Pair standing on the front lines to meet with those who needed my directions. Heretia followed me quickly. As we reentered my tent, I felt my adrenaline kick in and my hands shook.

"I can't do this," I whispered as Heretia came to stand next to me, surveying the map that was still laid out on the table before us. Little dots scattered all around, figures that represented regiments and battalions.

Heretia sighed heavily and turned to lean against the table, facing me.

"We don't have a choice anymore, Mia. We are here for a reason. The Mother Goddess wouldn't have put us here if she wasn't sure we could handle something like this. It's overwhelming and it's not going to be pretty, but this is why we are here. What we have been preparing our entire lives for. The Mother Goddess needs us in this battle, and we must listen to her," she soothed.

Her words lit a spark in my head.

"The Mother Goddess," I whispered as an idea came to mind. "That's it. I'll go talk to her again. See what she wants us to do. She has to be watching this. I'll just ask her what needs to be done."

Heretia righted herself.

"It would take too much time for you to go see her in the Forest. Besides, she told you to never go there again. It would rip apart the fabric of this world for you two to be near each other like that. Once was risky enough. You can't do it again," she advised.

"But she told me that I could call out to her, and she would be there!" I began pacing the room.

"If I can just find a place to meditate myself into a space where she and I can actually communicate, I can get help and direction. This encampment is too noisy and full of anxiety. Where can I go for peace?" I asked her. Heretia wrung her hands together, thinking.

"I have an old meditation garden that may be able to block everything out. But that's some higher-level meditation to get direct access to her. Can you do that?" she asked me. My eyes shone with hope.

"No, but I know someone that can help me get there."

It took the better part of an hour to track down the one person I wanted to help me reach the Mother Goddess and mere moments to convince her to help.

"Of course! Let's go!" Alyssa exclaimed, grabbing her thin shawl and wrapping it around her head.

Thomas barely even got a second glance as we raced out of their tent and back up to the looming High Castle. The obsidian face growing darker as the dust from the advancing army began to black out the sun. I looked behind me only once as we quickly made our way back into it's cool walls and out of the heat. I could see the dark mass that was coming towards us, unable to discern the shape of the Cannibals that made it up, but they were moving slowly. It would take time for them to arrive, a luxury I couldn't take too much advantage of. I saw our Kingdom's men lining up and readying themselves.

"This way," Heretia called out, and I focused my attention on the task at hand.

Alyssa placed her hands in front of her in a walking meditation stance, I followed suit. Heretia led us quietly to a door that was further into the center of the Castle than I had ever been. She slowly opened it and beyond lay a simple garden of green and filtered sun.

"I'll make sure you are not disturbed," Heretia whispered as Alyssa and I entered, falling deeper into a meditative state.

"Thank you, Heretia," I nodded back and she shut the door behind her with a quiet snick.

I waited, with my eyes closed, and listened to the garden around us. Complete focus was the key to communicating with the Mother Goddess and calming my nerves was the first step.

"Let's be seated," I heard Alyssa instruct.

I instinctively plopped myself down in a cross-legged fashion and waited for her to speak further.

"We're going to have to delve deep into your inner conscious for this journey to the Mother Goddess. I've never done this before, but your link with her should be enough to succeed," Alyssa began. "Three deep breaths."

I opened my eyes to find myself inside of the Mother Goddess' sanctuary all the way in the Forest again.

"Amelia," I heard her call to me.

I turned to see her standing over a small garden that was in the corner of her place. She looked the same as before. Just as ethereal, breathtaking, and tired.

"Mother Goddess," I bowed my head in reverence.

"I see you found the work around to us being together," she smiled at me gently, still tending her small garden with care.

"The war has started," I cut to the point, not knowing if we had limited time or not with this connection.

"I know, I have seen Michelo moving across the desert. I still can't see in, but I can see that they've begun moving towards Purge." She waved towards her living map and even from where I stood, the black mass that had been further out and away from the High Castle was now practically almost to its gates. How long had it taken me to meditate? I moved to peer over it some more.

"It won't be long now. You will have to lead the Kingdoms against Michelo's army. I trust you have prepared everything?" she asked me, floating to my side.

"That's just it, Mother Goddess. I'm not really sure what to do now. I've never been in war. I've never led an army. I'm not sure how to proceed with this," I admitted. The Mother Goddess smiled again.

"Do you have to tell your body to breathe? Do you instruct your heart to beat every time?" She waved towards the army that the Kingdom's had erected. "You have Generals to tell you that. The most important thing I have discovered in my eternal existence is that delegation is key. Why do you think I created my children? I could do everything myself, but how exhausting would that be? You must rely on those around you. You lead them and let them lead the rest. As long as you remain the head on the shoulder's, the rest of the body will follow the way it works best."

I sighed. This wasn't as helpful as I wanted it to be.

"But what if it comes down to me fighting to? How am I supposed to do that? I'm not physically ready and my magic has limits," I pleaded.

"It will come down to you fighting, Amelia. It has always come down to you fighting, but your purpose will be to end it," she breathed.

I whipped my head around to face her, "Then why can't I just do that? Why do people have to die before I step in?"

The Mother Goddess just shook her head. "That's not the way war works. Even if you did your best, innocents would still perish. But you have two options," she sat at her chair. "You can either let the war play out in its normal course and thousands will perish with a possibility you will lose, or you can end it quickly."

"Of course, I choose that option! End it quickly, how do we do that?" I begged.

"That option will ask everything of you. It may even end you, but it will be the only way to guarantee the survival of Medeis and its people," she replied.

I bit my lip, "End me?" I asked hesitantly.

The Mother Goddess nodded, "It will mean your ultimate sacrifice."

I looked down at the ground, and scuffed my foot lightly, leaving no imprint on the soft moss beneath my feet.

"How do I do it?"

190

CHAPTER TWENTY-TWO

"Mia?" I hear Alyssa's soft voice call for me as I find my way back from the connection the Mother Goddess and I shared.

"Mia?" she called my name again. I held on to the last string of connection that I grasped tightly, before letting go completely, my mind set in what I had to do.

"Amelia!" I realized suddenly that Alyssa was screaming my name, shaking me back to the meditation garden with her.

"Amelia! We must go! The attack has started!" I heard her report as I opened my eyes.

A massive explosion burst through the air the exact moment I awoke, knocking us both backwards.

"I've given you all the time I could, Amelia. But we must hurry. The war has begun and it's already bad. The generals have been beating down the door and it's taken everything Heretia and I had to hold them back. We must go now! Hurry!" Alyssa pulled me up from the floor and together we raced for the door.

Just beyond the door, two angry men stood there arguing with Heretia, but she held her ground.

"The Druid must not be disturbed!" she was shouting above the noise of another explosion.

"Our men are dying out there! We need her magic!" King Ludwig of Lotho screamed back, red faced in anger.

"Then I suggest you get back out there and help them, too!" Heretia placed her body back in the middle of the hallway, preventing their shoves past her. Ludwig, not used to being bossed around by others, dropped his shoulder to shove the small Queen out of his way. I decided this had gone on long enough.

"What seems to be the problem here?" I called out and all three sets of eyes turned from their argument to watch me exit the meditation garden.

"Druid!" the one general bowed his head in respect. "You're needed at the front." He began but Ludwig had already lost his patience along with his tact.

"Where have you been?!" He shouted, stepping into my personal space. I felt Alyssa, Heretia and the other general tense, but all waited to see my reaction.

"I have been communing with the Mother Goddess." I answered him coolly. I could see Ludwig losing his mind.

"The Mother-?" he spluttered in shock and then gritted his teeth, leaning down so close that I could smell his hot breath. "What good is that going to do us? She's not going to just show up and end this war for us, she's useless! Why waste time on that old crone with nothing to lose?" he seethed.

Everyone waited in silence for my reaction.

Slowly, I lifted my hand up and firmly placed it on Ludwig's shoulder, giving it a hard shove backward.

"This is exactly why I am the Druid and not you, Ludwig." I answered him and took a step into his own personal space. Last time I had attempted this brazen move, it hadn't ended well for me back in the Second Uprising encampment. This time, however, I had my magic and I wasn't afraid of Ludwig.

"Until the day the Mother Goddess shows up herself and grants you that right, taking it away from me completely, you are not the one in charge. I am." Ludwig blinked in surprise at my words.

"So, if you would excuse me. I have a job to do and frankly, I have more important matters to think about than you're disregard for my decisions."

With that, I grabbed Heretia's hand and together we headed down the hallway towards the exit. Once, outside, Alyssa parted from us to check on her own spouse, who must be going mad not knowing where she was.

I felt around for Theo, casting my magical net out wide and attempting to dodge the worst of emotions amongst the warriors below. At first, I couldn't find him, but as I stepped out into the darkness, his found me first.

In front of me, the battle raged. The noise was intense. Screams and clashing of swords could be heard all around and my nose caught the tang of blood. I could see the two armies colliding in an ugly mass ahead, but in the darkness and due to the distance, I couldn't see who was winning or how well we were doing.

"Hurry!" Heretia shouted above the noise and together we rushed out into the labyrinth of tents.

Far ahead, I could feel Theo straining and moving. Battling with both sword and power through the front line. My heart skipped a beat, and my feet began to move.

"I want my armor!" I shouted above the clamor and continued to race ahead.

"Surely, you're going to use magic, and not sword, Druid. That battlefield is no place for you!" The other general called from behind me, Ludwig having been left well behind us.

Many heads turned as I threw back the flap and stepped a confident foot into the den of Kings and Queens waiting for me.

"I said, get me my armor. No questions, just go!" I shouted.

Two women began to run for the chest of armor that had been made and brought out for me. I stepped behind a partition and began to shuck off the dress I had been wearing and waited for Heretia to bring the cloth undergarments that would sit underneath the metal plates that had been designed for my body.

"Druid! We need your magic, not your sword!"

I rolled my eyes and kept placing straps where they needed to go. I was careful to make sure the amulet was still with me, even as it's heat grew with the energy surrounding us.

"Everyone out!" I commanded. One woman began to hesitate, but a nasty glare from Heretia had them scurrying like mice from my tent.

"Are you sure about this?" Heretia asked me privately.

"I'm as sure as the Mother Goddess is. I have to join this fight to end it," I answered her solemnly.

"How are you going to do it?" she continued. I stood with my back to her, strapping a light sword on my hip.

"Just watch!"

Heretia stood back as I walked through the tent and back into the battle. Hundreds of heads turned to see me as I waited and surveyed the battle laid out beyond. Theo was still fighting, but he wasn't tiring yet. Above, Gabriel swooped and swirled, throwing out magic as best he could against the flying Wild Beast Tailong. I could see of to my left a giant horse-like creature, at least twelve feet tall, stampeding and battling its way into our midst. That must be Antamba, the one who gave in willingly.

"Gabriel!" I shouted above the noise, knowing he would hear me. Gabriel launched a few more blasts of Death magic and then turned to find me in the crowd. As he touched down, his eyebrow rose, taking in my silver-plated armor.

"It's a good look for you," he complimented.

"Get me to the center, get me to Michelo," I commanded.

Gasps could be heard in the crowd that had collected behind me, but I blocked them out.

"As you wish Druid."

And with an elegant bow, Gabriel and I took off into the skies and into battle.

CHAPTER TWENTY-THREE

Below me, the battle looked as if ants were fighting over a mound, but the cries and screams were very much human. As we began our flight, Tailong yet again saw his intended targets and attacked.

"Mia!" I heard Gabriel shout in warning, but I had already expected this move. I ducked to the side as Tailong's tail whipped out, attempting to strike me from the air. The feathers at the tip snapped with a loud and precise crack where I had just been standing. It might not have killed me, but that hit would have sent me flying backwards all the way into the wall of the High Castle where I surely would have died on impact from the unyielding obsidian surface.

"We have to get past Tailong first. Antamba can't do anything to us up here but this one is our biggest problem." I instructed Gabriel.

"I've been hitting it with blast after blast, but it doesn't seem to slow down. It is a Wild Beast, not a human and therefor much stronger." Gabriel answered me. I furrowed my brow to think, still in constant motion so as to keep Tailong from striking out again.

I was beginning to come up with a solution when Tailong reared back and, with a roar, sent a stream of fire in my direction. I gasped and threw my hands up, creating a wave of water to douse its flames.

As the impact hissed and the steam floated away from us, I moved closer to Gabriel with a plan.

"I don't think just dousing it in water will do it, but if we drown it, it may work." I called out. Gabriel nodded in understanding and flew off to my left to take up position. I was clearly the intended target and I planned to remain so.

Tailong flew in another circle, preparing to lash its tail out once more. As soon as the Wild Beasts back was turned, I inhaled a deep breath and grounded my nerves. I felt the power well up inside of me as I collected my Water magic deep in my chest. When I opened my shining golden eyes, water exploded from my being, as large as any fast-moving river I had ever seen and channeled it directly towards Tailong.

At the same time Gabriel created his bubble of magic that had been a mechanism of freedom for the orphans and wrapped it around Tailong. I pumped the entire bubble full of water and when it was completely filled, I gasped for breath. I watched as Tailong squirmed and beat against the bubble of Death magic, and I threw a secondary bubble up just outside of Gabriel's, just in case.

After only a few moments, Tailong locked eyes with me and my breath caught. For a fleeting second, they were no longer empty and unaware, as all Cannibal eyes had been. They were filled with a multitude of emotions. I held my breath as Tailong gave me a last second thanks with its expression, a moment of consciousness before it was gone forever. A moment later, Tailong closed its eyes peacefully and moved no more. No longer was Tailong to be imprisoned, it was free of the destruction it would cause under someone else's' volition. I looked to Gabriel for confirmation, and he nodded, Tailong was now gone to whatever afterlife the Wild Beasts could go to.

"Thanks, I've been kicking his ass for three hours now and just couldn't get the edge on him!"

I frowned, thinking about the loss of such a noble creature and the look it had given me the seconds before it's death.

"I don't like this. Don't thank me for that, it's sad and I am sorry Tailong had to suffer for the actions of the same witches it wanted to protect so nobly," I muttered, making Gabriel blink twice at my sentiment.

"Tailong was easy to kill because it didn't want this. It didn't want to be a puppet of an evil witch. It was waiting for us to kill it and went happily, knowing it couldn't hurt anyone else."

"Well, if you look at it that way," he mumbled and then followed my flight to help me find Michelo amongst the thousands of bodies hacking away at each other. From above, I could see blasts of magic and flashing of steel. As the sky grew darker, it seemed as if I was watching a firework show on the ground from above.

196

"There's the center of the fight, but if Michelo is as cowardly as I believe him to be, he will be more toward the back!" Gabriel shouted above the noise coming from below.

I ground my teeth in anger. Below somewhere in that turmoil was my Pair, my friends and my people fighting to save their existence, and Michelo didn't even have the courage to wield a sword himself . Instead, he sent his Cannibals to die for him. People who had no will to resist or to understand. This set my blood boiling, and I took off for the rear of the fighting. Twice I had to dodge a magical attack that had misfired straight into the sky and once was startled when a group of Earth witches created a sandstorm on the left flank.

"They're fighting hard!" Gabriel pointed out as we neared closer to my intended target.

"They won't have to much longer. I'm going to end this now before this goes any further," I answered him. Gabriel pulled up in front of me, causing me to stop mid-flight.

"What is your plan exactly, Druid?" he asked me, the serious tone of his voice creeping in.

"What the Mother Goddess told me had to happen," I responded. Gabriel attempted to press further but I shot around him, and dead headed onward.

"Mia!" Gabriel shouted after me, but I pushed myself faster, refusing to be stopped. "Amelia!" he called again but much quieter now that I was overtaking his own speed. The wind began to whistle in my ears, and I threw out an Air tracking spell, something that I had been working on since I had seen Tim do it subconsciously. Within a moment, I found my intended target.

"Michelo!" I called, using Air to amplify my voice. It was quieter on this end of the battlefield as the fighting hadn't yet completely reached this spot. I waited, hesitantly, searching with my eyes instead of magic for the man who had the audacity to cause this bloodshed.

"Mia!" I heard Theo call for me, and I felt his presence near. He had seen me, which meant everyone else could too.

Finally, a small circle spread out, creating a blank space in the field save for one individual. Large and clad in black armor, Michelo stared back at me waiting, a wicked grin spreading across his face. I heard Antamba whinny in the distance as Michelo seemed to be calling for it.

"Michelo Unda!" I called again and lowered myself slightly to hover above him.

"End this now and save yourself and what's left of your army. Give yourself up!" I demanded.

Michelo flung his hands out to his sides and looked around.

"Why should I? I can easily win this, and then once I take Purge, the rest of this world will fall. What is a simple witch like you, who knows nothing of magic, going to do to stop me?" he asked.

I touched down onto the soft, sandy ground, my feet barely kicking up any dust. I unsheathed my sword and let it sit in my hand, pointing downwards.

"Turn your army around and give yourself up. This path won't end well for you. The Mother Goddess has deemed you unfit, and my orders are to stop you!"

Michelo belched out a gut turning laugh. Cannibals around him stood still, but kept their weapons pointed at me. With only a thought, he could have each and every one of them attack me, yet he did not.

"Unfit? Her? She is one to talk, hiding out in her little Forest. Not coming to help those who ask for it. Where was she when my entire family deserted me?"

I felt Theo and the rest of the Elite Guard approaching slowly, hacking their way to my side. I turned to see Theo at the front, slashing his way over and around bodies, sweat dripping from his brow.

"No one deserted you! You were out of line with the laws of Lotho and your father had every right to pass the Throne on to your sister. It was your twisted thinking that caused the rift," I retorted, thinking back to the story Tim had admitted to me a while back. Michelo's face hardened into a frown.

"She had no right! She had ruined herself. That Throne is mine!" Michelo roared in resurfaced anger.

"If you're problem is with Lotho, then why go to all this length? Your sister isn't even alive, her son now sits there," I attempted to reason.

This didn't work, which I hadn't thought it would.

"If I can't have Lotho, I will have it all. Don't speak to me of that bastard brat! He isn't even deserving to clean out stalls like his father, let alone sit on a High Throne of Lotho!" Michelo seethed.

I winced at the statement. I had only ever known Thomas to be kind, gentle, and wise in my few months here. While I had never

198

known Michelo's sister, I did know his nephew, and Thomas deserved his place in Lotho, twice over.

"Michelo, stop this. Direct the Cannibals to cease, come to the Mother Goddess in humility, and let's find a way to resolve this peacefully," I ordered.

This man had taken me hostage, tortured me and beat me, but it was the Mother Goddess' will. She had wanted me to give him one last chance to try and make amends. It was killing me personally to offer this token to him, this advice, but it was my duty to do so. Even as a nurse, my job was to treat even the worst of criminals, and the nastiest of people. It was my oath, and I was extending that oath to this situation. Putting my own conflicts aside with Michelo, I gave him this last hope.

Michelo seemed to pause for a moment, and his eyes even flicked side to side, as if thinking through my offer. For a heartbeat, I thought maybe he would take it. I hoped for the possibility for redemption, but that was quickly squashed when he bared his teeth at me, the scar on his face turning ugly again.

"Never," he hissed.

I sighed, "Then we must end this. You and I, no one else. If you want this world, you're going to have to take the Druid out of it, because with me still here, I will always find a way to stop you." I sliced my sword up before my face and readied my stance.

"Call off your Cannibals. Just you and me, Michelo, to the death. Winner take all."

I threw the verbal gauntlet down and held my breath. His wicked grin widened, and the Cannibals ceased to move. It took a moment for the soldiers surrounding us, including the Elite Guard, to realize the Cannibals weren't fighting back. Even the Antamba had ceased its charge, and the area around us went silent.

"Mia!" Theo called for me, but I blocked him out. I blocked everyone and everything out. I closed my eyes and removed the amulet from its constraints near my chest, the black gem glowing deep within it.

"I knew you had it!" Michelo shouted, and with a mighty leap, he came crashing down over me. I side stepped, parrying out swords once with a clang, and together we danced.

In and out, up, and down, our swords sang again and again. I dodged repeatedly, attempting to evade the worst of his blows. The sand beneath my feet slipped and more than once I had to catch my fall, barely in time to roll out of the way of Michelo's swing.

In a sickeningly short time, I was panting. Try as I might, I ran through every little thing I had been taught by my friends, but the sand was too much. I was losing my footing and every time I had a harder time recovering. I couldn't overpower Michelo. He was too strong, too skilled, and frankly just better at battle than I was.

"Already exhausted, little Druid? That's too bad, I'm just getting warmed up!" he shouted and launched a blast of water down at my feet, causing the sand to become mud. I fell backwards, managing to hold on to my sword, but it left me scrambling to right myself. An idea flashed through my mind, and I threw out a command for the Earth beneath my feet to change to solid ground.

Instantly, the sand and patch of mud turned to rock and stone, creating an arena of sorts. Great for me, even better for Michelo. He now had better footing and his attacks came faster and faster.

I took a pot shot at him of fire and it barely grazed his right arm as he leapt out of the way. My Life magic was working overtime to heal my bruises, calm my aching limbs, and reinforce my muscles as they wore down blow after blow.

At one point, Michelo swiped at my knees, and I leapt into the air to miss it, but lost my balance and came down hard on my knee. I screamed out as I felt the knee shatter underneath the weight and angle of my fall directly onto the stone arena.

"Mia!" many voices shouted, and I had to stop myself from searching behind me. The Cannibals had created a protective barrier around our fight, and no one was going to get through. I had to keep everyone away for this. I had promised Michelo a battle between just us, and if I let them come to my aid, it would all be over.

"Stay back!" I commanded to those who could hear me. Michelo barely looked winded as I attempted to stand back on my knee, but it gave underneath my weight and I cried out, falling back to the ground. He began to approach me, sword glinting from the firelight that was all around us. In desperation, I flung out spell after spell, but Michelo threw up a water shield. Earth turned to mud, fire fizzled out, and air turned to shards of ice that rained down on the ground at his feet. Michelo began to laugh as he watched me struggle to rise again.

"Ready to yield, little Druid?" Michelo taunted. "Be ready, because I take no prisoners."

I channeled Life magic into my knee and righted myself, feeling more drained than I should. Every time I threw out a spell, I pumped magic into the amulet, filling it with the power it would need for my final move. I had been doing so quietly since I had left the meditation garden. The amulet was hot with power now, practically burning my chest even through the armor. If I looked down, I would probably see scorch marks on my leather breast plate.

Finally, as I stood completely on my legs, I felt it reach its capacity and I knew it was time. I took a moment to look behind me, and locked eyes with Theo. He was still trying to jump through the ring of Cannibals, but he was too far back. I cast him one last, apologetic glance and then turned back to face Michelo, who had begun advancing on me once more.

I gathered my strength, calmed my will, and took in a large breath to steady myself. With a battle cry, I charged Michelo and leapt into the air, holding my sword back to deal one last blow. As I came down, guided by Death magic to the right spot, I saw Michelo reach up with his own sword. I faltered ever so slightly, and my trajectory was suddenly skewed, leaving me a full four inches further than originally intended.

I gasped as I fell back down to the ground from the pinnacle of my flight, unable to stop myself in time. With a flash, the point of his sword pierced my belly, and I felt the cold steel slide into me. My ears were surrounded with the sound of slicing flesh and spewing blood as I realized what was happening.

The pain lasted for only a second as the sword made its way through my entire body. I screamed one last time as it severed a vertebra of my spine, and then I felt no more. The sword in my now numb hand clanged to the hardened ground useless. I tried to inhale, but my throat welled up with blood and I began to choke under its tang. Air rushed away from me, my lungs hurt, and my heart stilled. I opened my mouth, but the only thing that came out was a gurgling noise, my throat completely closed off. I was drowning from the inside, but I felt nothing anymore. My head spun, and the edges of my vision went black. I heard screaming, but that was quickly numbed as my eyes closed one final time. The last thing I saw before my world went black was Michelo's shocked face, realizing that he had finally done it.

He had killed the Druid.

CHAPTER TWENTY-FOUR

THEO

Theo's soul ripped in two as he watched the love of his life, his Mia, drive herself on accident into Michelo's sword. She had been going for a beautiful kill, but because of a miscalculation on placement, she had instead impaled herself.

"NO!" Theo screamed.

Wynnie, at his side began to thrash about, still trying to climb her way through the barricade of Cannibals that were at least four rings deep. They watched as Michelo lowered his sword and, with his Mother-forsaken boot, kicked Theo's Pair off of it and his heart shattered. It welled up inside of him, feeling as if his own magic were choking him out, drowning in sorrow for the loss of its other half. Theo couldn't breathe, couldn't see. He just wanted Mia, to feel his arms around her, needed to know she was going to live. But Theo knew from experience that no one could survive an attack like that.

Gabriel and Heretia floated above it all, having arrived only moments before to see what was going on. Heretia could be heard wailing against Gabriel's chest, and Theo looked to see the same war inside of himself, written on the magic of Death's face.

In anger, Theo unsheathed both his blades and began hacking at the bodies in front of him. He cared no longer that the Cannibals weren't fighting back, that they couldn't. He only had a certain amount of time before Michelo woke himself from the shock of what Mia had done and he ordered the death of the Kingdom's armies. Wynnie, seeing Theo spring into action, did so herself. Together they created a road of dead bodies beneath their feet. Michelo was still standing there, seemingly slightly surprised at the outcome, but as the two broke through the last Cannibal, he launched his hands into the air in triumph and the Cannibals erupted in cheers.

"Medeis is ours!" he chanted above the noise.

Theo paid no attention to him. His swords clattered down to his side as he reached to pull Mia up from the ground. Wynnie took off in Michelo's direction for vengeance as Theo cradled her head in his hands and the tears that he hadn't known were falling from his face, kissed the now pale cheeks of his Pair. His beautiful Pair, the one person who the Mother Goddess had created for him. Her usually lovely dark-brown locks were caked with dirt and sweat, her face once so pink and alive were now ashen and covered in droplets of blood. Theo mourned the idea that he would never see her perfectly golden eyes radiate out into the crowd and glow when she was angry.

Theo heard the clang of steel continue around him as the Elite Guard came in to try and hold back the line of Cannibals from him, but he couldn't focus on anything but Mia. He cared no longer if one of them stuck a sword through his heart. It would mean he would be with Mia, gone to a place that he could not reach her in now.

"Gone to a place," Theo muttered and then stopped. "Gone to a place?" He wheeled around, searching the skies for Gabriel. He was nowhere to be seen, probably having taken Heretia back to the camp and to safety. He would be the one to rally the soldiers now, along with Heretia and the rest of the High Rulers. Now that Mia was gone, the two of them were the strongest among them all, but Theo had to ask him a question, he needed to know.

"Gabriel!" Theo called out, looking for the Death magic in the crowd. Within moments, he felt Gabriel silently descend next to him in the sand.

"Is she gone?" Theo cried and held out the limp body in his arms. "Only you would know?" Gabriel made a grim face.

"Is she really gone? Dammit Gabriel, answer me!" Theo screamed and pulled Mia's lifeless body back to his chest and leaned over her, seeing the answer written on the auburn-haired man's face.

Through his grief, Theo felt a warm hand touch his shoulder, "From this body, yes she is gone."

Another sob racked through Theo's chest, but he suddenly stopped mid-cry.

"From this body?" Theo asked out loud and turned to see Gabriel standing straight up, head facing the West and his golden eyes glowing brightly, outshining even the brightest Mia's eyes had ever shone.

"From this body, she is gone," he repeated, staring off into the horizon.

Theo went quiet and looked to see what Gabriel was staring at, slightly raising his head. From the West came a glow, dim at first, but quickly gaining luster. The dark night sky began to lighten, as if day was breaking from the wrong direction. Soldiers stopped battling, even the Cannibals slowed at the command of Michelo whose attention had also been caught. Theo stared in wonder as the glow grew to overtake half the sky.

"From this body, she is gone," Gabriel said one last time, and then turned towards Theo, eyes still glowing brightly. "You might want to step back." He grabbed the grief-stricken man's elbow, wrenching him away with a strength Theo didn't know he had from Mia's body.

"No! She needs me!" Theo fought back and tried to break from the grasp, but Gabriel was too overpowering even for the best of warriors.

Theo was about to kick Gabriel in a really unsavory location to get away when a voice called out from beyond the glow. It was right in his ear, but everywhere as well. Ethereal yet grounded, it resonated inside and all around each person on the battlefield.

"Phoenix! Arise!" a deep female voice called out from the clouds and the earth beneath their feet shook heavily. Many dropped to their knees in reverence, for this was clearly the voice of the Mother Goddess. No one alive had ever heard her, but all recognized it deep within them. Written into their very body, their bones, and their magic was an understanding of the Mother Goddess and her might. Each soldier felt their magic quake at its presence and bow down to its power.

Theo stared in awe as the earth quaked with even more fury, the fires from the camps and torches all around blazed higher, the wind picked up into a gale, and the sound of water rushing through a stream was like a hurricane in their ears.

"Look!"

All eyes, including Michelo's, turned to see what was causing the commotion. To Theo's amazement, Mia's body was floating upright in the exact spot he had just been drug away from. Her armor was now gone. In its place was a bright yellow light that encased every inch of her skin, save for her head.

"Amelia!" he called out with joy, but Gabriel refused to release his steady hold on him.

"Let me go!" he punched out at the Mother-forsaken magic, connecting fist squarely with hard face, but still Gabriel did not budge.

"Wait. It's not Mia," he warned, never breaking his gaze on the spectacle unfolding before Medeis.

"Michelo, you have been charged with heinous crimes against this world, against the Druid, and against the Mother Goddess. You have been judged guilty and unrepenting. I have given you a chance and you still rebuke me. I sentence you to death without afterlife!" Mia's lips moved, but it was not her words nor her voice. The Mother Goddess was Projecting through her, a form of magic outlawed centuries ago, as it was invasive and devastating to the witch whose body was used as the conduit.

Michelo's knees began to shake, "Why should I care what some glorified witch thinks of me? When have you ever helped those in need?" he argued, but still something about him was terrified that everyone around, including Theo, could see written on his scarred face. Michelo took two shaky steps back, lifting his sword slightly in case of another attack.

"Phoenix! Arise!" The Mother Goddess called again, and Mia's body began to rise into the air. Theo watched as his Pair grew brighter. His heart dropped as he looked closer, squinting through the shine, and realized that Mia's body was now on fire.

"Someone help her!" he cried out, searching for a Water witch who could put her out.

Mia's arms stretched out wide, the flames now evident as they licked her skin and grew hot. The soldiers below shielded their faces from the heat and backed away. Theo couldn't move. He was rooted to his spot in the sand beneath the feet of this awesome power. Suddenly, Mia's head tilted back, and she let out a terrible screech. It was a sound no human witch could make, no instrument could repeat, and no ear would withstand without covering. A scream never heard before in the history of witches and never to be heard again. It was the mourning cry of the Phoenix, it's last note before it died within its own flame.

Tim was suddenly beside Theo in all the madness and chaos of soldiers running and others falling to their knees, attempting to keep the sound from their ears. He grabbed Theo's shoulders, turning to face him.

"We couldn't find the Phoenix because it was right before our eyes the entire time." He explained as the knowledge of what he was witnessing dawned on him, on all of them.

"Mia *is* the Phoenix," he spoke in a loud clear voice, so that those around could hear and hopefully understand what they were witnessing.

As the mourning cry ended, Mia's entire body gave way to a burst of flame, causing everyone to duck in fear of igniting themselves. When they returned their gaze, Mia was no longer above them. Instead, to their wonder, was the Phoenix, the Wild Beast created by Life and hidden away by the Mother Goddess in the beginning of time.

The Phoenix screeched again, and Theo realized the bird wasn't made of feathers, but of fire. It was a massive creature; larger than even Cetus had been. Phoenix spanned the length of its wings and the heat rushed all around them. Phoenix surveyed the crowd with the hollow sockets it had for eyes and came to rest on the figure of Michelo, slowly backing away into the crowd.

With a mighty cry, Phoenix swopped down, chasing the screaming man away. Phoenix was too quick, however, and in one grab, had Michelo within its fiery talons. Michelo roared in pain as the fire seared his skin around his torso and almost instantly, went limp. Phoenix wrapped its wings around its own body and that of Michelo, cocooning the man in its fire.

Theo wrinkled his nose at the smell of the burning flesh and had to cover his face in fear of vomiting. In silence, the soldiers watched as Phoenix cried one last time, and then, like a flash of a sun bursting in the sky, Phoenix imploded upon itself with a roar that seemed to echo throughout Medeis. Gabriel forced Theo and Wynnie down with his arms, covering their heads and attempting to duck away as well.

"Get down!" he shouted as the boom of the explosion sent a shockwave and knocked everyone off their feet.

Theo's ears were still ringing when he looked back up to find ash raining down on the heads of all those still on the battlefield. Those who had been pushing their way through the ranks to see what was happening, had to right themselves back on to their feet, unsure of what had just happened.

Theo searched the sky frantically, seeing nothing but darkness and, once he blinked a few times, stars poking out to join watching the scene below.

"Mia?" he asked hesitantly, but she didn't answer. He scanned faster and his eyes came to find a pile of ash resting in the center of her magical makeshift arena.

"Amelia!" he cried once more over the growing murmurs of questions. Racing to see if she had survived, Theo stumbled over the swords that had been dropped, slicing a palm open in his haste.

"Oh, please, be alive," he whispered to himself and began to dig through the foul-smelling ash. Scoop after scoop, Theo dug faster until finally his hand reached the rock below and he stopped, his heart sinking. He whipped around and dug through another portion, but the pile was barely bigger than a single body, let alone big enough to hide it in multiple places.

"Amelia!" his sobs flowed once more freely over his face.

Heads hung in sorrow all around him. They may have been rid of Michelo, but they had lost their Druid in the process. Medeis was once again all on its own, now suffering the loss of its greatest blessing.

Slowly, Theo's friends stepped forward, hoping to help him away and spare him this scene. Wynnie knelt down on his left, Tim on his right, and Will placed both hands on the man's shoulders giving what comfort he could. No one was without tears as the realization of what they had lost set in.

"She was the best of us," Tim started.

"She was the bravest of us," Will joined in.

"She was the kindest of us," Wynnie finished.

Theo said nothing. He couldn't say anything. They may feel her loss as her friends, but his entire soul was ripping into shreds. Only Wynnie would ever possibly know this pain and Mother-willing it would be a lifetime before she did. Theo wasn't sure he was going to survive the next breath without Mia. Sobs began in the crowd of soldiers around them, still littered throughout with Cannibals that had yet to move from their spots. Michelo was no longer there controlling them and soon, just as those in Purge had done, they would start moving aimlessly under their own volition but with no purpose.

Shouts of confusion could be heard further back towards the camp outside of the city, followed as well by cries and shouts of disbelief. Theo couldn't take this any longer, he wanted rid of this noise, and of these people. After a few moments, he finally opened his eyes and blinked back tears as his attention was caught by something in the ash pile.

Laying there, hard to see in the darkness and under the gray ash, was the black Death amulet he hadn't noticed her wearing. Confused, Theo sniffed back another sob and reached for the amulet, wondering why she would have had it. Gabriel was supposed to be wearing this, not her.

He brought the amulet closer to him to look it over. He noticed that there wasn't a scratch on it. The amulet had absolutely no indication that it had been in the fiery inferno Phoenix had created.

"Why is that there?" Wynnie asked aloud for Theo, ever the voice of the group.

"I-I don't know," Theo answered her, turning the amulet over again. Theo suddenly winced as the heavy amulet opened the wound further. He hissed from the pain and moved it to his clean hand to keep looking at it.

Gabriel came up behind them to see what they were looking at.

"Did you know she had this?" Theo asked him, trying not to sound accusatory. Gabriel nodded, "I thought it would help a little."

"Fat lot of good it did, she's still gone," Theo muttered and went to throw the hunk of metal away when suddenly he stopped. His eyes went wide, and he pulled his arm back down.

"What's wrong?" Tim asked, noticing his friend's reaction.

"It's warm. The amulet, it's warm. It wasn't warm a moment ago," he whispered and stood up to his feet, the amulet still cradled in his hands. The army's attention was shifting back slowly at Theo's words, curiosity overwhelming their sorrow. Theo looked up to see the Generals, High Rulers, and even Heretia edging their way through the crowd. Heretia and Gabriel locked eyes and she hurried over to him, throwing her arms around his neck.

Theo returned his attention to the amulet, which was growing warmer, clearly not from his own body heat. From deep within, Theo thought he saw a glow, a small pulsating glow. As he peered closer, that glow grew, and it was indeed pulsating. He sucked in a breath and brought it closer to his face.

"Is that," Wynnie began. "A heartbeat?"

Sure enough, Theo realized as he timed it with his own, the pulsating was indeed a heartbeat.

"Gabriel!" he shouted and showed the Death magic the amulet. The auburn-haired man looked it over and finally he met Theo's eyes, wide with wonder.

"It can't be," he muttered and looked back down.

"What? What is it?" Theo demanded.

"Get back!" Gabriel suddenly shouted, and with a quick toss, threw the amulet into the air above everyone's heads. Most ducked, but those closest, ran to catch the amulet as it began its descent back to the ground.

"What the hell-?" Theo rushed to catch it first, but there was no need. As he placed himself under where the amulet would fall, it stopped in the air and hung there motionless. Theo paused, stunned.

As if it were a living thing, the amulet began to glow and grow before his eyes. It took an oblong shape before coming back down slowly to the earth. By the time the top of the shape reached Theo's eye level, it began to take form. Slowly, agonizingly, the light grew brighter, and Theo had to take a step back in hopes of not being blinded. A flash erupted amongst the crowd, and everyone turned their heads. When they turned back, jaws dropped.

There, before them, stood Amelia Vida Wardman, dressed in a white tunic that glittered and shone as if it were made of moonlight itself. Her hair held a luster that it never before had shone with, her eyes glowed golden, and her skin seemed to radiate sunlight. Her arms were open wide, and her smile outshone her own radiance. Theo stared, slack jawed and without words for only a moment before his feet began to move for him and he raced to his Pair, not stopping until he held her in his arms again.

His heart fluttered in recognition, and he held her close, leaning his weight into her before losing himself in tears. Thankfully, they were of joy this time. Mia knelt him to the ground and allowed herself to be surrounded by his shock for a moment before pulling back and staring into his eyes.

"You're here? You're really alive?" Theo whispered, tucking her hair behind her perfect ears, and gazing down at her.

"I'm here. And this time, I'm not going anywhere," she promised him.

A roar went up amongst the soldiers within moments. It seemed as though the entire city was cheering as well. The Elite Guard, Gabriel, and Heretia swooped down upon the couple and lifted Amelia into their awaiting arms for hugs.

As the cheering grew louder, a clap of thunder rang out across the sky, startling everyone with its nearness and they all went silent. Mia pulled herself from the arms of her loved ones and walked out into the desert alone.

"Mia?" Wynnie asked, watching her go slowly by. It was if she had been called by the thunder and could hear nothing more. Theo moved to stop her, as he wasn't ready for anything more to happen, or be away from her, but Gabriel stopped him with a gentle touch to his shoulder.

"It's the Mother Goddess, she wants to speak through her," he warned. Theo wisely hung back. Mia looked up into the sky and then turned back to the awaiting crowds, everyone silenced.

"Medeis, Be Blessed," The Mother Goddess' voice came, once again, from Mia's mouth.

"Be Blessed," many muttered back and bowed their reverent heads.

"You have conquered and shown your bravery, as has the Druid that I sent for you. I am proud to call you my children, and will, therefore, give this desolate land beyond the border of Purge new life. It will be a new Kingdom, ruled by the Druid and her descendants and it will be called Vida, Life."

"Yes, Mother Goddess." The crowd responded as one in obedience.

Theo couldn't take his eyes off of Mia. He wasn't ready to lose her again. No more came from the Mother Goddess, and with a sigh, Mia blinked twice and began walking back towards him. She reached her arms out with a smile, and Theo happily gathered her back up into his arms and kissed her.

CHAPTER TWENTY-FIVE

The next few days went by quickly after I was reincarnated. I had never felt more alive, in control, or powerful. Before the rest of the Cannibal army could be rounded up, Ez had already begun to administer the Cure potion, and one by one, they were all released of their bonds. The process of discovering which ones had gone willingly and which had chosen this path for power was rough, but eventually, we would have all those who had chosen behind bars. What to do with them afterwards was another question, as it seemed every single one regretted the decision.

Gregor had been searched for briefly, and his body had been found in a tent far back from the battle site. He was dead, seemingly an accident during a last failed attempt to steal magic from a witch.

"I know it's not right to lose a soul, but good riddance," Heretia had sneered when she heard the news.

I had to agree with her on this one. I wasn't in the habit of killing as a punishment, and I didn't want to start with such a lowlife as Gregor. Antamba had been released as well, but being a Wild Beast, it was up to the Mother Goddess what to do with it.

The shockwave during Phoenix's death had sent out a blast of magic so great it seemed to have reincarnated the other Wild Beasts. To everyone's surprise Tailong was now flying around the skies of Purge, assisting in moving objects back to the Eastern ports for the kingdom's return home. I could only assume Nandina, Cetus, and Aqrabuamelu had also been reincarnated. No word on them had been reported yet, but I assumed Suravia would have its hands full looking for Nandina and shoving it back in the cave it had originally been banished too for bad behavior.

Theo never left my side in the following days, which was a hard task, as I felt as if I had slept for years and the energy I had to burn was limitless. Ez had suggested I slow down some just in case the magic coursing through my veins was finite, but I didn't listen very well. I had a job to fix and secure Medeis, and I was going to waste it all on that if it was being wasted. Maria was overjoyed to see me as well, and commented on my hair and eyes, which now constantly glowed yellow instead of only when I was emotional.

My parents even mentioned how well I looked, but they still weren't over the fact that I had died to get that way. They checked on me constantly, pitching in and offering to help in any way they could.

Slowly, Purge and all of Medeis began to right itself again when I was asked a question, I wasn't ready for.

The High Rulers had requested a special audience with me four days after the battle. I had, of course, agreed and met with them in Heretia's Throne Room as before. As I entered, each and every one bowed lowed before me.

"Druid," they said in unison.

I begged them to rise and be seated.

"We have asked you here in the question of your new kingdom, Vida, that the Mother Goddess has ordered."

I nodded my head at my Uncle Michael, as he was the one speaking. I knew this was coming. I wasn't the most sold of being a High Ruler of a new kingdom. For one, I had no subjects, but furthermore, I knew nothing about it. I hadn't even really led the people of Medeis into battle, I had just ended it.

"We, as the Five Kingdoms have been discussing amongst ourselves, and we have come to believe that the only way for Medeis to survive is to regrow it's Life witch population. And since, the name Vida has already been given to the land, we were hoping that it would be a place for Life witches to come and regain what they lost so long ago."

My pulse quickened. They were giving me subjects! I was stunned, and also touched.

"I believe that would be a wise idea. It is beneficial to Medeis to take back what it lost twenty years ago, and I would be happy to take all those Life witches who wish to come under my protection," I responded gracefully.

My uncle beamed and sat back down in his chair, seemingly pleased with himself. It was Thomas then that cleared his throat and stood. I raised a confused eyebrow at my friend and now colleague.

"The next bit, you may want to think over," he began, and I squirmed slightly in my chair.

"We, as the High Rulers of the Five Kingdoms, formally request that High Queen of Vida, Amelia Vida Wardman, be proclaimed as Empress of Medeis until her own natural death. Which is hopefully many years to come."

My breath caught in my throat as I stared out at the twenty-one men and women sitting around me.

"We need a strong, centralized leader right now as we recognize and renavigate our relationships with one another. We need a figure we can go to that is above and beyond our understanding of magic as the Mother Goddess wished. We want you, Mia, to guide us," he finished grandly, and with a wink to boot.

My jaw fell, which was very unladylike, and I had to tell myself to inhale and exhale a few times before answering.

"Is this truly what you all wish?" I asked quietly and each, in their turn, nodded their agreement. Even Theo's father and the reluctant Rulers of Maravette did without question.

"Then I must accept," I answered, and then a thought occurred to me.

"Now, I don't want to overrule you. You are still the chosen Kings and Queens, and you know your own people better than I. But I am okay with guiding, assisting, and advising in any way I can," I clarified quickly.

"We wouldn't have it any other way," Vanessa remarked sweetly from her place in the small crowd.

Telling Theo that night was a different story. He sighed heavily and looked out the balcony window in the new room we had been given now that everything was settled, and Rulers were returning to their Kingdoms.

"They want to hold a coronation in a month and begin building Vida sooner than that. I suggested we use the prisoners to begin the framework of the city and then create a plan of growth from there once the Life witches arrive," I continued on, seeing that he was upset.

"Am I ever going to get you to myself?" he asked, arms braced against the balcony railing. The cool night hair played havoc with his brown curls on top of his head, and I forced back a smile as I tucked them behind his ear.

"I don't think that was ever the Mother Goddess' plan dear. I was always meant to be for the people. She was preparing me for that before I even knew who she was."

Theo signed again, "I just want you to be with just me for a while. Start a family, have a life of our own," he groused.

"I get that, I really do. But we wouldn't be together if the Mother Goddess hadn't thought we weren't truly the right people for the job. We will find time for all of that. We are still young, and the world is starting new. It will be hard, but I know we are up for the task. What do you say?" I asked him, looping his pinky finger in mine. Theo turned and looked deep into my eyes and my heart melted all over again for him.

"I don't think I would have been happy with anyone else but you. So confident and fearless. You astound me every day, Amelia Vida Wardman."

He reached down and kissed me soundly. Beyond us in the desert, Tailong swam through the clouds and the stars shone like twinkling shapeless lights above our heads. The city below was finally coming alive with music, chatter, and laughter.

"My Princess of Life," he whispered one last time, before scooping me up and shutting the balcony door behind us.

The End

About the Author:

Stephanie Welch is a businesswoman, educator, dog fancier, wife, and mother to two amazing girls. She lives in Warner Robins, GA where she spends days chasing dogs and kids and nights bringing her characters stories to life.

Dear Reader,

Thank you for the final time for joining me on Amelia's journey. This has been a ride, one that I will always hold dear, and I hope you enjoyed it with me. While Amelia's story has ended, other worlds and characters await in the future. Please like and follow me on Facebook, and Instagram and keep up to date with my happenings and future publishing's.

From the bottom of my heart, Thank you!

Stephanie Welch

The complete works of the

INTO THE DARKNESS

SERIES

by

STEPHANIE WELCH

STONES OF DESTINY

CHAINS OF DARKNESS

ASHES ARISING

www.ingramcontent.com/pod-product-compliance
Lightning Source LLC
Chambersburg PA
CBHW070731280626
47159CB00023B/3084

* 9 7 8 1 9 5 6 5 4 4 0 4 6 *